DIVORCING JACK

DIVORCING JACK

COLIN BATEMAN

ARCADE PUBLISHING • NEW YORK

FIRST U.S. EDITION

Library of Congress Cataloging-in-Publication Data

Bateman, Colin, 1962–
    Divorcing Jack / Colin Bateman. —1st U.S. ed.
        p.   cm.
    ISBN 1-55970-310-5 (hc)
    ISBN 1-55970-359-8 (pb)
    I. Title
    PR 6052.A773D58   1995
    823'.914 — dc20   95-17773

Published in the United States by Arcade Publishing, Inc., New York

Distributed by Little, Brown and Company

10 9 8 7 6 5 4 3 2 1

BP

PRINTED IN THE UNITED STATES OF AMERICA

For Andrea

DIVORCING JACK

I was upstairs with a girl I shouldn't have been upstairs with when my wife whispered in my ear, "You have twenty-four hours to move out."

If I'd broken off then, chased after her, perhaps things would have turned out very different for everyone. But I didn't. I was lost in an erection powered by alcohol, unable to say no. The girl was aware but unmoved by the interruption. She was clamped to me like a limpet mine. We weren't even in bed. We were in my study, standing silhouetted in the doorway, the party booming beneath us, kissing, only kissing, like school kids behind the bicycle sheds. Innocent, almost.

I have never been a ladies' man. Perhaps in my private moments I liked to think of myself as a sexual wildebeest — no body as such, but a lot of horn — but it was a delusion born of marriage. Patricia was my first girlfriend, lover, my wife. I had never wandered before. Neither, to the best of my knowledge, had she. I had never considered being unfaithful, or, at least, not with anyone I had any remote possibility of getting; fantasy is the justifiable preserve of the married man. This girl was a toe in the polluted ocean of romantic betrayal.

In that moment I lost one beautiful woman and gained another, an acquaintance of a few hours who would change my life, and lose her own.

1

1

The waiter had permed hair which was turning grey. He slammed the chopsticks down on the table and said in a better Belfast accent than mine: "This is a Chinese restaurant. No bloody knives and forks."

I managed a weak smile for Maxwell and under my breath cursed China in general and Patricia in particular.

I have two troubles in life, and sometimes they converge. I have always had a problem with foreign food. I was brought up with Protestant tastes. Plain and simple. Nothing fancy. Of course I could see the attraction of Chinese food: the taste of the Orient, that whiff of intrigue you get in a Chinese restaurant. The same as with an Italian restaurant: you always have that thought at the back of your mind about whether they are tied up in some way with the Mafia. Were the Chinese, with their incessant gambling and blood-curdling yells from the kitchens, really gangsters? It's a relief that they never moved into the hairdressing business. It would be difficult to take seriously threats issued by the Curling Tongs.

My problem with foreign food — sometimes I can't even manage a German biscuit — coincides with manual illiteracy. I cannot change a fuse, a tire or a light bulb. I cannot build a wall, unblock a sink or complete a jigsaw. The reason I have my garden paved over is that I know if I attempted to combat the jungle that was, I would somehow contrive to cut off one of my feet in the process. Chopsticks, long silvery gripless ones, are a pain.

Maxwell looked happy enough. He was already playing with his, picking up a little saltcellar with consummate ease. He was plump, maybe edging fifty. His black blazer hung over the back of his seat. He wore a white shirt that marked him out as a bachelor: the front was ironed perfectly but the sleeves were badly creased and the collar stuck out at mad angles. His front six teeth were capped, a vanity that did not sit well on him. His accent wasn't Belfast, but it wasn't country enough to be annoying. He drank Ballygowan Spring Water. I ordered a shandy.

He looked a little surprised. "Your column makes you out to be a hard-drinking man," he said.

I shrugged. "Artistic licence," I said. "I'll maybe go to an artistic off-licence on the way home."

He grinned. "Quick. I have a good sense of humour, you know. I read *Punch* and *Private Eye*."

I nodded. Frankie Woods didn't have a sense of humour either. He was, indirectly, responsible for me making a fool of myself with a pair of chopsticks.

Frankie, God love him, spiked me. I had this idea about swapping the terrorist wasteland of West Belfast for the Guinness Brewery in Dublin. They could have our troubles and we could drink theirs. I mean, it was only an idea. I put it in writing, but Frankie killed it. He said he was trying to build up the circulation in the west of the city. I told him he paid me to write stuff like that and he said no, he paid me to write stuff that was funny. It's all a matter of taste, really. Anyway, to cut a short story shorter, Mike Magee saw me in the dumps and suggested a different way for me to make a bit of money. I liked Mike. He looked like a rugby player who'd done too much drinking at the bar; squat, with the hint of a double chin. He wore a crumpled cream sports coat with wide collars and a cream open-neck shirt. His trousers were brown cords, fading at the knees. Nike trainers. His voice was verging on BBC plummy, but he would lose that under pressure. He poured me a cup of coffee from the percolator at the back of

4

the newsroom. It was quiet. Cleaners were moving between the rows of computer terminals. Only a couple of them glowed green. The computers, not the cleaners.

He offered me the cup. I shook my head. "You know I never touch the stuff."

He tutted. "Sorry, Dan, I forgot you were a Coke and Twix man. Any joy with the Coke machine yet?"

"Blank wall. I tell them it's a health drink — says right there on the can, made with vegetable extracts — but I'm getting nowhere."

"Don't give up, Dan, we're all behind you."

He put both cups down. "How's Pat?"

"Fine. Fine. Y'know. Can't live with them, can't live with them."

"Yeah," he said, shaking his head ruefully, "I know the score."

"You'll have to come to the next party."

"You threw me out of the last one."

"I threw everyone out."

"That's true. Things did get a bit out of hand."

"Par for the course."

A sheepish grin slipped on to his face. "I couldn't help over-hearing Frankie having a go at you."

"Ah, not really. You know Frankie. About as funny as a fire in an orphanage. Still, looks like it's cream crackers for dinner."

"That bad?"

"Nah, not really."

"How's the great Ulster novel coming?"

"Great Ulster sonnet at the rate I'm going, Mike. Too many distractions, y'know?"

"Tell me all about it."

So he got to talking about working for the Government. He did a bit of it himself, but he had a full-time job on the *Belfast Evening News* and couldn't make much of a go of it, but he reckoned a freelancer like myself was tailor-made for it.

With the elections just round the corner the city was being

swamped with foreign journalists looking for a story, so a bit of local knowledge was at a premium. I knew the city like the back of my hand, and the rest well enough to bluff my way. The Government press office — or the Central Office of Information as it styled itself — was on the lookout for dependable people to guide visiting journalists round the country, advising on background and generally putting across the Government's optimistic views on the chances of this latest initiative working. I have never been described as dependable, but I was interested.

I got straight to the point. "What's the money like?"

"It's not bad. You won't make your fortune, like, but it'll probably appeal to you for the same reason it appeals to me — it gets you out from under the wife's feet and the food and drink go on the expenses. Get plastered for Ulster, Dan."

He said it wasn't just a matter of a twenty-minute briefing. More shadow work. All day and all night if need be. I nodded enthusiastically and he fell for it and offered to arrange an interview for me. "A word of advice," he cautioned as I went to move on, "if you get it — one, you owe me a pint or two, and second, in the interview, presuming I can swing it for you, they're not just looking for knowledge about the North. Show them you know something about another country. Remember you'll be dealing with foreign correspondents. A bit of repartee goes a long way."

Patricia thought it would be a doddle. But she didn't have to do it. She had visions of moving out of the Holy Land. The interview was set up; Patricia got me a junior guide to the disintegration of the USSR and told me to learn it. America was too obvious. It took me a couple of hours, but by the end I reckoned I knew enough to hold my own with an above-average five-year-old.

You can walk almost anywhere in Belfast worth walking to in twenty minutes. I went down the Ormeau Road, fighting a biting wind the whole way, then through the Short Strand on to the Newtownards Road. Traffic was stalled at the foot of the road; soldiers were lazily checking IDs. There was rarely much trouble in this Protestant heartland and they knew it. As I dodged shoppers I tried to concentrate my mind on the fall of the Communist

6

empire: on Gorbachev, Yeltsin, Stalin, Lenin, big fat women and black-market vodka. An old man fell in beside me. He wore a battered ulster and clutched a brown paper bag containing a bottle of Concorde. The fool.

"Can you lend me 20p for a cuppa tay?" he asked, his voice nicotine rough.

"If you can show me where you can get a cup for 20p, I'll join ye, mate," I replied, and quickly regretted it. I felt curiously nervous. I gave him a pound, but he wasn't that easy to shake off. He puffed along beside me.

"Did ye see the match last night?" he rasped. "Them Brazilians are magic, aren't they?"

"Didn't see it, mate," I said. I took advantage of a break in the traffic to nip away from him. When I looked back he gave me the fingers.

I turned left onto the Holywood Road. The Dragon Palace was about halfway up. It was garishly, freshly painted. Outside, workmen were completing a bargain basement improvement to the sidewalk, changing cracked concrete slabs for gentrified cobbles, row upon row in sickly yellow, like a giant Caramac bar. My old dad would have called it mutton dressed as mutton.

My stomach rumbled for the first time as I opened the door, which I thought was pretty good timing. A swarm of flies flittered about the glass like anxious relatives at an incubator. A scowling waiter took my coat, his hands lingering long enough on my body for me to realize I was being searched. It was a bit of a surprise. It didn't happen much, except on the way out.

Neville Maxwell wasn't fooled by my shandy or my artistic licence. "A hard drinker and a confirmed Unionist," he said lazily, still tinkering with his chopsticks. "You think that's a suitable background to be showing folks round the country with?"

"You're judging me by my column again. Like I say. It gets a laugh."

He ordered for both of us. I thought things progressed well. He'd ask three or four innocuous questions then slip in a serious one. I could tell they were important by the way his pupils receded to tiny points as he sized up my replies. We passed on

7

starters. I thought it wise to pass on another drink. I was thinking of the money.

"Your column seems to have quite a following."

"Yeah, well, y'know. What can I say?"

"But you'll agree it portrays an image of you that . . ."

"I don't think your visitors would be aware of that."

"True."

"I mean, I don't mind a drink. But it doesn't interfere with my work."

"I had a chat with Frankie Woods."

Oh-oh. "Dear old Frankie."

"Full of praise."

I nodded.

"Surprised?"

I laughed. "Not at all. Nice guy, Frankie. Honest."

"He says you're only part time."

"Yeah. I don't like to be tied down."

"So what else do you do. Freelance?"

He looked like he already knew. "Yeah. Anyone that pays. Can be *The Times* one week, *Sewers and Sewerage* the next. The rough with the smooth. Like I say, anyone who pays, within reason."

"What's within reason?"

I shrugged. Nobody had yet tempted me to something without reason. Getting a cheque had its own kind of reason. "Well," I said, "I wouldn't work for *Republican News*. But then I doubt they'd ask me."

"That's what I'm trying to get at, Dan," he said, jabbing his chopsticks towards me, "you're not really impartial, are you?"

"Who is? I have my views. I don't let them get in the way of my work — apart from my column, which is supposed to have a particular viewpoint. Unionist with a sense of humour, if you like. It's balanced by the fascist on the opposite page and the loony Republican at the back." I leant forward. He withdrew his chopsticks. "I'm a professional journalist, Mr. Maxwell. I wouldn't work for *Republican News* because it supports terrorism. Simple as that."

8

He sat back in his chair and absentmindedly scratched at a permanently furrowed brow. "You think you could stick to the Government line?"

I shrugged. I gave him a little grin. "Up to a point, Lord Copper."

His mouth widened into a grin. It made his face look like a split melon. "Cry havoc and let slip the dogs of Waugh," he said.

I nodded appreciatively. "Matched and maybe beaten. Very good. I like that. Tommy Waugh, of course, used to play for Linfield."

He took a big gulp of his water, I sipped my shandy. "With your reputation . . . ," he began.

"Such as it is . . ."

"Such as it is . . . you wouldn't be worried about going into Nationalist areas?"

"Not at all. I get more flak from Unionists. More tightly strung. The other lot enjoy a good argument. Although they do tend to have you shot afterwards."

He shook his head slightly. "Like I say, I've a sense of humour. But I keep it under control. You can do that?"

"Absolutely."

Laughter erupted from behind me. I glanced round. A group of six business types were cackling over something. One banged the table with his fist; another took off his glasses and rubbed his eyes. Maxwell said, "Tell me, do you have an interest in any other country besides Northern Ireland?"

Gorby. Trotsky. The Baltic states. Yeltsin. "Yes," I said confidently, "Brazil."

I looked him dead in the eye and thought passionately about leaving the table and punching the first pensioner that hobbled into view.

"That's an unusual choice."

I reached up to push a dank strand of hair from my brow. As I brought my hand down I cracked my glass and it toppled over. I watched helplessly as the dregs fanned out across the table towards Maxwell. I mumbled an apology and began to dab at the mess with my napkin. I trained my eyes on him again, staring the

9

way I had at girls as a youth to overcome my shyness. It hadn't worked then either.

"Uh, yeah, Brazil. A great football team. I'm really keen on football."

Maxwell set his chopsticks down in front of him. They formed a little dam before the sop of shandy. "That was a great match the other night, eh?"

"One-a-the-best."

"Did you think it was in?"

"No shadow of a doubt."

"Then if you do join us, the first thing we'll get you is a pair of glasses," he chortled.

I was pulling it round.

"What about Germany?" he asked.

Football or politics? Trivial or serious? The effortless goal machine or European inflation? I shrugged. "What can you say about the Germans?"

"That's what I'm asking."

"Well, you have to take them at face value."

"What do you mean exactly?"

The food arrived. A pork dish. Lots of noodles. I lifted my chopsticks for the first time. Smooth as silk. I dropped one. Maxwell was already tucking in. His eyes didn't leave me.

"I mean . . ." A piece of pork nearly reached my mouth, it was stretching out its arms to me and my lower lip was curling out to grasp it when it fell, bouncing from my left trouser leg. ". . . That there's very little pretence about them, whether you're talking football or European Parliament." As nonchalantly as possible I reached down to retrieve the pork from my shoe.

"Have you met many Germans?"

"Enough."

"Where was that?"

"Oh, I've been around Europe a few times. You can't help it. They own everything."

"You have a point there." He set his sticks down. He was half finished and food hadn't yet crossed the border of my lips.

10

"You're not very comfortable, are you?" he asked sympathetically. Sweat was dripping down my brow like irrigation on a hillside paddy field. "I should have checked this was okay for you. Not everyone can use them."

I put my chopsticks down. "I'm fine," I said. "My hands are slightly arthritic. You might have noticed." Jesus.

2

When I was thirteen I woke up in the middle of the night and found my brother pissing in my typewriter case. I decided there and then that there must be something wonderful about alcohol. As my artistic interest grew I discovered that many of my heroes had had impassioned affairs with what my old da referred to as the devil's vomit: Brendan Behan, Dylan Thomas, George Best, Pete Townshend. It had not adversely affected any of them, with the exception of the first two, whom it killed.

It was the most natural thing in the world for me to hit the pub as soon as I finished lunch. My embarrassment with the chopsticks needed diluting.

I headed back into the centre of town, then up the Dublin Road to Shaftesbury Square. I turned left into a dusty alleyway and entered a brown doorway at the top, Lavery's back bar. It was the kind of spit-and-sawdust pub that was becoming increasingly rare on the ground in the city; most of the rest had adopted themes. Maybe Lavery's had too but never let on: not so much mock Georgian as take-the-piss hard-man. There were a few ageing punks at the bar, a couple of students in a corner and an old drunk studying the jukebox. Willie Nutt was behind the bar. He winked over as I came in. He poured me a pint of Harp without asking.

"Howdy, Dan, how's it going? What's the headline tonight?"
I shrugged. "God knows. I only work there."

He leant on the bar as I put my money down. "Did you hear the forecast, Dan?"

I'd heard the forecast, but I'd hear it again. "Cloudy," he said, "with widespread terrorism."

He gave a big belly laugh, scooped up the money and wandered down the bar.

I sat with my pint. Had another. Two or three others. A couple of shorts. There was a nice atmosphere. Relaxed. Towards teatime it began to crowd up. Still not many suits. Tax Inspector Patricia would be at work for an hour yet. I bought some cans at the bar and headed up the few hundred yards to the Botanic Gardens. The wind had dropped and there was a pleasant warmth in the air; the change in temperature had brought crowds of youngsters out of the bushes and they sat on the green in groups, half-shielding bottles of cider. Ah, my youth before me.

I found a bench and began drinking. Save for ordering drinks I hadn't spoken to anyone since Maxwell, and I wasn't worrying about him. It was out of my hands now. The money would be handy, but moving house was a pain I could do without. I thought about chopsticks and how ridiculous they were. I thought about the waiters and how ignorant they had been. It was a trait that would in time make the Dragon Palace one of the most popular establishments in the city.

I took a gulp, closed my eyes. I felt the tension oozing away. It was shaping up into a beautiful evening.

I opened my eyes. I was on the ground. I looked at my watch. A quarter to ten. It was getting dark.

A voice at my side said: "Are you all right?"

I looked up. A girl. Maybe twenty. Her hair was long, crimped at the front, dyed black. She'd a long angular face, pretty in a starved kind of way. Her eyes were close together, but not so close as to suggest Catholicism, and they were as electric blue as eyes can be at dusk. I said: "I'm fine. I'm a gravel inspector for the Department of Stones. Undercover." Snappy, precise, slurred.

She smiled. A nice thin smile. "Do gravel inspectors always sleep on park benches for two hours, allow wee lads to steal their drink and then make sudden dives on to the ground?"

I sat up, wiped loose stones from my knees. "Always."

She giggled and turned to leave.

"You been watching me?"

She stopped. "I was across the way having a drink."

"It's not safe here by yourself."

"I was with friends. They're away on." The top of a bottle of cider peeked out of a deep leather handbag that hung from her shoulder.

"You wouldn't care to join me?"

"What, down there?"

"Nah, for a drink. Down the road. No strings attached." My tongue felt fuzzy, my brain fuzzier.

"Do you not think you've had enough?"

"No such thing. Sure I've had a wee sleep. I've drunk myself sober."

"I shouldn't really . . ."

But it was a shouldn't with a hint of should. If I'd been a girl I'd have said no, but she looked me up and down and must have seen something vaguely appealing. God knows, it wasn't my physique — she later described me as the Adonis of Auschwitz. But she nodded and stretched out her hand to help me up. "Just for one, and that only 'cause I'm interested in stones."

I said: "Do you always pick up strange men in parks?"

"Nah, I usually do it in public toilets. You get a better class in there."

She was nice. Chirpy with youth. Only a wee slip of a thing. I said: "Are you a student?"

"Aye, but not up there." She nodded back towards Queen's University, which bordered the gardens. The little smile jumped back on to her pale lips. "I'm up at Jordanstown. I study geology."

"A fortunate choice of words then. It must be fate."

We went back down to Lavery's. She chatted animatedly on the way, nothing of any real substance, or perhaps there was and I was far too gone to notice it. There was a slight slur in her voice; it didn't make much difference to my drunken ears.

The back bar was packed and the drinkers had spilled out into the alleyway which was brightly lit now by a large, bare bulb high up on the side of the wall. It took me fifteen minutes to negotiate my way to the bar and get served. By the time I got back she was chatting to a couple of spiky-haired youths. I stood behind her with two pints in my hands, feeling old. She turned to me, took her pint and then recommenced her conversation with the punks. I took it as a hint and started to move on. She came skipping after me.

"Hey, hold on. I'm sorry, I hadn't seen them for ages."

"No problem," I said.

"Don't be like that."

I shrugged. And I thought to myself, Christ, I've known her five minutes and I'm jealous. "How can I fall out with you if I don't even know your name?"

"Well, there's a point." She seemed about to hold her hand out, but suddenly did a basketball pivot, reaching up to kiss me on the cheek, spilling part of her beer on my coat as she did so. "I'm sorry," she said, and I wasn't sure whether she was apologizing for turning her back on me, spilling her drink or having immediate second thoughts about the kiss. "I'm Margaret. Margaret McBride."

I leant down and kissed her back. No, not her back, her cheek. It was cool and white and smelt of mandarin oranges. "And I'm Dan Starkey."

"Oh, I know who you are. I've seen you in the paper."

"Ah."

"And I've seen you with your wife."

"Ah."

"It was at a party. You were drunk under a table. You had to be carried to a taxi."

"I've never been carried to a taxi in my life."

15

"Well, you certainly had help."

"Maybe help. I've never been carried."

"You don't look much like your picture in the paper."

"Disappointed?"

"You don't look as hungry in real life."

"It was taken on a particularly bad day. You like the column? Be honest. I'm not fishing for compliments, but if you don't answer in the affirmative I'll break your nose."

"I like it. Sometimes. Better than the other crap."

"I like that. Better than the other crap. Put that on my gravestone."

A lank, dank guy ambled up to her and offered her a pull on a joint. She shook her head. After a moment's hesitation he begrudgingly offered it to me. I shook my head as well. He moved off into the shadows.

"Friend?"

She shrugged. "I know him to see. It's nice of him to offer. I don't mind a smoke actually, but not here, the half of them are probably undercover anyway. You should know that."

"Aye, I know."

"And when I say I don't mind a smoke I'm not talking to you as Daniel Starkey, journalist, but Dan Starkey, drunk. All strictly off the record."

"Of course, of course. I will have no memory of this in the morning." Or I would remember it all, or remember it all wrong. It varied.

It didn't start out as anything more than a few quiet drinks with a stranger, but the drink and the time flew in. Patricia would already be out on the town. It was a Friday night tradition. Eight or ten of our friends would call round to our house after tea, have a carry-out and a smoke and then head out to a bar. Patricia was accustomed to my occasional non-appearances. If I didn't meet them in one or other of the bars we favoured with our custom I'd see them back at the house later where the drinking would continue. It was teenage partying on adult paycheques.

By 1 A.M. the bar was closed and Margaret started to make vague noises about going home, but I took her by the arm and

16

gently insisted that she come back to the house for a drink. She should meet my friends. She'd maybe meet a nice man. You never know who might be there. It seemed like a good idea at the time.

"I know your wife'll be there. What would she think you turning up with me?"

"Nothing. She's used to it."

"Thanks a lot, like, you make me sound so special."

"Don't be silly, I mean she doesn't mind me bringing people home for a drink, man or girl. She likes meeting people and she trusts me. She's no reason to mistrust me. And I don't mess around."

She looked unconvinced. "Unless you get the chance."

"Come for one. What harm's it going to do? It's only up the road."

"And you promise you won't write about me in the paper?"

"Don't be so paranoid."

She hemmed and hawed for a while, but I won her over, using charm and drunken logic. We went up Botanic Avenue and turned into the Holy Land, a tangle of terraced streets off the university that had mostly fallen under student occupation. It was late, but there was still plenty of life about, most of it drunk. We were home in five minutes.

There was music booming out of the house, barely muffled by wood and brick. It was a big house, three floors and an attic. We'd had it for three years and it still smelt like the student flats it had been, kind of musty and unshaven, an air of potential about it stifled by laziness. I opened the front door. Directly ahead of us in the kitchen Mouse was piling food into the microwave. He was thirty-two, powerfully built, an old mate. He turned as the door opened.

"BOUT YA, DAN!"

"Hi, Mouse. Pat here?"

He pointed towards the lounge. I could feel the throb of a bass through the door and people jumping up and down. I opened it and led Margaret in. The Rezillos' "Flying Saucer Attack" was blasting out of the speakers. Half a dozen of my friends were bouncing around to it, wearing album covers on their heads. They

17

looked like druids. It was a tradition. There was a stack of cans in the corner. I grabbed two and gave one to Margaret. She sat down on the arm of a ripped leather armchair. Immediately Gerry and Dawn pounced on her and had her up dancing. I wandered into the adjoining room.

Patricia was sitting on the Magic Settee. We called it that because most every time we sat on it in daylight we ended up making love. We hadn't sat on it for a while.

"All right?" I ventured.

She had her knees folded under her and a glass in her hand, vodka and orange.

She smiled. She looked brilliant. Save a line or two round her eyes she looked as beautiful as on the day she had asked me out.

I kissed her.

"Sleepy," she said.

"You want me to throw them out?"

"Nah. We're not here that long. I'm waiting for my second wind. Who's that you came in with?"

"Another victim for satanic sacrifice. Margaret. Young and maybe virginal. She'll do fine."

"Just the one? You usually manage a couple."

"You know how it is. I didn't have much time, what with the interview 'n' all."

She put a hand on my arm. "I take it things didn't go all that well. Moscow let you down?"

"Brazil let me down, but that's another story. Apart from that it went okay. I'll tell you in the morning. Party time."

I went back into the lounge as Patricia nodded off where she was. Someone had found an old glam compilation in the depths of our record collection and we formed ourselves into a circle for "Tiger Feet."

The needle jumped a couple of times and Mouse ripped off the album, throwing it on top of a burgeoning pile of sleeveless plastic. I took advantage of the momentary silence to quit the circle and follow Margaret into the kitchen. She opened the fridge and pulled a bottle of cider out, hugging it to her chest as she turned to me.

"Strongbow — brilliant." She held the yellow label up to me. "Two big bottles of this and you wake up in the morning with a pile of vomit in your slippers and six hours pregnant."

"That's a profound thing for a youngster like yourself to come off with."

"Youngster? Ha! I'm not as young as I look. How old would you say?"

"I'll start off at thirty-seven, then everything below that is a bonus."

"I'm twenty-two."

"Dead old. I'm old enough to be your big brother."

"You're old enough to have a lot of old records. It's like going into a time machine in there."

"You can't beat quality. That old punk stuff . . . timeless."

"Witless. I can't picture you as a punk. Did you have spiky hair? Bondage trousers? The whole heap?"

"Nah. Not really. Punk was more an attitude than a look. That's what so many failed to understand about it."

"You mean your mum wouldn't let you dye your hair blue."

"Yeah, a bit of that as well."

"I was eight when the Sex Pistols released their first single."

"Jesus."

She took a long swig from the bottle and offered it to me. I declined. Beer and cider do not for a good hangover make. Mouse had obviously discovered my Ramones live album. I grabbed Margaret's free hand and led her back into the heart of the dancing. You're never too old to rock 'n' roll.

The dancing was chaotic and by the end of the song I felt the spins coming on and headed for the door. I stumbled up two flights of stairs and found the bathroom mercifully empty. I locked myself in and was sick twice in the washbasin. White, my legs shaking, my head resting on the rim, I reached up to turn on the cold water tap. It was warm and sticky where someone had already been sick on it. I was sick again. I leant over the bath and turned the cold tap on, flicking off the shower control at the same time. As icy water rushed out I put my wrists under it and let it burn cold against my pulse, then splashed it up on to the back of

19

my neck and on to my face. I sat for a while on the edge of the stained cream enamel bath, my head bowed, until I began to settle down. There is no greater feeling than regaining control of your body after it has been usurped by a friend you have willingly invited in. I stood up, steadied myself against the wall and then, without breathing in, washed the sink and taps. I am nothing if not a responsible drunk. The draining water caught the rear end of a slater as it endeavoured to escape the smoothness of the sink, flushing it down the plughole. After a moment the little round shell of the woodlouse reappeared and began to ascend the curved sides of the basin again. I turned both taps on it and it disappeared again. Ten seconds later it reappeared and began its journey anew. I laughed and let it go. I hoped I could come up after going under for the second time.

I was just starting down the stairs when I noticed a light on in my study at the end of the hall. Margaret was standing just inside the door, looking at the books that lined the wall. I get fidgety when people are in my study. I don't like them looking for works in progress because mostly there are no works in progress. I'd been working on a conversation-based novel, like *The Graduate* or *The Commitments,* but my characters kept turning out shy and tongue-tied.

She looked round as I approached.

"You've good taste in books," she said.

"That makes me sound like I eat them."

"Devour them maybe. Do you? Devour them?"

"I haven't read them all. A lot are review copies, from the paper. Take any you want. There's a laugh-a-minute guide to macroeconomics up there or there's a biography of Skippy the Bush Kangaroo. Take your pick."

"I heard you being sick." I nodded. "I beat you to it. Feeling better?"

I nodded again. "My mouth tastes like a horse's arse."

"You want a mint?" she asked. I nodded. A wide grin split her face. When I looked closer there was a mint jutting from between her teeth. "My last one," she said, clamping down on it, her voice strangled like a ventriloquist's. She angled her face up towards mine, proffering the sweet. I bent to take it. My lips wrapped round the public half. She smelt good, I could feel her heat. My teeth tightened on it, but she wouldn't let go. We were both grinning inanely as we pulled at the mint. As I went for a better grip my lips touched hers and her mouth widened. The mint became a flapping border gatepost, there but unguarded, as our tongues met around it. In a moment it fell from our mouths and we remained clamped together, lost.

I did not think of Patricia. It was as if she did not exist for those few seconds, that my love for her was of a different time and place, that there and then there was only Margaret in the world and she was all that mattered.

When her voice came it was quiet, collected, like an exchange with a dying, unfamiliar relative. She could be a violent, argumentative, tantrummed woman; that was why the calmness of her discovery was all the more frightening.

"You have twenty-four hours to move out."

And then she was gone. I tried to pull away, but Margaret held me for precious seconds as Patricia walked sadly down the stairs.

Finally I pushed her away. I turned to follow my wife.

"That was nice," Margaret said. I looked back. I have never seen a more attractive brightness in a girl's eyes.

I turned away again. "I'm in trouble," I said. "I have to go."

3

Patricia's twenty-four-hour expulsion threat evaporated in the time it took for her to consume a triple vodka. It was replaced by a physical assault that Lizzie Borden would have been proud of. I tried the appeasement route and it worked as well for me as it had for Chamberlain.

My left eye was beginning to close and there was a thin trickle of blood running from my nose. It looked like brilliant sap leaking from a skeletal tree. That's how Margaret described it as she led me through the Holy Land; she had a good turn of phrase, for a drunk. I was in mumble mode, little of it favourable to Patricia. She had done more damage to my nose in three years of marriage than twenty years of amateur football. My nose had always been big, but it had not bent perceptibly to the left before I started going out with her. Besides that, she had a singing voice that could pickle eggs.

"As I believe the song says, the best part of breaking up is when you're having your nose broken," Margaret sang, putting a consoling arm round my shoulders as we crossed on to Botanic Avenue. "I think maybe I've gotten you in a wee bit of trouble."

"You could say that."

"I thought she didn't mind you bringing people home?"

"She doesn't. I've just never snogged with them before."

"Or just never got caught?"

"I'm telling you. I don't mess around."

"Nah, you go straight for it."

Margaret waved down a cab outside the York Hotel. I climbed into the back. She joined me. The driver turned to look at me. He was chubby-cheeked and had bushy eyebrows. He said: "Don't bleed on the seats, mate."

"Nah, I'm dryin' up," I said; it was a rare taxi to get at that time of night, so I held off on the abuse.

"Where to?"

"Antrim Road."

"Which part?"

"Up past Fortwilliam Golf Course. Ben Madigan."

"That's okay." He put the car into gear and moved off. "We're not allowed to stop lower down. Too risky. One of our boys got topped up there last month. They always seem to pick on fuckin' taxi drivers. All we're trying to do is earn a fuckin' livin', y'know?"

He was the type could talk himself into getting shot. We didn't try to feed his fire by continuing the conversation. I don't quite know when it was decided I was going to Margaret's.

Traffic was sparse. The lights were on in the city centre, but there was nobody in. A metaphor perhaps for our times. We crossed Carlisle Circus and were at the top of the Antrim Road in maybe ten minutes. We turned into Lancaster Drive. All the streets round about were named after different types of bomber — RAF as opposed to IRA. Margaret paid off the driver then led me to an electric-bill-red front door. I stumbled against it as she fumbled for a key.

"Coffee for you, I think," she said.

"It's been proved that coffee does nothing to sober you up."

"What would you suggest then?"

"Another beer, maybe."

"I thought you might be thinking that. Just as well I'm all out."

Just as well too, I thought. You could only take bravado so far. She led me into the lounge. It was small, uncluttered, one wall dominated by a large portrait of herself, the hair jet black, her face more pinched than in real life, but her eyes had the same deep-pool brilliance that had first captured me.

"A self-portrait?"

"How'd you guess?"

I shrugged. You didn't often get the chance to compare self-portraits with the self; but I knew most painted themselves thinner. There was a shuffling, sniffling sound from the kitchen. Margaret went and opened the door slightly and an elderly Jack Russell pressed his face through the gap. I could see a stump of a tail, maybe an inch erect above his hindquarters. He was snarling at me. He reminded me of Patricia.

"That's Patch. I won't let him in. He'd kill you."

"Don't worry, I like dogs. Dogs like me."

"He's not a dog, he's a fucking monster. At least that's how the police described him."

"He's not wanted, is he?"

"He's not wanted by anyone. That's the trouble. Nah, he got out a couple of weeks ago and bit a couple of kids. But of course the cops drag me down to the station. Three hours I was in there arguing with them."

"I know the form. First the good guy, then the bad, then the good, then the bad guy comes in and gives you a severe beating with a large orange spacehopper. It's common practice."

Margaret pushed Patch back into the kitchen and closed the door behind her. I heard her rifling. She opened the door again and flashed a garish box at me. "Pizza okay? In the microwave?"

I nodded. Probably do me good. It was one of those genuine Italian pizzas from the supermarket, the ones with the chef's own hair included.

I sat down by a mauve armchair and began sorting through her record collection. She had maybe fifty albums. A lot of Van Morrison, some Bob Dylan. A worrying series of Status Quo records. There was a Chris Rea album which was also a bit of a minus. I preferred diarrhoea; it wasn't very enjoyable either, but it didn't last as long and you could read a good book at the same time. At the back of the pile there was a pair of Loyalist flute band records, The Pride of Whitehill and the Wellington

24

Young Defenders. Bandsmen in silly uniforms with embarrassing plumes on their caps sat in rows on the cover like psychedelic soldiers.

Margaret came back into the lounge, carefully closing the door behind her. I held up the flute band records. "Lapse in taste here, I think."

"Oh, for God's sake. I forgot they were there. Not mine. They're my da's, I brought them with me by mistake when I moved in here."

"Well, what's he doin' with them? Is he mad?"

"Where we used to live, they came round the doors with them. You more or less had to buy them or you'd get a brick through the window. They were raising money for new band uniforms."

"Quieter ones, I hope."

"Guns for the boys, I presume."

"I dare say."

Margaret knelt beside me. She selected a Cocteau Twins record and slipped it on to the turntable. I'd seen them once in concert, a lot of years before. All syrupy guitar and high-pitched vocals. The sort of music you should buy on CD, then smash. Still, I was in no mood to argue, with throbbing nose and closing eye, and besides, as she sat back she collapsed into my arms and she kissed me long and soft. I tried moving my hands, but she pinned them behind my back. I didn't struggle.

We came apart with the pinging of the microwave. She jumped up and ran into the kitchen. I heard a low groan and a minute later she appeared at the door with the pizza neatly cut on to two plates. She said: "I think I may have had it in for too long."

She was right. It was like eating a discus.

We made love on the floor. It was nice. We had a bit of an argument about the lack of a condom. I volunteered to use my sock. She thought that idea was: a) disgusting; b) stupid. Socks weren't watertight, or whatever. She said, "You wear a sock, not only will I have a baby, but it'll come out wearing a bloody jumper." We compromised on my withdrawal.

I didn't. We British don't withdraw from Ireland.

25

*   *   *

Later, in bed, she said, "What are you going to do about the wife?"

I shook my head. I didn't know. There was a knot in my stomach; I didn't know whether it was guilt or satisfaction. We both drifted off to sleep.

I woke in the morning with a frightening headache, the sort of throbbing that demands that you wash your hair in liquid aspirin. My first thought was: oh shit. My second: get me out of here.

Margaret was still sleeping. We'd neglected to close the curtains and the sun was streaming in through the window. She'd thrown her half of the continental quilt off her some time during the night and her pale body gleamed like a baby's. I reached out to touch her, but pulled back. It was madness.

She began to stir. Her eyes opened, fluttered, closed, opened. "Hello," she said. Her voice croaked.

"I'll get you some water," I said. My voice croaked worse. I got out of bed and pulled my suit trousers on. They were a crumpled mess and they smelt of smoke and beer and there was a gravel scrape down one leg. I went into the bathroom, used the toilet, opened the window and looked at myself in a small round mirror that was attached with some Blu-Tack to the window frame. It was at the wrong height for me. I bent into the sink and washed my face in cold water. Still half bent, I examined my face again in the mirror. One eye was black and mostly closed. There was a hint of dried blood round my right nostril that the water had failed to dislodge and a slight bruise on the bridge of my nose. My hair was dank and tangled, but I didn't much mind that as long as I still had some.

There was a box cabinet on the wall to my left. It was mostly filled with makeup, but I found some paracetamol and swallowed four and a mouthful of water from the tap. I straightened up slowly, trying to close my throat to make sure they didn't come up again. They didn't.

I went downstairs and into the kitchen. Snarling greeted my entry. Patch sat in a brown wicker basket in the far corner in front

26

of an elderly twin-tub washing machine, his ears erect, grey muzzle pointed at me, eyes keen. I crossed to the back door, unlocked and opened it. Patch was up and out into the back in a flash. I didn't much mind who he bit, as long as it wasn't me.

Back upstairs, with two pints of cold water. Margaret was sitting up in bed, the quilt pulled up to her shoulders. Her hair was tousled and her eyes half-closed still, but she looked better than she had a right to. I handed her one glass and drew the quilt back so I could get in beside her. She moved her hands shyly to cover her breasts as I manoeuvred my way into the bed without spilling a drop. I was an old hand.

She said: "You're staying?"

I said: "You don't want me to?"

She smiled. "It's not that. Most men after a night like that — and all married men — want to make an early break for it."

"I'm not entirely sure I'm a married man."

"It'll be okay."

"What, you'll go round and patch things up for me?"

"The last man was here said he had to leave because he had to see the Cup Final. It was eight o'clock in the morning. He said he wanted to see the teams leaving for Wembley. Can you imagine doing that to someone?"

"Depends who was playing." I leant over and kissed her lightly on the lips. "Besides," I added, "I've nowhere to go."

The bedroom was small, warm. The floral wallpaper looked like it had been pasted in the sixties; maybe even the fifties. It was a single bed but it fitted us well; neither of us were fatties, yet. At the end of the bed there was a simple wooden dresser with a round mirror. There were a couple of cheap-looking jewellery boxes and some fluffy toys on the left. In a gold-effect frame on the right there was a colour photograph of a red-headed woman in upper middle age; resting against it was a much smaller colour snap, beginning to curl at the edges, of a young man, probably in his twenties. They didn't look dissimilar.

"Mother and brother, right?"

"Mother and friend."

"Her friend?"

27

"My friend."

"Boyfriend?"

"Ex."

"But still has a place in your heart."

She shrugged.

"What happened to him?"

"It's a long story."

"Shorten it."

"You don't give up, do you?"

"I'm a journalist."

"Is this off the record then?"

"No." I lifted the quilt and snatched a look at her body. "And I feel a column coming on."

"You're a dirty bastard," she said, poking me in the ribs, but it was a good-natured poke and she fell to kissing me next and in a minute we were making love again and it was every bit as good as the first time. When she was finished, and I most certainly was, she said: "You don't let your troubles interfere with your love-making, do you?"

"A trouble shared is a trouble halved." I had no idea what I meant, but it sounded quite appropriate.

We nestled back into the bed. It was a little after eleven. It was a Saturday morning and I'd no work until the evening. Patricia would maybe be wondering where I was, and maybe she wouldn't. I cared deeply, but I couldn't bring myself to do anything about it. I would phone her later, let her stew for a bit, let her realize she'd jumped to conclusions a little too quickly. It was only a kiss. A wee kiss. She didn't need to know about the rest. I could bluff it through. I was in bed with a woman who wasn't my wife. The first time. Ever.

"Tell me about the guy in the photo."

Her chin rested in the crook between my arm and chest, her thin hand on my stomach. "I had an abortion. I had to go to England for it. He didn't want me to have it. We split up."

"Okay," I said.

"I'm not looking for approval. I didn't want the baby."

"I didn't say a word. Your life."

28

"Yeah."

She said it with what might have been a melancholy sigh or a stifled yawn, or both. It was the first hint of bubblelessness she'd displayed, if it was the former, and about time if it was the latter.

"You still see him?"

"No. He's in prison. The Maze. He's a bad boy. Or he became one."

"Because of you?"

"I don't think so. He was going that way anyway. You've maybe heard of him. Pat Coogan?"

"Cow Pat Coogan?"

"Cow Pat Coogan. Yeah. The Paper Cowboy."

"I haven't heard that one, Paper Cowboy."

"You know the old joke. He was done for rustlin'."

She turned her head up towards me, held me with her eyes.

"Jesus," I said. "I kissed the mouth that kissed the mouth of Cow Pat Coogan. Mother would have me shot, were she still alive."

Coogan wasn't quite a legend — most all of them were dead — but he was a name, a character, in a largely characterless war. Reckless or stupid, he'd added a bit of life to the papers a couple of years back with a series of daring armed robberies round the country, north and south of the border. He'd briefly been the most wanted man in the Province, not so much for the viciousness of his crimes as for the extent of them. He was branded a Republican, but he always seemed more interested in money than freeing Ireland. When he was finally arrested he faced thirty-nine charges — thirty-eight for armed robbery on the word of a paid informer and one for stealing cattle. He was only convicted for the cattle.

"So how long were you going with him?"

"Not long. Six months maybe. Long enough to get pregnant anyway."

"Still hear from him?"

"No. And don't worry. He doesn't keep tabs on me."

"Who's worried?"

"It's quite hard to think of him being in prison. I keep thinking of sitting in the back row of the flicks with him, holding hands, sneaking a kiss. I think I was quite smitten. Then we split up. You know how it is. You think you're over someone then you hear he's taking a girl out for dinner and you feel all right about it, but then you hear he's meeting her again and you're in tears for seventy-two hours. Miserable. I hated him for doing that to me. He's a good-lookin' fella. There were a lot of broken hearts along the Falls when he went inside, and it wasn't for the love of Ireland."

"You'd not go out with him again then?"

"I don't know. I suppose in a way I still love him. But things would have to be different." Margaret ran her fingers through her hair, then through mine. "You're nice, y'know? A lot of men wouldn't like to hear a woman they've just slept with talking about old boyfriends."

"As long as they don't come through that door with a shotgun I don't mind who we talk about," I said. And I didn't. I had enough problems of my own without worrying about anyone else's, but I could listen all day. "Well, I take it you're from at the very least a fairly Loyalist family — I've seen those records, and they aren't a pretty sight — what did they make of Cow Pat Coogan? It must have been like bringing the Pope home for dinner."

"We may be Protestants, but we're not bigots. Mum got on with him all right, I suppose. Dad never met him. He's not home much."

"What's he do?"

"Don't ask."

It was a don't ask that was a do ask, but I took her at her word and left it. It was getting late and my head had cleared and my stomach was rumbling.

A high-pitched whine, gradually growing in annoyance, enveloped us as we lay in sunny silence.

I said: "I let the dog out a while back. I gather he wants in."

"If there's blood dripping from his mouth, you're in big trouble." Margaret jumped from the bed, her small bottom a marvel of tightness. She pulled on a T-shirt with Mickey Mouse on the front and hurried down the stairs. I heard the back door open and a scampering of paws.

When I went downstairs about ten minutes later Margaret was making a fry-up. Sausage, bacon, egg, fried bread, soda bread, potato bread, mushrooms, pancake, tomato; I liked the way she took it for granted that what I most needed after a night on the tear was a fry. She made me wait in the living room and we ate in there on the settee with the plates on our laps.

When we'd finished she went to wash up and I ordered a taxi. We sat awkwardly in the lounge for ten minutes until it arrived. What, after all, do you say? A pump of a horn from outside, and I stood up and slipped my jacket on. She stood up with me and followed me to the door in silence. She opened it and then stood back, looking up at me.

"Well," I said.

"Well," she said.

"This is it then."

"Yeah. Uh, thanks, I'd a really good night."

"Yeah, so'd I. With certain exceptions." I touched my eye. Margaret reached up and patted the side of my head lightly, then, on her tiptoes, kissed me on the lips.

"Y'know," she said, "apart from the bruising, you look like James Stewart when he was black and white."

I smiled and left.

4

The knot in my stomach was still there. Guilt. Satisfaction. The pizza. The fry. A mixture of all four. I felt uncomfortable. As the hangover receded, the worry set in. I have an inability to lie well. My face reddens and I talk nonsense. My wife is aware of this.

I had a faint hope that she might remember nothing. Awaken from her drunken stupor just wondering where I'd gotten to. I'd breeze in like nothing was wrong: I'd continued partying elsewhere. It had happened before. But then she'd look at her hands, feel them sore and bruised from striking me. And then she would remember. But a furtive kiss never hurt anyone, did it, Patricia? It was an aberration of alcohol. A whispering in the mouth of a fleeting acquaintance. She would have a vague memory of us fighting and an even vaguer memory of me upstairs with Margaret. A furtive kiss never hurt anyone. She'd been guilty of the same every Christmas as long as I could remember.

The city centre was already crowded with Saturday shoppers enjoying the sun. As we passed the city hall we had to slow down to allow a hundred or more Linfield supporters, all decked out in red, white and blue scarves and hats, and for the most part skinheads and Doc Martens, to cross the road, shepherded by about two dozen cops with Alsatians straining enthusiastically on chain leads. They would be off to cause havoc with local rivals, Glentoran, near the shipyard. Two winter-grey armoured police Land Rovers moved slowly against the flow of traffic behind them.

When I got home there was a letter waiting for me on the kitchen table. The envelope was plain white but my name was written in block capitals on the front in thick red strokes. It was either a note from Patricia or a final demand from the Blood Transfusion Service. I took it into the lounge and sat down amongst the empty beer cans. She hadn't bothered to tidy up.

> Dear Dan,
>
> I think we have a major problem. We're having too many fights. And we're drinking too much. We should think about what we want to do.
>
> I've gone to Mum's for a few days. Hope you enjoyed yourself with that girl. Bastard.
>
> Your wife.
>
> PS A man called Maxwell called. Wants you to call him. Said you had his number.
>
> PPS You know your mint-condition copy of the Sex Pistols' "Anarchy in the UK" (EMI label) you say is worth £300?
>
> I melted it under the grill.

And she had. I pulled the grill out from the cooker. The disc, hardened into black plastic stalactites, hung pathetically from the thin metal rungs of the grill.

I made a charge for the record collection. It was still haphazardly slung around the stereo system, most of the albums out of their sleeves, but it only took me a moment to realize that all of the records particularly valued by Patricia had already been whisked away. She knew me too well. I sat down to let my anger subside; I thought briefly about crying, but instead I started giggling. It had been a smart move on her part. She hadn't let her fury crowd her judgement, she knew how to strike where it hurt most and protect herself against reprisals. I wondered if she was laughing herself now.

I set about tidying the house. There were two or three half-full cans of Harp sitting about and I drank them as I worked. They were a bit warm and a bit flat, but I was trying to wean myself off Coke and I didn't reckon they were half as bad for me. I finished the tidying and adjourned to my study, the scene of the previous night's passion. It was shielded from the sun, pleasantly cool and dim. I tinkered with a few lines on a short story but didn't have the energy for it. I lay down on our bed and dozed off thinking about Patricia and about Margaret. Taking what must have been a thumping hangover into account, Patricia couldn't have left the house until quite late, so she'd still be on the road to her parents' house in Portstewart, a holiday-resort-cum-retirement-town up on the northwest coast. She couldn't stand her parents or Portstewart, all three of them old and decrepit and buffeted by the Atlantic gales, so she must have been pretty bloody angry with me to go to them. I'd call her later.

I woke with a start after maybe an hour and went downstairs to watch the football results come across the teleprinter on BBC1. Liverpool won, United lost, a good omen. I phoned Neville Maxwell. It was his home number, but he answered it on the second ring.

He said: "Maxwell."

"Hi. Dan Starkey. You called."

"Ah, yes, Starkey. Good man." Five words in and he'd already complimented me. "How are you?"

"Fine. Practising chopsticks. I think I've got them cracked."

"Ha, yes, mmmm. Listen, Starkey, I have a man coming in on Monday morning and I thought you might like to meet him and show him around."

"Sure."

"You know the form, Starkey, we've been over that. Let me know what you think of him and if he's up to scratch we'll maybe try to arrange for him to meet the Big Chief himself."

"Big Chief himself?"

"Brinn."

"Ah. Right. Got you now. What about him being up to scratch?"

"You know, sympathetic. He's an American, by the way, and we're quite keen for some positive coverage on that side of the ocean. A lot of money in it, if you know what I mean."

"For me?"

"For the country, Starkey, for the country."

"You didn't manage to find me a Brazilian then?"

34

"Ah, no. Not this time. Maybe another time, eh? Man's name is Charles Parker, no relation to the jazz person of that name, works for the *Boston Globe*. He'll be arriving at 10:30 on a puddle jumper into Sydenham. He's staying at the Europa. I've arranged for you to meet him there at 11:30."

"Okay. Sounds good."

"Charge all sundry expenses to me, I have an account there, and get receipts for everything else."

"No trouble."

"Oh, and Starkey?"

"Yeah."

"Americans tend to have an odd attitude to things. They may not appreciate all of your witticisms. Try not to be too much of a smartarse."

"No fear."

He put the phone down. I resolved to spend the next day swotting up on American history. I already had *The Alamo* on tape.

I got out of my dirty suit and showered. I pulled on my black jeans and a white short-sleeved shirt. I meandered between my tweed jacket and my stone-washed denim. Tweed got it. By the time I hit the street there was a pleasant early evening coolness settled on the city, blowing in off the lough, successfully battling the stench of the River Lagan. I called into the Empire Bar, housed incongruously in an old church beside the railway station on Botanic Avenue, and had half a pizza and a pint and then headed into the *Evening News*.

The daily paper and the Sunday paper were put together by two distinctive groups of journalists and editors who enjoyed an occasionally friendly rivalry. I was a columnist for the daily and a sub on the Sunday, so I fell between both camps. Sometimes they all hated me, and distrusted me, other times they all loved me, and distrusted me. But they seemed to like what I wrote, apart from those who didn't.

I was late. Sloth and Slow Ltd.

Paul McDowell, editor of the Sunday, saw me slope in.

There were five or six disks sitting by my terminal, all of them containing football reports.

McDowell was thin and pale-skinned; he looked kind of wasted even though he was an abstemious Christian. I knew rockers who'd OD on every drug they knew to get an effortlessly decadent look like his. He shuffled over as I took my seat and switched the screen on.

"Hi, Paul," I said.

"About time."

"Sorry." I pointed to my face. "Bit of an accident."

"You okay? What happened?"

"Car."

"Glad you could still come in."

"Wouldn't have missed it." Paul was a real softie for most of the time, but when the occasion demanded it he could run the tightest ship in the country. I flashed him a painful smile and turned to the screen. Half an hour was enough to turn them into English, then I dropped them down to the process operator to be run out for lay-out on the stone. It could have all been done on my own computer screen with a little extra investment, but times were hard and the unions were causing trouble.

While I waited for the stories to appear on the stone I wandered into an empty office and phoned Patricia's parents in Portstewart.

Her dad answered, his voice ragged.

"Hi, Joe," I said, "it's Dan. Your throat sounds bad."

"It is bad. Bloody sea air."

"You'd be better off down here."

"Don't I know it."

"Is Patricia there?"

"Aye, I'll get her," he said and then hesitated for a moment. "Listen, Dan, everything all right?"

"Sure."

"She seemed a bit . . ."

"Upset?"

"Yeah, upset. She hasn't said, of course, but it's nothing serious, is it?"

"Nah, Joe, never worry. Y'know women. Wrong time of the, if you get my drift."

I could almost hear him nodding at the other end of the phone. And to think I was once equality officer for the union.

"Ah. Understood. I'll get her for you."

I heard the receiver being set down and her dad limping away on the hardwood floor of their cottage. I could just about hear the wind whistling in the background.

More footsteps and — "What?"

"Now, there's a pleasant greeting."

"What do you expect?"

"What about 'Hello, darling, missing you terribly'?"

"Catch yourself on."

She wasn't finding me terribly amusing. I tried another tack.

"I'm missing you."

"I noticed that last night."

"That was nothing."

"You mean there's worse."

"No, I don't mean that. It was stupid. You know how plastered I was. I'd just been sick in the bathroom. She just grabbed me."

"Sure."

"Honestly. Jesus, Patricia, I could have been kissing a Jack Russell for all I knew. It shouldn't have happened, I know that. I'm sorry. Jesus, if you could see the state of my face you'd know I've already paid the price for it."

"It serves you right."

"I know."

There was a moment of silence. I said: "Will you come home?"

Silence still, then: "I don't know, Dan." Again: "I don't know."

"Jesus, Patricia, over a wee kiss. You've done as bad yourself for Christ's sake."

"It's not just her. Look — I just need a bit of time away from you, and this is as good a time as any when I have a bit of an excuse. I just . . . feel like I should be doing something else. We

37

need to change. We're getting older, Dan, and we're still running around like kids."

It is too easy to argue with loved ones. That is the attraction of strangers. You're on your best behaviour. I bit my lip. "Patricia, look, I'm not going to suddenly develop an interest in bloody gardening. I'm not thirty yet. You're not twenty-eight yet. We are young. Jesus, 'Trish — we've gotta have a good time while we can — you never know when that giant piano is going to fall on us from the sky."

"I know that. You've always said that. It's just that I don't know if what we're doing constitutes having a good time. Drinking, dancing, having a laugh, is that a good time if you do it every single bloody week with exactly the same bloody people? You saw last night what it can lead to."

"Well, what do you want to do? Stay in Portstewart? It's where old people go to die."

"Of course not. I don't know. But that's why I'm here. I want to have a think. Just a wee think. Give me a few days, eh? Then we'll talk. Just a few days."

"Do you still love me?"

"You know I do."

"Good."

"You still love me?"

"Yeah."

"Okay then."

Paul McDowell appeared at the office door and signalled me back to the stone, I nodded and stood up from the edge of the desk where I'd been sitting.

"I'll have to go. I'm in work. I'm needed. Someone needs me."

"Okay. Oh — Dan? Did you sleep with her?"

Sneaky. Suspicious. Tread softly.

"Don't be ridiculous. I hardly knew her."

"Well, where did you stay all night?"

"I tramped the streets for a while until the blood stopped." Easy, go easy. "Then I went round to wait for Mouse to come home. You know I did. I always do when we have a fight."

There was another pause. She said quietly, "I'll see you."

"Bye, love," I said and put the phone down.

I should have left it at walking the streets. Always the tendency to say too much. Glancing up, I saw McDowell had his back to me out at the stone, so I tapped in another number.

Mouse answered. He said: "YES?"

"Hi, Mouse. It's me."

"AH, MR. POPULARITY."

"Very funny."

"I'M SERIOUS. WE HAD TO RESTRAIN PATRICIA FROM TAKING A CARVING KNIFE TO YOU."

"Yeah, well, these things happen."

"NOT TO ME THEY DON'T."

Mouse never argued with his wife. I wouldn't argue with her either. She wasn't large or particularly overbearing, but she had a presence that was unnerving, a mental strength that enabled her to beat me at arm wrestling despite lacking any discernible muscles.

"Listen," I said, "I need you to do me a favour. If Patricia calls can you tell her I stayed in your place last night? It's important."

"LOVE TO HELP, DAN. PATRICIA CALLED FIRST THING THIS MORNING, LOOKING FOR YOU. UNFORTUNATELY MANDY GOT TO THE PHONE BEFORE ME AND TOLD HER SHE HADN'T SEEN YOU. I WOULD, OF COURSE, HAVE HAD THE PRESENCE OF MIND TO SAY THAT YOU'D BEEN AND GONE. BUT I DIDN'T HAVE THE CHANCE."

"Shit," I said.

"SORRY," Mouse said, and added: "DAN, NO HARM TO YOU, LIKE, BUT YOU SHOULDN'T MESS AROUND WITH WEE DOLLS. IT'S DANGEROUS."

"Thanks, Mouse," I said, "I'll bear that in mind," and put the phone down.

I'd have to think about this one.

Out on the stone things were progressing more quickly than normal, but I knew it wouldn't be long until some unfortunate occurrence pushed things into overtime. It happened every week without fail. The workers liked their overtime pay and didn't appreciate the benefits of getting the paper out earlier and improving circulation. Too long term. Within the next hour or so somebody would accidentally overload a computer, wipe out a disk or cause a power failure. The management knew all about it but couldn't do anything. It had always been like that.

The front page lead was fairly tame. A chapel had been burnt in the north of the city, not far from Margaret's home off the Antrim Road.

As I stood by the front page I said to Miller, who was pasting the story in, "So they've burnt another one." It paid to keep in with the workers. There was a photograph beside it with the charred building in the background and a priest carrying several planks of wood in front of it. There was no caption on it. I said: "What's he up to?"

Miller said: "He's building a temporary one."

"Good idea," I said, nodding sagely.

"They're all temporary," said Miller, turning narrowed eyes from the page to me.

"Right on," I said and moved. We still had to do some work on the bigot front.

From the front page, Miller shouted up the stone, "Paul, I need a wee piece of single column."

Behind me a voice replied, "I bet that's what your wife says too."

"At least mine speaks to me," Miller replied and laughter rumbled over the assembled workforce.

After work I bought a carry-out and went home. I sat in front of the box and watched a late-night film. Sylvester Stallone was in it. My old da always referred to him as Victor Stallion. For that matter he always called boxer George Foreman, George Formby. And once accused javelin thrower Tessa Sanderson of throwing a harpoon. And then I thought about Patricia again and how much I was missing her and how I'd dug my own grave over the phone.

Was all this wondering about her life just a reaction to me

kissing somcone, or had she been thinking this for a long time? I'd thought we were okay. Sure, things could be better. Every marriage could be better. She'd come round. Just because I wasn't at Mouse's didn't mean I slept with the girl.

And then I thought about Margaret. Young. Innocent, yet plainly experienced. Alone, perhaps, tonight. No, I told myself.

5

Charles Parker was two inches over six foot and built like a heavyweight, more Holyfield than Tyson. He wore a dark suit with narrow lapels and his trousers were very slightly flared. His shoes were brown leather, scuffed at the front. His hair, although clearly receding, was cut short. I was an hour and a half late arriving at the Europa. Illness, self-inflicted. Rolling Rock.

I put out my hand and he shook it warmly.

"You'll be Mr. Starkey," he said. A soft voice, curiously at odds with his appearance. The Whip and Saddle bar where we were standing is part of the Europa Hotel, the biggest hotel in Belfast. It was and is known as the most bombed hotel in Europe, an overused description and rather misleading. Not that many European hotels get bombed.

I nodded. "Sorry I'm late. Got held up." I pointed to my face . . .

"What happened to you? You look like shit."

"I always look like shit. Car accident. The prescribed medicine is an Irish whiskey. That should really be your introduction to Northern Ireland."

He smiled widely and signalled to the barman. "Nothing I like better than getting straight into some research, Mr. Starkey."

"My pleasure to be your guide, Mr. Parker."

He ordered two drinks and we adjourned to a side table of the bar overlooking Great Victoria Street.

"You're from Boston, right?"

"I work in Boston. I'm from New York."

"Big Irish interest in Boston, isn't there? Keen to see peace break out over here, I suppose."

"You could say that."

He lifted his glass to me, swirling the half-finished drink. "It's made nearby, I understand," he said.

"Aye. Up the road. Bushmills. It's popular with tourists."

"I've had it before — but I'll have to admit it tastes better in Ireland."

"Like Guinness tastes better in Dublin. And stick to calling it Northern Ireland, although you'll hear variations. If you're a Loyalist you'll call it Ulster, if you're a Nationalist you call it the North of Ireland or the Six Counties, if you're the British Government you call it the Province."

"And what do you call it, Mr. Starkey?"

"Home."

Parker came complete with a fancy hire car, a grey Saab which I drove round the city for him. I took him on the usual terror tour, up the Falls Road to see the Republican wall murals, up the Shankill to see the Protestant equivalent, past the shipyard, out to the old government buildings at Stormont and finally down to City Hall. He looked underwhelmed by it all.

"Smaller than I thought," he said.

"Lowest crime figures in the UK."

"Unless you count all the killings."

"Mmmm. You could say that."

Around 6 P.M. I nosed the Saab into a car park in front of the BBC's headquarters on Ormeau Avenue where I'd arranged for us to watch an interview with prime minister candidate Brinn being recorded. I thought he might find it interesting.

"Will I have a chance to speak to Brinn?"

"No. Not today. I'm working on that. Maybe tomorrow, maybe the day after. You in a rush?"

"No rush, just keen."

"Keen is my middle name," I said.

43

We were checked and searched by three elderly security men at the entrance and two of them guided us to a lift. They gave Parker a wary glance as he stepped into it. "You know there are only about six black families in the whole of Ireland?" I asked him, punching the floor number.

I smiled pleasantly at the security guards as the door slid across. They glared back.

We were met at the top of the stairs by a small grey-haired woman immaculately dressed in a light-green trouser suit. Kay McCrory. She'd been in charge of the press office at the BBC since I'd first entered journalism, and for several decades before that.

She introduced herself to Parker, then turned on her heel and led us down a corridor.

"Nice to see you again, Kay," I said.

"Likewise."

"How have you been?"

"Fine."

She opened a door and showed us into a small viewing room. There were a couple of musty-looking settees, a colour TV, and a tray of sandwiches and some bottles of beer and a bottle of wine on a small table in the corner. The TV was switched on. I could see Brinn having makeup applied to his face.

"They're due to start recording in about twenty minutes," Kay said to Parker, "and it should last about half an hour. I'll come back towards the end. If you have any questions then about the programme I'll be glad to answer them."

Parker shook her hand again. "Thank you for your help," he said.

"No trouble at all."

She closed the door behind her without looking at me.

"Good friends, are you?" Parker asked.

"She doesn't like what I write about her programmes."

"You a TV critic?"

"An everything critic."

"And what do you say about her programmes?"

"That they're all crap."

44

"I can see why she mightn't like you."

I shrugged. "Par for the course."

I walked over to the table and opened a couple of bottles of Harp. I handed one to Parker, then tapped the TV screen lightly with my own. "And this, God bless him, is our next prime minister."

"Yeah, I recognize the face. Mark Brinn. Leader of the Alliance Party. Widely seen as the best hope for Northern Ireland: an acceptable compromise to both the Unionists and Nationalists. That's what my file says. What do you make of him?"

"It doesn't matter much what I make of him. That's not why I'm here."

"You're a Unionist writer, I'd be interested in the Unionist view."

I took a seat in front of the TV and a slug from my beer. "Who told you I was a Unionist?"

"My file."

"Must be some fucking file if it has me in it."

"Hey, I'm a journalist. I'm paid to know these things."

"Keen as well."

He shrugged his shoulders. "Well?"

"You want a personal opinion I'll give it to you. If you want one from your official guide I'll give you the official opinion."

"The official opinion I know. He's the good guy."

"Right."

"You don't agree?"

"I don't disagree."

"But?"

"Personally speaking, off the record?"

"Of course."

"I just love him to bits." Brinn had finished having his makeup applied now and was staring patiently into the camera. He had a thin face, sallow despite the makeup. His nose was long, slightly bent, but he was not unattractive in a middle-aged successful executive kind of way. "I love him because he's such a salesman. Politically and literally. What do you know about his background?"

45

"Uh . . ." Parker thought for a moment, his eyes dulled and then suddenly bright as if he'd just remembered an awkward date in a history exam. "Right . . . born in Cookstown, County Tyrone . . ." He pronounced it Tie-rhone.

"Tyrone . . . pronounced Ter-own . . ."

"Yeah, whatever, Ter-own . . . to Protestant father and Catholic mother, educated locally . . . didn't go to college . . . into business, successful, injured in a terrorist bomb attack on local restaurant 1974, in which eight people died, suffered severe burns . . ."

"Although you wouldn't know it."

". . . spent six months in the hospital, on release resumed business and joined Alliance Party. His status as victim and peace campaigner quickly catapulted him into the limelight, became local councillor and then Member of Parliament in 1980. Elected leader of the party in 1987."

"Dead on. You want to know what says more about him than any of that, than any speech or anything you'll hear him say in a minute?"

"Of course."

"His name."

"Brinn? Mark Brinn? What about it?"

"Your file probably has this, if it's any good, but doesn't understand it. Nobody understands it, 'cept me of course."

"Which makes you the smartest man in the country, or the stupidest."

"Exactly."

"Okay, so what about his name?"

"Until 1972 his surname was O'Brinn. Nineteen seventy-two was one of the worst years we've had. Major death and destruction. O'Brinn is ostensibly a Catholic name. When he opened his first furniture shop in 1972 he had his name changed by deed poll to Brinn. So nobody would know he was a Catholic."

"Is Brinn, as a name, Protestant?"

"It's not anything, it's neither one thing nor the other, you'll barely find another like it in the phone book. It's a compromise

46

name, like the Alliance is a compromise party. He changed his
name to make money by not offending anyone. A lot of people
wouldn't do business with you back then if you were a Catholic."

"That's changed?"

"Mostly."

"So what are you saying, you don't like him because he
changed his name?"

"Yeah."

Parker wiped his hand across his brow. Mockingly. "Well
thank God that was all off the record — that's too hot for me to
handle."

I shrugged, emptied the bottle, and fetched another two.
Parker finished his off and then accepted the second.

"You don't understand — it's the wee things like that that
mark a man out."

Parker took a long drink, watching the screen as the picture
shifted to the interviewer having a microphone attached to his tie.
"According to my file . . ."

"I must see this file . . ."

"Brinn has never been religious. Why should he lose business having a Catholic name if he isn't religious? It makes perfect
sense to me."

"Yes, but you're American."

"And exactly what do you mean by that?"

"Nothing. Here we go."

The interviewer had begun his introduction. I reached over
and turned the sound up as Mark Balmer started his questioning.
Balmer's thin grey hair glistened under the studio lights, his pink
skin looked sunburnt. "If I can take you back to your very earliest
days in business, Mr. Brinn," Balmer began, "you felt the need to
change your name from O'Brinn to just plain Brinn. Could you
explain that decision? It seems to me in some way you were
denying your Catholicism."

Parker looked across at me. "Two smart men in this country," he said.

"In a way perhaps I was," Brinn replied gently. "I think it

47

was possibly a way of expressing my resentment at the state of affairs in this country — the fact that just because there was an 'O' at the start of my name a certain section of the community automatically believed that I was, in some way, the enemy. In fact, although I was brought up a Catholic, I ceased to be a practising Catholic in my teenage years. I am a God-fearing man, Mr. Balmer, but neither Protestant nor Catholic. I simply believe in God."

I tapped the TV screen again with my bottle. "And butter wouldn't melt in your mouth."

"Seems a reasonable argument to me," Parker said.

"You come from a land of salesmen. He's just renounced his religion, but he's still going for the God vote."

"Perhaps people admire his honesty."

"Who ever admired honesty? Catch yourself on."

Balmer meandered through Brinn's career with an admirable thoroughness that had us both yawning. Near the end he came to the standard Brinn question and the standard Brinn answer.

"Your experience in the restaurant bombing had a tremendous effect on you, didn't it?"

"Uh, no, didn't change me a bit," I said to the screen. Parker shushed me.

"Of course, of course. You know I really don't like to talk about it, but it was, in some ways, a catharsis, the bomb itself, hospital, the sympathy and understanding of ordinary people from both sides of the community. It gave me hope and, I suppose, an ambition, an ambition to try to do something to stop such things happening again."

"Shite," I said.

"You really don't like him, do you?"

I gave him one of my better shrugs. "Do you want another drink or will I swipe this wine?"

Parker looked at me for a moment, his pupils darting about in his brown eyes like lemons on a fruit machine. Weighing me up. "How about we have another drink, then you swipe the bottle?"

"Sounds good to me."

48

I handed him the bottle and took one for myself. The screen had just gone blank as the door opened again and Kay entered. She smiled at Parker.

"That will be going out tonight," she said to him.

"I appreciate you letting me see the recording," Parker said. "It was most informative."

"No trouble at all."

I stood up, buttoning my coat so that she couldn't see the wine bottle under my arm. "Balmer come out of the closet yet, Kay?"

"You tell me, Starkey, you're the newshound."

"Newshound?"

"I think she means son of a bitch," Parker ventured.

"Jesus, a double act. What is this, *The Black and White Minstrel Show*?"

Kay took Parker by the arm and led him to the door. "Don't be offended by our Mr. Starkey, he doesn't know any better. You read any of his stuff? He's a national institution. Like rickets."

Outside it had started to rain, a fine cool rain that was pleasant to walk in. "Leave the car," I said. "Let's go for a drink, 'less you have something planned."

"Not me, I'm a stranger in town. Don't you have a wife to go home to?"

"She can wait."

"She must be an understanding woman."

"The best," I said, but as I walked she slipped from my mind like a one-night stand and I found myself thinking again of Margaret.

6

We were in a bar in the centre of Belfast, somewhere I didn't know. It was jam-packed, sweaty. The Clash were singing "White Man in Hammersmith Palais" out of the biggest jukebox I'd ever seen. I spent twenty minutes trying to get a drink, but every time I squeezed my way to the bar I got squeezed out again. It went on and on and on.

Parker was in a big black baggy suit. He wasn't having any trouble getting a drink. The people just melted away in front of him, but he wouldn't buy me one. I kept asking but he kept saying I'd had enough. He looked uncomfortable in the heat; sweat stood out on his high forehead and every minute or two a little tear of it trickled down his cheek.

And then there was a breath of fresh air as the doors opened and the crowds began to ooze away, called to another bar by some unheard siren, some Lady Vodka.

I made it to the bar. I got a drink. Parker was beside me. I said, "It's starting to thin out a bit."

His face went all serious, his brow furrowed like a potato field. "Are you calling me bald?" he demanded.

I shook my head, started to explain the expression but he put a big hand on my shoulder and squeezed tight. "You call me that again and I'll break your face," he said.

I turned away from him, taking a giant slug from my glass.

Jesus. Touchy, touchy. I decided not to hold it against him. We'd both had a lot to drink and he'd done most of the buying. I'd buy him another, he'd cool down.

Before I could order, my eyes met Patricia's. She was walking the length of the bar towards the ladies' toilets. God, she looked good. She walked straight past me.

I said, "Patricia?"

She stopped, turned uncomprehendingly towards me, her eyes focused in, widened in recognition.

"Fuck off," she said.

She walked on. I stared after her, mortified. My wife. Fuck off. I turned to Parker, gave him a knowing all-men-together smile and said: "Her loss."

"Hair loss?" Parker shouted and before I could make a run for it he knocked the glass from my hand and caught hold of my arm. He produced a big shiny pair of scissors from his pocket and cut off two of my fingers and stuffed them in his ears. "Explain that to your mum!" he cried and loped off towards the men's toilets with a big grin on his face.

And then I woke up.

Noise.

Distant at first, then closer, insistent. As the fog lifted I recognized the sound of the phone mixed in with something closer, just as repetitive but faster, more annoying. I stumbled from bed, naked but for my socks, and made for the phone. I stopped on the way past to lift the needle from the record player where it had been stuck on the third verse of the Skids' "Working for the Yankee Dollar" for just over seven hours.

I lifted the receiver and said hello. Nothing came out. I cleared my throat and tried again. "Huh?" I said.

"Hello, could I speak to Daniel Starkey please?"

I recognized the voice.

"You've got him."

"Ah, Starkey, good man, didn't recognize the voice."

"A bit of a sore throat."

"Well, yes, that time of year, isn't it?" What was he talking about? "Just checking on yesterday. How did it go with your Mr. Parker?"

"Fine, no problems at all."

"Good, good, fine. You're seeing him today?"

"No." In fact, I couldn't remember what we'd arranged. All I could remember was that both of us had trouble speaking by the time he paid for my taxi home. "I've to phone him. He's out on his own today."

"What did you make of him?"

I shrugged and for a moment I was puzzled by his lack of response. "He's keen," I said quickly. "He seems to know his stuff."

"Good. We've had a cancellation, so I've been able to set up a meeting with Brinn for him. Tomorrow, 3 P.M., Red Hall. Can you get him there?"

"Of course."

"Good man."

"Do I get to sit in on the meeting?"

Maxwell was silent for a moment. "Okay — but with conditions. You're there as an observer only, nothing he says goes into your paper."

"If it's going into his . . ."

"Nothing in yours."

"Okay."

"And you get him there sober."

"Parker has a drink problem?"

"You know what I mean."

I shrugged again. "What are you implying?"

"I'm not implying anything. I'm telling you. Don't go hitting the drink tomorrow. This is serious. Leave the expense account alone for tomorrow."

"Why give me the job if you don't trust me?" I asked. I could feel a sulk coming on.

"Starkey, do you have any idea how many foreign journalists there are floating round this place at the moment?"

"I . . ."

52

"Hundreds. We have to use who we can as guides. And don't take that personally. You know yourself you're no one's idea of a public relations executive."

I sat at the bottom of the stairs, cradling the receiver in the crook of my neck. There was a thin layer of dust on the telephone stand. "Okay," I said, "maybe I'm a little rough round the edges, but you can depend on me."

"I know we can."

I opened the fridge and took out a couple of eggs and a copy of the previous night's *Belfast Telegraph*. I must have been drunk to buy the rival paper. There wasn't much worth reading. I scrambled the eggs and took them through to the lounge. I put on the Ceefax. It had been another night of fun and games across the city. Two taxi drivers had been shot for being Catholic. One was on his first night on the job. He'd been called to an address off the Lisburn Road and his car sprayed with automatic fire. His wife's first husband had been murdered by the Ulster Volunteer Force twenty years before. Two Unionist election workers pasting up posters had been attacked and badly beaten by a gang of skin-heads off the Ormeau Road. A string of hoax bombs had been left in various shopping centres on the outskirts of the city. For all we'd known, meandering drunk through the city centre, it could have been another world.

After breakfast I left a message for Parker at his hotel. He was already out being keen. Then I phoned Patricia. As I dialled, I saw her face as it had been in my nightmare. Cold. Beautiful. She answered on the third ring. Her voice sounded small, remote, down.

"It's your favourite husband," I said, cheerily.

"Your joviality is misplaced."

"I'm sorry."

"It doesn't matter."

We lapsed into half a minute of silence. She wasn't going to be the first to break it. "When're you coming home?" I asked.

"I've already told you, Dan. I need some time."

53

"Ach, come on. Come on home. I need you." It felt strange to say it. I hadn't said it for a long time. Maybe never.

"No."

"I'm not as bad as you think I am." Her hair would be pulled back into a bun, the way she always had it when things were serious. Smoking a cigarette, but not enjoying it.

"I didn't say you were bad."

"No, but you're thinking it."

"I've already said what I'm thinking. I just want you to leave me alone for a while, Dan, please."

"You don't want me to come up and see you? I could be up in a couple of hours."

"No."

"Will you call me when I can see you?"

"Sure." It was difficult to detect any note of affection in her voice. She was hiding it well.

"Dan?"

"Yeah?"

"You know when you do something like that, like what you did, it puts a wall up between us, a very big wall. It can be impossible to get over."

"Walls are there to be got over. They got over the Berlin Wall. They pulled it down."

"You're asking me to build something out of rubble. It can't be done."

"It can be done."

"You just get another crazy wall."

"Maybe you get something better."

"I doubt that." Her voice was starting to crack. I wanted to put my arms around her and say sorry. "I have to go," she said quietly and put the phone down.

I sat on the stairs for a minute, holding the receiver. I thought about driving up to see her, regardless. I would be irresistible in the flesh. I replaced the receiver. My head was aching, my hair felt sore, my throat was sore. I drank from the tap in the kitchen, then went back to bed. I would go and see her when the hangover had gone.

I was just drifting off to sleep when the phone went again. I rushed downstairs. "Patricia?"

"Uh . . . no. It's me. Margaret. I've been trying to get in touch with you for ages."

Margaret. I had a vision of her naked. "I've been out a lot."

"You weren't avoiding me?"

"Of course not."

She gave a little chuckle. Nervous. Cute, but nervous. "I think you'd better come and see me."

"I . . ." I wouldn't. I shouldn't. I can't. I can. Pregnant? No. Too soon. An interesting sexual disease? No. I'd be itchy. She's in love. Not beyond the realm of possibility. More sex? Jesus. I was sweating.

"She's caused a lot of trouble."

"What? Who has?"

"Your wife. She didn't tell you?"

"What do you mean? Tell me what? She's not here. She's left home. She's in Portstewart. Tell me what?"

"Come and see me, Dan. It wouldn't do it justice telling you over the phone."

"I . . ."

"Please . . ."

She put the receiver down before I could reply. I thought of Patricia and my Sex Pistols single. What could she possibly have done to Margaret? I sat with my head in my hands. My first instinct as ever, in time of crisis, was to run away.

I put on Dr. Feelgood live. Turned it up loud. I needed the fast urgent blues beat of the Feelgoods. Pick-me-up music. I went upstairs and put on some cleanish underwear and a pair of black jeans. I selected a faded Tintin sweatshirt from the wardrobe. Pointy Head and Snowy were on the front with "60 Ans d'Aventure" emblazoned across the belly-button line, which was like the Plimsoll line save that it had seasonal fluctuations. Tintin's cheatin' heart, the adventure Hergé never wrote.

I went back downstairs and phoned for a taxi. A gruff voice at the other end said: "Yes?"

55

"Uh, I'd like to book a cab."

"Where to?"

"North Belfast. Lancaster Avenue."

"What's your telephone number?"

"Sorry?"

"Your number. We need your number."

"What on earth for?"

"Security."

"I can't go giving my number out to complete strangers."

"Okay."

He put the phone down.

I rang back. "What do you mean, security?"

"I mean, too many of our drivers have been shot up there. We have to check out our passengers."

"Fuck, times are getting bad."

"Fuckin' more dangerous being a cabbie than a peeler these days. What's your number?"

"Of course by revealing my number, it could end up with anyone."

"It could. It won't."

I gave it to him. He phoned me back and I ordered. It arrived within five minutes. A middle-aged woman was driving, a cigarette hanging out of her mouth.

"Starkey?" she asked, her voice an angry rasp.

I nodded. "That's me." I climbed in. The back seat was thick with dog hairs.

"That's some fuckin' crap you write in the paper."

"Thanks."

"Mind you, the husband loves it."

"Good."

"But then he's a stupid fucker."

"I see."

"But not stupid enough to drive a fuckin' taxi, that's for sure."

"No."

"Not that stupid to know he's on to a winner by gettin' me to drive the fucker 'cause he's scared of getting topped."

56

"No."

As we turned onto Great Victoria Street she wound down her window and spat. Not so much a question of Finishing School as never having finished school. She was maybe forty. Gnarled-looking. She wore a creamy-white cap-sleeved T-shirt that revealed a blotchy tattoo: the letters UVF, only her arm was so thin that the F was lost round the horizon and all you could really see was UV, like she was advertising a sunblock. Her hair was wild and greasy, tinged red. Or maybe it was the world's first nicotine-stained hair.

The Belle of Belfast City dropped me at the corner of the estate. "I'm not going into that fuckin' Fenian hole," she said.

I thanked her and walked down towards Margaret's. Even from the end of her street I could see that every window in her house had been smashed.

Jesus, Patricia.

7

She had tears in her eyes. She threw her arms around me and hugged me tight and before I knew what I was doing I was hugging her tightly back, like we were long-term lovers not the remnants of a one-night stand. We had hardly exchanged more than a few words in sobriety. But it felt right. Margaret kissed me lightly and I could taste the salt on her lips. She took me by the hand and led me into the lounge. Her portrait stared down at me and if I hadn't known better I'd have sworn that those oily eyes followed me across the room to where she sat me down in an armchair beside the record player. It was like being in an episode of *Scooby Doo*. I could hear Patch growling from the kitchen.

Margaret said: "I'm sorry."

"What on earth have you got to be sorry for?"

"I should have left you alone."

"Rubbish — I'm as responsible as anyone." She sat on the floor, her legs folded under her and looked up to me, her black eyeliner smudged, tear stains on her cheeks like a dried-up river bed. My hand rested on her shoulder, I raised it to her cheek, held it lightly, then bent towards her and kissed her. Lingering.

"Tell me about it," I said when we had finished.

She was wearing a short black skirt over black tights and a black sweater; her hair was tied back, not as spiky as on our first meeting. Her pale face looked fragile. She took a tissue from her sleeve and blew delicately into it.

"There was a knock at the door on Sunday morning and she was just standing there. I didn't know what to say. I just stared at her. I was in shock. She said, 'It's taken me a while to find you,' but it wasn't angry, really cool, really calm. She had this bag with her, like a shopping bag. She opened it up and took this potato out."

"A potato?"

"A potato. She held it up to me and said: 'This is a Comber potato. If you're going to sleep with him you can bloody well cook for him as well,' and she heaved it through the front window. I just stood there. I didn't know what to do. Then she took another one out and fired it through the top bedroom window. She did every window in the house."

"Jesus."

"I just stood there the whole time, frozen. All the neighbours were out but they didn't go near her, just stood around watching. When she finished the potatoes she turned and went to her car — then she turned and said: 'He likes turnip as well. I'll be back to-morrow.' I just went in and bawled my eyes out.

"I cleared the glass up later and some friends of my dad helped me board the place up. I wouldn't let them put glass in. I didn't want her coming back and doing it all over again. But she didn't come back. Not yet."

"Did you call the police?"

"No."

"Why not?"

"I couldn't have your wife arrested. I couldn't. Dad told me not to. He said it would be too embarrassing for him if it got into the local papers."

"God love him."

"No, it would, he's having some sort of trouble at work, he wouldn't say, but I could tell he needed me in bother like a hole in the head."

"I don't care about his troubles, I care about you."

I was looking at Margaret, but I could see Patricia. Stony-faced, a cool white anger masked by steady determination. Outside the house, bag of potatoes in hand. A novel revenge, calculated to cause the maximum of embarrassment and expense. She would have guessed that Margaret wouldn't go to the police. She'd discovered my lie, fumed in Portstewart, then calmed down sufficiently to work up a meaningful revenge. Indeed, she would have shopped around for the cheapest potatoes. Carried out the attack and driven back up to the coast. And no hint of it when next I spoke to her. I took Margaret's hands and said softly: "I'm sorry, I'm really sorry. I should have handled things better."

"What could you have done? She had a right to be angry."

"She had no right to do that. She should have punished me."

"Maybe she did. Maybe she thinks that if you care about me, the best way to hurt you is to attack me."

"I assured her I didn't care about you."

Her fingers tightened in mine.

I let her hands go. "What do you want me to say?" It came out sharper than I meant. I sat back. Confused. What was I supposed to say? "I've only known you a few hours." And I knew then it was long enough, but I couldn't say it. I couldn't say anything.

"I don't expect you to declare undying love, Dan. But I know what I feel." And her eyes were wide and beautiful and magnetic.

"Margaret . . . I don't mean I don't feel for you . . . but, Jesus, we've only known each other a few hours . . ."

"What difference does that make? You know from the start. As soon as you meet someone you know whether they're the right one. What's the point in taking five years to get to know someone you know you're not going to end up with?"

I got up and walked to the window. The hardboard across it gave the room an odd feeling, like we were in a children's fort, playing at being adults. Maybe we were, with all the petty jealousies and fights of pre-pubescence. And at the end of the day we'd all be friends. I'll say.

"What'd you tell your dad?"

"I wasn't going to tell him anything. He just arrived round. He nearly had a heart attack."

"I'm sure he did. What'd you say, redecorating?"

"A jealous boyfriend. He chewed me out, like, but he's paying for it. He couldn't be too nasty about it, the only reason he came round was to give me my birthday present."

"Happy birthday."

"Thanks, but it's not for another two weeks. He brought it round because he didn't think he'd be here for it. Said he was going abroad on business."

"Ah, well, it's the thought that counts."

"Thought nothing." Margaret leant over to the record player and removed a cassette tape from a shelf just above it. She tossed it to me. It was one of those cheap compilation tapes made up of classical music that had been used in popular television commercials. "I'd rather listen to static. Keep it."

I shrugged and slipped it into my pocket. "If you insist."

"That's how well he knows me, a shoddy bloody tape like that."

"I gather you're not too close then."

"Close isn't the word for it."

"Maybe your mum will get you something nice."

Margaret smiled. "Optimist." She wiped at her eyes with the back of her hand, making the makeup worse in the process, but it was a small sign of recovery at least.

I walked back over to her, knelt down, put my hand on her shoulder.

"I love my wife, you know?"

"She's a hard bitch."

"She can be. She doesn't believe in hiding her feelings. But I do love her."

A thin smile played on her lips, those eyes bored into me again.

"What are you saying?"

"I'm not saying anything. I'm just telling you. You should know. Whatever happens between us, I love my wife."

"Are you saying you can't love me?"

"No. I don't know. Maybe I will. Maybe it's in the future. All I'm saying is that no matter what I've done to my wife, no matter what she's done to me, or to you, I love her."

"Maybe you can love two people."

I nodded slowly. "Maybe."

She took my hand in hers, stood up and led me upstairs to her bedroom. I was a sucker for subtle seduction.

Later, she persuaded me to go out and get us something to eat and drink. There wasn't a lot of arm twisting involved. She fancied chips, so I trotted up to a row of shops a couple of hundred yards away to a place called Victor's she had raved about, but it was closed. A sign written in the thick black marker strokes of a child or an educationally subnormal person said CLOSED DUE TO VARI-COSE VEINS which under normal circumstances would have been enough to put me off food, but I was physically drained and needed the calories. Another hundred yards up there was a pizzeria. They took a note of my order and told me to come back in twenty minutes.

I crossed the road to a phone box and was pleasantly surprised to find it in working order. I phoned Patricia. Her dad answered. He said she wasn't in and after some persuasion he told me she'd said she was going down to Belfast to collect some things but not to tell me if I phoned.

The pizzeria's twenty minutes turned out to be forty-five and even then they didn't look particularly concerned.

"Hey, sometimes you've got to wait for quality," a spotty guy behind the counter said when I complained. When I was going out the door I heard him say quietly, "And sometimes you've got to wait for shite too," but I was too hungry to punch his lights out. And too small.

On the corner of Margaret's street a small, thickset man with a thick moustache and short black beard stopped me and asked for a light.

"Sorry, I don't smoke."

"Never worry, mate," he said, moving past me with a curly, annoying grin on his face, "stunts your growth anyway."

Margaret's front door was slightly open. I pushed it and walked into the darkened hall. I shouted: "The pizza man's here!"

up the stairs and headed for the kitchen. There was no reply. I turned the light on in the lounge and stopped dead in my tracks. It had been turned upside down. Seats ripped, drawers emptied, records out of their sleeves strewn across the floor. Margaret's portrait had been slashed and hung in tatters from the wall. I dropped the pizzas and ran up the stairs in the dark to Margaret's room.

It was lit by the dull orange glow of her heavily shaded bedside lamp. Margaret was in bed, the thin cotton sheet pulled up around her neck, just as I'd left her. Her eyes were focused on the far wall, on nothing.

I said: "What the fuck's going on?"

Her eyes shifted to mine, her lips parted slightly and she made the nearest sound possible to a human whimper.

I ran to the bed. As I touched the side of it her face contorted in pain.

"Jesus, Margaret, what's . . . ?"

I pulled the sheet back. She was naked underneath. Her upper body was soaked in blood. It oozed from three or four black-tinged holes. I felt her whole body vibrate. I tried to pull her to me, hold her safe, but it was like trying to pick up a spider's web intact, blood fell everywhere and she let out a little helpless cry. I let her back softly on to the pillow, her eyes wide now, pleading hopelessly. She raised her arm slightly, touched me, pulled me lightly towards her. She kissed my cheek. Lips hard, cold. Her head moved sideways to my ear and I could barely hear her whisper above the tom-tom thump of my own heart.

"Dan . . ."

Barely a voice at all.

"Dan . . . div . . ."

Another tremor shook her.

"Margaret . . . shhhh . . . let me get . . ."

"Dan . . . no . . . no . . ." And her words were slurred. "Dan . . . divorce . . . Jack . . . divorce . . . Jack . . ."

And then her head fell back and she was silent. She took a couple of shallow breaths. And then she was dead.

I stared at her for I don't know how long. I pulled the sheet back up over her, tucking it in under her chin so that only her calm, white face showed. Her eyes were closed and she looked like she was only asleep.

Suddenly my whole body was shaking uncontrollably, great rolling waves of shock that rocked the whole bed. I gripped the side of it till they stopped, my blood-soaked hands putting eerie prints on the sheet.

I stood up but my legs buckled under me and I crashed to the floor unconscious.

I thought people only fainted in films. And then it was only women.

I don't know how long I was out. I didn't dream. I was still on the floor beside Margaret's bed. For a brief moment I hoped it had been a dream, but then I saw Margaret's face again and the tears began to roll down my cheeks. I scurried away across the floor and into the bathroom.

I was sick in the washbasin, retched until there was nothing left to come up, then washed my face. I sat down on the toilet seat to stop myself shaking. Margaret was dead in the other room. Dead in the other room. Dead. Dead.

And then I heard it.

A soft, stealthy creaking from the stairs; soft, but not soft, like a dormouse in jackboots. In my rush to be sick I hadn't turned the bathroom light on and the hall was still in darkness. The bathroom door was three quarters closed. The only light came faintly from Margaret's room. I could barely make out a small shadowy figure making its way cautiously up the stairs.

I tried desperately to control the vibrations that were racking my body, my leg was tapping against the cool ceramic of the toilet bowl like some kind of spastic Morse code, shouting out, HEY, I'M IN HERE. My breath only came in rasping flurries, welcomed on each occasion by a manic waving of my arms like a mime artist on acid.

The figure drew nearer. Margaret was dead. Margaret was

dead and I knew in every inch of my shuddering body that I was next, this dumb spinning top of a body was going to die on a toilet seat in his lover's house.

And then I was up from the seat, possessed of a madness born of desperation, determined to go out fighting, a last gasp at life that was about to be taken from me for a reason I would never know. I felt the hot blood course in my veins, all that vibrating shock distilled now into a surge of vengeful violence. I flung the door open and with arms flailing like Chinese table tennis paddles plunged into the darkness.

We collided at the top of the stairs, he with a high-pitched wail of shock, me screaming a death scream, and we tumbled together, his taut body cushioning me down to the bottom steps where I bounced off him and thumped against the door.

I lay there for a moment in stunned silence, then pulled myself into a crouch ready to plunge back into the fray. But there was only silence.

I hissed into the darkness, "Come on then, you fucker!" all the time waiting for the flash of a gun and the searing heat of a bullet that would finish me the way it had finished Margaret, but the only response was a low growl from the kitchen.

After a few moments I stood up and carefully crossed to the lounge door and pushed it fully open; the light blinded me and it took a few seconds for my eyes to adjust.

A dark form lay motionless at the bottom of the stairs, folded uncomfortably, like a widower's sandwich.

I approached cautiously. Prodded. Poked. Got a look at the face. Dead. It looked like a broken neck.

I walked into the lounge and sat amongst the chaos in the chair by the record player. The smell of the pizza made me feel sick again.

My head was pounding. I was soaked in sweat and I could feel the dull throb of panic creeping into my body. Visions from the last few days flashed through my mind: fucking up my interview, meeting Margaret in the park, getting beaten up by my wife, making love to Margaret. Upstairs Margaret was dead, shot, murdered in the space of a few minutes while I was out buying food.

I sat and thought of lovely Margaret. I had heard the last words she would ever speak, she had died in my arms. I wondered what she would think of me now, would she still love me now that I had pushed her mother down the stairs and broken her neck?

8

I woke up in a room with two corpses and a radio alarm which almost delivered a third.

Seven or eight times during the night I lifted up the phone to call the police, only to put it down again. What could I say? Uh, my girlfriend has been murdered and I've killed her mother by mistake? I knew that every minute I put off phoning them I was getting myself into deeper water, but I could see no way out. If I admitted one I'd be a dead cert for the other. There was no way they would accept her mother's death as an accident. I'd reported enough courts to recognize a crap story when I heard one. Why hadn't her mum just said something instead of sneaking up barely lit stairs? Just hello, anyone there? Just called her daughter's name like any reasonably sane individual would do? She must have taken for her role model those dizzy blondes who always entered dark caves in horror movies when the obvious route was to get the hell out.

Some time around midnight I lifted the pizza from the floor and picked my way through the mess of the lounge. The kitchen had been turned over as well. Patch was out of his basket, ears pricked, snarling, advancing slowly but aggressively towards me. He was limping. He'd been whacked but he wasn't in a mood to appreciate being alive.

I stuck out a finger towards him and shouted with as much

viciousness as I could muster, "You fuckin' move and I'll kill you!" He stopped. The ears went down. He sat. All bark no action. I went to the back door to let him out but then stopped. Who could tell what was outside? A sensible killer would be long gone, but since when were killers sensible? He could be lurking in the garden, or out front, waiting for a chance to kill me as well and then I cursed myself for switching the kitchen light on and alerting him to my presence, and then I cursed myself again for being so bloody stupid because I knew if he had wanted to kill me he'd have killed me by now. And then I thought what I hadn't dared to think and the thought put me into a kind of daze and I opened the back door slowly to let Patch out, then closed it and locked it.

Patricia. My Patricia. Not my Patricia.

Patricia had always had a violent streak.

Patricia had attacked Margaret's house.

Patricia was not home when the attack took place.

Patricia wouldn't have a notion where to lay her hands on a gun.

I love Patricia.

I betrayed Patricia.

Hell hath no fury like a woman scorned.

Who was Jack and why was he getting divorced?

I put the pizza in the microwave to reheat. Then I went out into the hall and lifted the cold body and carried it upstairs to Margaret's bedroom. She was a small woman, but she had the weight of death upon her. I pulled the sheet back and, averting my eyes as best I could, laid her beside her daughter and pulled the sheet up over them entirely. I went back downstairs, let the dog in, found some food for him and then removed the pizza. I found a six-pack of Harp in the fridge and took it and the pizza into the lounge and sat down. My hands were shaking badly but I forced myself to eat and drink. When I finished the last of the beer I took the empties into the kitchen and put the plate in the sink. Patch was looking at me curiously now, his head cocked to one side. I clicked my tongue at him and he growled. Patch, the Jack Russell. Divorcing Jack? Nah.

I opened the fridge again and found the half-bottle of chilled Polish vodka I'd spotted on my first visit. I took it upstairs into Margaret's room and sat down against the bedroom wall and sipped slowly from it until I didn't remember anything.

Then the cool light of dawn was streaming through the spaces around the edges of the ill-fitting hardboard window and a Radio 1 DJ was shouting the news about inflation and I was lying on the floor, my heart steamhammering towards breakdown. When it slowed down I sat back against the wall and cried my eyes out.

It was misty and exactly 7:30 A.M. when I let myself cautiously out of the front door. The street was quiet. The milkman had called about twenty minutes before. He left one bottle. I'd opened the door a crack and watched as best I could the houses opposite until everyone who was going to get their milk early had taken it in. Then I reached out and pulled it in quickly and drank it down. Wiping my mouth, I stepped out and walked towards the main road with my head bowed.

Traffic was still light. The mist put a refreshing chill into my body as I walked. A police Land Rover passed after about five minutes and my legs almost gave out beneath me; I steadied myself against an uninhabited bus stop until it and my palpitations were history.

It was just over an hour later when I got home. I opened the front door quietly. Three items of that morning's mail were sitting on the telephone stand, all bills.

I called softly: "Patricia?"

There was no one downstairs. I raced up to our bedroom. I hadn't made the bed since she had left; now it was back in neat order. My clothes had been tidied. The bathroom cleaned.

Back in the lounge I found a note.

Dear Dan,
I spent the night here, alone. How's the whore? I burnt your signed photo of Sugar Ray Leonard.
Patricia.

69

I crumpled the note and threw it into the grate; the remains of a fire were smouldering. I looked at myself in the mirror above the fireplace and shuddered. My hair was matted, my face bruised, there was a dark stain on my shirt which I knew was blood but which anyone else might have mistaken for cheap wine or, indeed, blood. The stain would have been covered by my coat on my walk through town, but if I'd been a cop I'd have stopped myself for questioning just out of curiosity.

I phoned Mouse at his work. He worked for Short Brothers, making and testing missiles. Last time I'd spoken to him about his job he said his most recent prototype went wonky in the Arizona desert and landed on an extremely rare colony of insects, wiping them out.

I said, "This is the Insect Protection League."

He recognized the voice. "YOU'VE GOT NOTHING TO LAUGH ABOUT, YOU STUPID FUCKER."

"You're telling me?"

"I'M TELLING YOU, DAN."

"You've seen Patricia?"

"YEAH. SHE CALLED AGAIN LAST NIGHT."

"What time?"

"WHO CARES WHAT TIME? SHE'S STILL PISSED OFF. SHE'S BEEN TO SEE THAT GIRL OF YOURS."

"What time did you see her, Mouse? It's important."

"WHY?"

"Will you just fuckin' tell me?"

"DON'T GET STROPPY WITH ME, SON. YOU HAVEN'T GOT THAT MANY FRIENDS."

"Mouse, I'm sorry, I'm sorry. I need to know. Look. I'm in some trouble. It's important I know what time you saw her at."

"GIRL TROUBLE?"

"No. Yeah. Sort of. Serious trouble."

"YOU KNOW SHE PUT YOUR GIRL'S WINDOWS IN?"

"I know. What time did you see her?"

"I DUNNO. ABOUT TEATIME. SIX, MAYBE EARLIER. YEAH, EARLIER. I WAS JUST IN FROM WORK. SHE WAS ALREADY BITCHING AWAY TO THE WIFE."

"When did she leave?"

"NOT LONG AFTER. I DIDN'T GET INVOLVED. BUT THE WIFE SAYS SHE WAS FUMING, STILL FUMING."

"Did she say where she was going, Mouse?"

"I THINK BACK TO YOUR HOUSE FOR A SHOW-DOWN. NO SHOW, EH?"

"No show."

"YOU OKAY? YOU SOUND A BIT STRANGE."

"Yeah, sure. Okay." I laughed. Mouse, be in my shoes now.

"WHAT SORTA TROUBLE YOU IN, KID?"

"You don't wanna know, Mouse. But listen. I don't know what's going to happen in the next few days for me, but I don't think it's going to be very pleasant. I may need some support. You there for me?"

"OF COURSE."

"Thanks, mate."

I put the phone down. I sat down in front of the TV, watched a discussion programme without taking anything in. I was lost. Floundering. How long did I have before they caught up with me? Maybe only a couple of hours. Margaret's mum must have said to her husband where she was going. He'd be worried about her failure to return. But there'd been no phone call. Maybe she planned to stay the night with her after hearing about the attack on the house. Then he wouldn't be worried about her until the following day. Or maybe he'd already gone abroad. So they'd find the bodies. Launch a murder hunt. Who would the chief suspect be? The mad woman who'd smashed all the windows in the house. How long would it take to identify her? All the neighbours had watched her attack the house and then drive off. One was bound to have had the common sense to take down her number. So they wouldn't be long in getting her. She had a motive. But no murder weapon. Probably an alibi. Then they would come for me. My fingerprints were all over the house. A taxi to the house. Meeting a neighbour outside. Drinking a pint of milk. Feeding the dog and myself. How do you explain to the police, to anyone, how you behave after finding a lover murdered, and accidentally killing her mother?

71

I put the bloodstained shirt in the washing machine and turned it on. I went upstairs and sat under the shower. If not Patricia, who? And why? She hadn't mentioned anyone called Jack to me. She was surely too young to have been divorced from him. The only people she had mentioned were her mother and father and Pat Coogan, ex-lover and Paper Cowboy. Coogan was in prison, I'd killed her mother. That left her dad. Perhaps if I explained to him before the news broke . . . no, madness, madness, he would probably kill me himself. I was down shite street without a petrol bomb.

The door bell went. I pulled on a pair of trousers and a T-shirt. They clung uncomfortably to my damp heat. I walked slowly downstairs. My arms felt heavy as I went to open the door, like they were handcuffed already. It hadn't taken them long.

I opened the door.

Parker said: "Morning, Mr. Starkey, ready to meet the prime minister?"

9

Brinn stood with his back to us by a large bay window as we were shown into a musty book-lined room. Red Hall, built back in the twenties, had been acquired by the Alliance at a knock-down price from an aspiring newspaper tycoon who'd overesti-mated an Ulster interest in free newspapers and beat a hasty retreat back to London, where they appreciated his kind of prod-uct. It wasn't quite a mansion, but it looked good and had fine gardens. The Alliance offices took up most of the space, but Brinn and his family occupied a suite of rooms on the first floor.

Security was lax. There were two men on the big rusty gates who checked our ID, but neither appeared to be armed. Down in the hall we'd been searched, but it was the haphazard patting of coats and trousers that you used to get on the way into shops in the city centre. The sort of body search you could sneak a bazooka through.

Brinn looked out at a concrete marina bristling with masts. Seagulls stood lazily in the sun. Without turning he said, "You know they said they were going to landscape that marina when they built it. It looks like the Maginot line."

He turned towards us and strode briskly across the room. He put out a hand to Parker, shook strongly.

"You'll be Parker," he said. "Good trip?"

"Fine, thank you, sir."

He crossed to me.

"And you'll be Starkey." A warm handshake. His paleness, his thinness were accentuated by the strong sunlight coming in from the window. "I must say I enjoy reading your column. Very smart. Could probably do with a little humour in some of my speeches, eh? What do you think?"

"Never does any harm, Mr. Brinn."

"Mind you, I'm not entirely sure all of your humour would go down with the voters that well. What was it you said about this town last year? 'The cosy gold coast of Northern Ireland where paramilitary organizations hold coffee mornings, with an Armalite in one hand and a packet of Jaffa Cakes in the other.' That was it, wasn't it? I was very impressed with that. Summed up the place just about right, I thought. Used to be a great wee town this, great place for holidaymakers from Belfast, Mr. Parker. Used to get on the train, be here in twenty minutes. Like Rockaway Beach in your New York, Mr. Parker, eh? An Armalite in one hand, hah! Might be on something of a sticky wicket if I used that line, eh?"

I hemmed. He knew his stuff. Probably had as big a file on me as Parker had. Bigger. I wondered how warm his greeting would be if he knew what I'd been up to. Prime minister has tea with double murderer.

There were three chairs arranged in a semicircle in the centre of the room and we sat down, bathed in the sunlight, and I immediately felt sleepy.

Parker said: "I'm glad you could spare the time to speak to me." He produced a micro-recorder and set it on a flimsy table before him that looked to be on its last legs.

As if he could see what I was thinking, Brinn said: "I refer to it as my decaffeinated coffee table." He didn't smile, but dared us to and we accepted.

Parker said: "A lot of people back in the States are very hopeful that a solution to the Irish question might be just around the corner."

Brinn touched his chin for a moment, trained his eyes on Parker. "I understand," he said, "that you used to be in peanut butter."

Parker's mouth fell open. "Excuse me?"

74

"I understand that before you became a journalist, you worked in a peanut butter factory."

Parker looked shaken. His eyes darted to me for an instant. "Why, yes, briefly."

Brinn nodded. "A peanut butter factory. A motor factory. Started writing for a union newspaper, picked up by a weekly newspaper outside New York, then moved to Boston."

"Yes, I . . ."

Brinn abruptly stood up and crossed to the window again. With his back to us he said: "You see, gentlemen, the value of accurate information, of detailed information. It is the secret of good journalism, and it is very certainly the secret of good politics. Information can be the making or breaking of a man, the making or breaking of a campaign."

He lapsed into silence. Parker looked across at me. I shrugged. He shrugged back. We shrugged together.

Brinn turned towards us again. "My point, gentlemen, is that we're both in the same business, one you don't need any qualifications for at all, except a little experience in life, so let's not beat around the bush."

There was a wide smile now that seemed to breathe colour into his face and an animated look in his eyes. "Let's dispense with all the usual crap. Let's start with your toughest questions, then we can relax and have some tea."

Parker, giving a little appreciative nod, drew a small notebook from inside his jacket and began to rapidly flick through several pages of questions. Brinn had taken the initiative masterfully. He may have been talking nonsense, but it was masterful nonsense.

I said: "Do you believe in capital punishment for murder?"

Parker gave me a look that said: butt out.

"For terrorists?" asked Brinn.

"All murder is terrorism."

"But not all terrorism is murder."

"Are you playing with words or answering questions?"

"I'm playing with questions. Do you know what my party policy is on capital punishment?"

75

"Yes."

"Well?"

"I'm not asking party policy. I'm asking your views."

"But you're not suggesting my view could be more important than that of the party?"

"It could be. I believe your party's success is as much to do with you as its policies."

"An interesting point of view." He turned suddenly to Parker. "Found your question yet?"

Parker's head snapped up. "Exactly how much of your body is covered in burns, Mr. Brinn?"

"Does it matter? Are you not more interested in mental scars?"

"Are you going to admit to mental scars?"

"I'd be a fool not to."

"So what mental scars do you carry?"

"Well, I'm not very fond of fire."

Brinn returned to his spot by the window. "You know," he said, "I have a small boat out there. Sometimes I go and sit in it for hours at a time, just listening to the wind and the rattle of the masts. It's very relaxing. Maybe that's a mental scar. I never used to appreciate things like that. That bomb made me appreciate the finer things in life. And most all of them are free. The wind, the rain, the sea. With the exception of marina fees, of course."

"You do much sailing?"

"Never left the harbour. I just like sitting in my boat. I'd drown myself for sure if I got as far as the waves."

Most of the books that lined the walls were paperbacks, which was either a nice common touch or a piece of bad public relations. A lot of orange-spined Penguin Classics. A whole row of Hardy, complete Shakespeare, even a Bukowski. The bottom two rows near the door were children's books. Hopefully his son's.

"Are you going to talk to the terrorists?" Parker asked.

"No."

"Simple as that?"

76

"Yes."

"What if they renounce violence?"

"Then they won't be terrorists."

Parker got him on to the importance of American economic aid. My eyes started to flicker. I'd heard it all before. Parker listened intently, his eyes darting nervously to the microcassette from time to time to check that the tape was still rolling. Several times my head nodded forward and I shook myself awake . . . I tried sitting back, out of the sun, but it made no difference. It was as if the rays were chasing me round the limited circumference of my seat and instead of imbuing me with life they were sucking it out of me.

Brinn stopped in the middle of a sentence. "Are you all right, Mr. Starkey?"

I gulped and said: "Uh, yeah. Sorry." But even with that I could feel the bile in my throat and I swallowed hard. I shivered, shook my head. "In fact, no, I don't feel all that good. Perhaps you could excuse me? This is your interview after all, Mr. Parker. I'll go for a wander round the garden and get some fresh air, if you don't mind."

I stood up. Brinn said, "Not at all."

Parker just glared at me.

As I closed the door behind me I heard Brinn say: "He looks a bit under the weather, doesn't he? A hangover you think?"

One of the security men downstairs showed me to a small bathroom. I locked the door and bent forward until my head was in the pale-pink sink, the taps grinding into me just above the ears. I turned both taps on and enjoyed the cold water as it sprayed against my hair from either side, gradually growing hotter on the right until I had to jerk my head away to stop the burning.

I shook my head like a dog and looked into the speckled mirror above the sink. The droplets on the glass made my reflection appear out of focus. The way my life was. I pushed my sleeve across the mirror, but it made me look worse: fuzzy, indistinct, unidentifiable; the way I would have to be to escape, if it came to that. Where were they now, the police? Was Patricia being questioned somewhere, was she confessing it all? Patricia whom I had betrayed.

A phrase came back to me then, a phrase I had heard once and never forgotten. It had been another journalist, one of the first I'd worked with. A woman, maybe his wife, had accused him of having an alcohol problem. "Yeah, two hands and only one mouth," he'd replied. It had seemed hysterical at the time. Where would I be now if I'd not gone out drinking by myself after that stupid interview? Solo drinking, the sign of the alcoholic. Maybe they'd give me a reduced sentence for having a drink problem.

I dried my hair on a fading towel that might once have matched the pink of the bathroom suite and left the house by the front door. They didn't ask me about Parker on the way out.

I leant across the front of the car for a few minutes, wide awake now in the fresh sea air, and looked back up to Red Hall. I wondered if the Alliance appreciated the irony of having inherited a headquarters with a name like that. It was a party which espoused a milky socialism if you cared to read the small print of its manifesto. But its real message was reconciliation. It had failed to appreciate the historical lesson that if you try to kick with both feet you tend to fall over. I could see Brinn seated by the window, gesticulating animatedly, Parker's head nodding beside him.

A shrill scream twisted my head away from the hall. At first I could see nothing. There was a low wall about twenty yards in front of me that cut the garden in two, dividing the marching rows of flowers in bloom that shadowed the driveway to the front door from a rough lawn that was slightly overgrown and showed the crazy pattern you get from wind buffeting. The cry came again, sharper, and I realized it had come from the few feet of garden masked by the top of the wall.

Nobody else appeared to have heard it. I ran across to the wall and jumped on top of it. A boy, maybe four, was lying flat on his back, a figure bending over him.

I shouted, "Hey!"

A woman looked round. "What?" she said. The boy was laughing, screaming in mock pain. She had been tickling him. She was in her late thirties, maybe, small, not thin but not fat.

I said: "Sorry, I thought . . ."

She smiled and said: "No bother. We're only messing around."

I turned to go back to the car, but the woman said: "You're Dan Starkey, aren't you? He said you were coming. I enjoy the column."

I turned back to her. I sat down on the wall and smiled down at the boy.

"Thanks," I said.

It must have come out weakly. She said: "Are you okay?"

"Sure."

"Hangover?"

"Jesus . . ."

"I'm sorry."

I bit back the flash of anger. It wasn't her fault. I pushed a smile where it didn't want to go. "Nah, I'm sorry. If I write about alcohol all the time I can't really expect much more. No. Not a hangover. Flu, maybe."

She stood up and came over to me. Her brown hair was flecked with grey, but it looked well and she'd a good strong face that lacked any discernible makeup. High above her, coming out of the sun, a seagull swooped down towards the shallows of the marina.

"Can I get you anything?"

"No. Thanks. I just wanted some fresh air. I take it you're Mrs. Brinn?"

"Agnes, yeah." Instead of putting up her hand she lifted the boy up on to her shoulder. "And this is Robert." Robert grinned like an angel. He looked like he needed a good slap in the chops. "You're staying for dinner, aren't you?"

"I'm not sure. No one said."

"Sure you are."

"What's for tea, Mum?" Robert asked, endearingly.

"Stewed bugs and onions," Agnes replied, tweaking his cheek.

"Mmmm," I said, "my favourite." The boy twisted his face away from us in mock horror.

Agnes put the boy down on the top of the wall and I gave her a hand up. We jumped down together on to the gravel pathway and began walking towards the house.

"You finished with Mark already?"

"No. It's not really my interview. My American friend is doing that."

"Can I make you a cup of tea before dinner? Come on into the kitchen, it'll only take a moment."

The boy ran on ahead of us and opened the big oaken door by himself. The security man gave him a cursory glance and ignored me altogether as we made our way through a series of empty offices and into a small canteen. Agnes said she had the dinner already in the oven upstairs but it would be quicker to make tea down in the work's kitchen.

I shrugged.

She said: "So are you as bad as you make out?"

I scrunched my eyebrows up at her. "How do you mean?"

"Drinking, womanizing, ultra-Unionist."

"I'm fond of drink, women and Unionism, ish. I don't think that makes me a bad man. Unless I find a drunk woman Unionist and then I'm lethal."

"I'm safe then."

"Oh, I wouldn't go that far."

Her eyes steadied on mine and I looked away. Stared into a glass-fronted coffee maker.

"You're flirting with the wife of the next prime minister of Northern Ireland."

I remained silent while she poured me a cup of tea from a pot that had already been on the cooker. She poured one for herself and poured milk for us both. She didn't ask me about sugar. She said: "You look as though you've been in the wars."

I shrugged.

"Want to tell me about it?"

I shook my head. "I don't think that would be a good idea."

"I'm a good listener. You could try me."

I looked into her hazel eyes and I could see that everything she said was right. I could see my own sick reflection, her own sincerity. Here she was with everything ahead of her; here was me with everything behind me, everything closing in on me. For a moment I saw her as Margaret, then as Patricia, then as herself. I half-chuckled. "I'm much better in print," I said. "You'd be much better off reading my confessions."

10

We didn't have stewed bugs for dinner. When we sat down, the four and a half of us, we ate chicken. There was a radio playing jazz somewhere in the background, blending in with the faint hum of an electric lawnmower. Parker, Agnes and I drank cool white wine from a box. Brinn said he was off alcohol. He and the boy had orange juice.

"I do too much rambling when I'm drinking," he said. "I don't want any cock-ups in the run-in to the election."

"You mean you've made some before?" Parker asked.

"None I'd tell you about!" Brinn laughed.

"Ach, go on," I said and Parker frowned at me as if the conversation should be exclusively his.

"You could tell them about the hospital, Mark," Agnes suggested.

Brinn smiled benignly at her. "That was nothing to do with alcohol."

"Tell them anyway."

He looked at us with mockingly narrowed eyes. "I trust this won't find its way into print, gentlemen?"

Parker shook his head. I shrugged then shook. Just to be awkward.

"It was nothing really." He put his elbow on the table, resting his chin lightly on the top of his knuckles and looked down, as if he was embarrassed. His nails were bitten to the quick. Despite the thinness of his face there was the hint of a double chin when he looked down. "I was on a hospital visit. You know those tours of wards politicians do to make them look as if they are deeply caring individuals? The City Hospital, wasn't it?"

"Royal Victoria," Agnes corrected.

"Anyway, there was a guy there had had his legs blown off by a bomb a few months before. He was cheery enough about it all, but there's not much you can say to someone like that besides make sympathetic noises."

Giggling, Agnes cut in: "So he asked him if there were many people in his shoes." She sat back and roared like she was hearing it for the first time; Parker and Brinn laughed with her. I joined in as well. Laughing murderer and the prime minister. He giggled over maimed bomb victims while his lover was autopsied.

There was no getting away from it. They were a nice couple. And he was a nice enough man. So why did he give me the creeps every time I came across him in an official capacity?

We finished the food, then lingered over the wine. I said: "I was given to understand you were booked up day and night with interviews. Yet we've been here for hours."

Brinn sat back, yawned. "You know," he said lazily, "we try to accommodate everyone as best we can. But there are always difficulties. For example, we had a Lithuanian reporter here the other day. We didn't have a clue what he was on about, so it was fifteen minutes and half a cream cracker, and he was lucky to get that. And then we do like to do something a little bit special for our American visitors. American support is very important for what we have in mind for this place. The Irish built America. I don't think we're amiss looking for a little bit of a return on our investment."

"In many ways the Americans are more Irish than the Irish," Agnes volunteered. "Remember that Saint Patrick's Day parade in Miami, darling?"

Brinn smiled. "How could I forget? Thousands of people, all in green, drinking green beer, barely a word of English between them. It was most bizarre."

"One of the big days of the year," Parker said. "I even get to feel a little Irish. Boston's the place to be, of course."

"And it's where the IRA gets a lot of its money from too," I said. "It's not all cutesy shamrocks and top o' the mornin' to ya."

"Which is exactly why we try to give people like Mr. Parker here a little extra help. There are a lot of Irish-Americans who think it's romantic to support a civil war, which is really the situation we're in, though the Government will always deny it. A lot of armchair terrorists in that land of yours, Parker. It's up to you to put them right on a few things."

Parker nodded. "You gave me some very convincing arguments in support of the Alliance today, Mr. Brinn. Power sharing, a largely autonomous state, freeport status, British but not British, Irish but not Irish. Independence with a safety harness. A Northern Irish Hong Kong really. Ideas that seem to be generally popular."

"All I am saying is give peace a chance." Brinn smiled, but it was a thin, cynical smile that said, yeah, I know they shot Lennon.

"You really think the IRA — the UDA, for that matter — will lay down their arms?" I asked.

Parker said: "We've been over this this afternoon."

"I'm only asking."

Brinn leant forward. "No. I don't think they will. The violence is too ingrained in them. They've had their own way for too long. They won't want to give up what they have. I mean, it's long past the political stage, the Nationalist or Loyalist stage, for most of them. Now it's down to money. The rackets. They have their political thinkers, but they know they're on a lost cause, because we've got the people, a lot of the people behind us, and there's a genuine chance that what we're attempting will work. No, you'll see those political figures progressively eliminated from both sides of the paramilitary line and then we'll be down to a straightforward game of cowboys and Indians."

"Which is which?"

"Depends on your point of view really. Depends whether you're a John Wayne fan or a *Dances with Wolves* revisionist."

84

I poured myself another glass of wine and tried not to think of Margaret. I felt ashamed suddenly that she had only flitted through my mind briefly during dinner. But I would surely go mad if I kept thinking of her. And suddenly I was giggling and I had to clamp my hand on my mouth but it squeezed out between my fingers like vomit.

They were staring at me.

I swallowed hard. Pulled my cheeks in.

"I'm sorry," I said, a little high-pitched. "I'm sorry," I repeated.

"Are you okay?" Agnes asked for the second time that day.

Brinn looked perplexed. Parker looked angry.

"Of course. I'm sorry, what with the wine and the flu, and that . . . it's just got to me. That's all."

"Maybe we should be going," Parker suggested.

"Well . . . ," Brinn said.

"No, stay," Agnes interjected. "I'll make some coffee."

"It's not the drink," I repeated. "It's not just the drink, I mean, I . . ." and I didn't know what I was going to say, I didn't know whether I was going to mention Margaret or Patricia or the way my world was caving in. Who better to tell than the next prime minister of Northern Ireland, and who worse?

There was a knock on the door. They all turned towards it, thankful for the relief.

It opened without a reply from Brinn and a man I recognized as Alfie Stewart, the Alliance security spokesman, walked quickly into the room. He was a big, impressive man with a ruddy Antrim farmer's face. I'd met him a couple of times at press conferences and been impressed; he reeked of sincerity and could maybe have given Brinn a run for his money if given the chance, but rumour had it that he had a bit of a drink problem, which was more of a handicap in his chosen profession than mine. He nodded to me as he crossed the room; his eyes, slightly hooded, widened momentarily at Parker's blackness. I'd seen him calmly breeze through the toughest of interviews, but his face now had assumed a daunting tautness, like the stretched leather of the devil's saddlebags.

Stewart said, "Excuse me," in a voice that was more of a bark than an apology and bent down over Brinn's right shoulder to whisper in his ear: a raspy sound like a wasp half-glued to sandpaper . . .

Brinn's face gave nothing away, but his knuckles turned white as he squeezed tightly on his glass of orange. Agnes's hand instinctively dropped beneath the table, finding its way to his leg, although she could have heard as little as me.

As Stewart finished, Brinn turned his eyes up to him and shook his head slightly, then contradictorily nodded it. When he spoke, his voice was cracking with emotion.

"Thanks, Alfie. Uh, I'll be with you in a moment." Alfie turned and left the room. Brinn turned briefly to Agnes. "I'm afraid I have some bad news, darling," and then his eyes flicked over us. "You gentlemen may as well hear it now. I understand it will be on the news very shortly. It's our finance spokesman, David McGarry. His wife and daughter have been found murdered in the daughter's house in North Belfast."

Agnes gave out a little squeal and buried her face in her hands.

I said: "That's awful."

Brinn was shaking his head slowly; tears appeared in his eyes but didn't fall. "I knew they could sink low. God knows we've seen how low they can sink over the years — but this? An innocent wife and child, just to get at me?"

He banged his fist down hard on the table. Several glasses fell over, spilling their contents. Agnes began to half-heartedly dab at the mess with her napkin. Parker helped her.

"I'm very sorry," Parker said. "You must have been very close."

"Very," Agnes said.

Stewart appeared at the door again and signalled to Brinn to come over.

He stood up and crossed over while Agnes continued mopping up. The boy, neglected through dinner, had woken up as the glasses were knocked over and was now demanding a drink. Agnes ignored him, her eyes glazed, as she worked at the stained tablecloth. Parker reached over and poured the boy a fresh drink and handed the glass to him, but he wouldn't take it.

Brinn came back over. Agnes put out a hand to him; the other held the tightly balled sodden napkin.

He took her hand. "I'm going to have to go. You'll be okay? I may be some time."

She nodded half-heartedly.

"You want me to come with you?"

"Better not. Things aren't going to get any better." He looked at us again. "David McGarry has been taken to hospital with a suspected heart attack."

Agnes slumped back in her seat. Parker was quietly pushing the remains of his dinner around his plate; he looked embarrassed to be there, aware that he was in a unique position of seeing a future prime minister's reaction to a friend's murder but aware that he didn't have the tabloid ignorance to exploit it there and then, where it mattered. But it was all right for Parker. It was all right for Agnes. It was all right for Brinn. They hadn't killed anyone.

Brinn let go of his wife's hand, and marched quickly out into the hall to the waiting Stewart and together they clumped down the varnished wooden stairs.

I went and stood by the window and watched them leave in a green estate car. As they emerged into the traffic two police Land Rovers joined them, one in front, one behind.

I walked to the other end of the dining room and looked out over the marina. The sky was overcast now and a bit of a wind had gotten up, rattling the masts of the boats.

Behind me Agnes said: "It never rains but it pours."

I nodded.

She said: "They were a lovely family."

"I know," I said.

11

Parker realized we were being followed shortly after leaving Red Hall.

I'd told him to stop the car up the road a bit from the Alliance headquarters so that I could use a public phone to call Patricia. I directed him into a shopping centre on the town's ring road and he pulled up in a no-waiting area in front and I hopped out. I found a phone just inside the door but I'd no change so I crossed into a jumble of bric-a-brac market stalls which preceded the main retail area. I stopped at a paperback bookstall and was searching my wallet for some paper money when I noticed a rack of cassette tapes for sale. I still had the tape Margaret had given me in my pocket, so I fished it out and asked the man behind the counter if he was buying.

He eyed the box vaguely, then wrinkled his eyes at it and for me. "Not much of a demand for crap like that," he said.

"I'm only looking for a pound."

"Keep looking."

"50p."

"Done."

"You drive a hard bargain," I said. It was all profit for me, of course. Killer profits from lover's music collection.

I called Patricia at her parents' house. Joe answered the phone. From in-law to outlaw in a matter of hours. No, she wasn't in.

"Uh, Dan, she's out. She went out."

"You know where?"

"You know her. She doesn't say. Even as a child, Dan — where you going? Don't know. What you doing? Don't know. What you want for dinner? Don't care. Says I, don't care was made to care. Says she, piss off. What can you do?"

"What sort of form's she in?"

"Okay. Bit mopey really. I expect she'll be home to you soon, son."

I felt a sick chuckle in my throat. Sure, Joe, sure. Home sweet home.

He said: "You okay, Dan? You sound a bit down yourself."

"I've been better, Joe. Listen, tell her I called, will you? And I'll call back."

I went back to the car. We drove back out onto the ring road. Parker had been giving me a hard time over what he saw as my poor performance at Red Hall. He said I shouldn't bring my obvious problems to work with me. I wasn't in a mood to argue; he'd really know all about it if I brought my stiffening problems to work with me.

It was getting towards dusk and the traffic was fairly light; a shepherd's delight sky gave a marvellous hint of summer and The Adverts' "Gary Gilmore's Eyes" was on the radio. It would have been quite pleasant if I hadn't been practically a triple killer. Somewhere out there Margaret's dad was on a life support machine.

Why hadn't she mentioned that her dad was someone important? David McGarry was a decent enough bloke. I'd interviewed him a few times. Even had a drink with him. He'd written a couple of plays which had enjoyed a quiet success in the Lyric theatre in Belfast though they'd been shot to pieces in London and Dublin. Knockabout comedy with a hint of social grime: Ray Cooney meets Václav Havel. She hadn't even given me a hint; she'd mentioned her dad a few times, even joked once about something being off the record. No photos of him in her house. Just her mother. An admirable independence of thought, perhaps: not wishing to take advantage of her father's fame or name, slight

89

as it was; determination to make it on her own. Maybe it was nothing of the sort. Maybe she thought his position might scare me off. Maybe she thought I might take advantage of her position to get to her father. Maybe it didn't matter much any more. She was on ice, her mother was on ice and the Alliance Party's finance spokesman was tugging at the door of the freezer.

Parker's unfamiliarity with driving on the correct side of the road meant he was keeping an eagle eye on the traffic around him.

He said: "I have an idea we're being followed." He said it very matter-of-factly, like it happened all the time. I could feel our car beginning to speed up.

I looked round and Parker shouted: "Don't make it so obvious!"

"Whaddya want me to do? I've no eyes in the back of my bloody head."

There were three cars behind us; two directly and one coming up faster in the outside lane.

"Two reds and a white. Which one? The red about to overtake us?"

He shook his head slowly, eyes in the mirror . . . "No, not the Jap. Not the Yugo. The Fiat."

"Either way it's a sad reflection on the state of the British car industry," I said and sat back in my seat. "Mr. Parker, never take your job so seriously that you think someone might want to follow you because of it. You're not that important."

And the little voice said to me: they're after me. It has started.

"I'm serious." His eyes were darting from front to wing mirror and our speed was still picking up. You can do a fair rate of knots in a Saab. The Fiat was keeping pace with us, which was odd for a Fiat. "I noticed it behind us just after leaving Brinn but paid no attention. Then it turned into the shopping mall with us and waited about a hundred yards down the parking lot. Then when we left it followed."

I tucked myself further down in my seat and turned slightly more discreetly back so that I could just see the car around the leather headrest. It was a Fiat Panda and it sounded like it had been souped up for rallying. There were four people in it. Four men. It was difficult to be sure, they were lying about thirty yards back, but they didn't look like police. Even fastidiously turned-out plainclothes cops look like cops, albeit fastidiously turned out.

"Maybe they've never seen a black man before."

The first shot shattered the rear window.

Glass showered over the back seat. Somebody shouted "Holy fuck" and it was a split second before I realized that that disembodied voice came from me. I could see powdered glass on the back of Parker's tight black hair.

Parker pulled the wheel savagely to one side and we half mounted the curb. We began mowing the wild grass shoulder at speed, Parker's foot full down now on the accelerator. He was hunched down beside the wheel so that his eyes could barely see the road before him. I was down there with him. In movies you sometimes hear amplified heartbeats at times of particular tension. There was nothing Hollywood about this. I could hear Keith Moon playing the bongos in my chest.

I chanced a dwarf glance back and saw the Fiat beginning to draw level. It had moved to the outside lane for the shot at us and was now angling in to stop us dismounting from the shoulder. A skinhead with a pistol was leaning out the window, waving the gun and shouting, but the roar of his own engine was taking his words away. He had the letters FTP etched on his forehead and a wild drunken leer on his face. He couldn't have been more than eighteen years old. But you don't need the key to the front door to kill someone.

Parker's white eyes, wide and scared, darted towards me, but his face cracked in a defiant grin.

"Traffic cops?" he shouted.

Before I could answer he threw the car sharply to the left to avoid a bus stop planted solidly in the centre of the shoulder and we were fully on the sidewalk; the Fiat moved closer to the shoulder as the skinhead raised the gun again to fire.

Abruptly Parker slammed on the brakes and we skidded to a

91

halt in a cloud of torn grass, brakes squealing like cows in an abattoir. The Fiat shot past us, tried to brake too fast on too little tread and somersaulted on to its back.

Parker clapped his hands together and yelped. The Fiat was still spinning when he pushed the Saab into gear and raced across the shoulder towards our assailants.

I screamed: "What the fuck are you doing?"

The car bounced down off the curb; he corrected the slight hitch in trajectory and aimed it dead centre at the Fiat.

"Hey," he said, "I'm from New York. We do this for breakfast."

We rammed the side of the car, slamming shut a door which had just begun to open. It crumpled inward and I heard a high-pitched scream from inside.

"They've got fucking guns," I yelled.

Once was enough for him. Parker slipped the car into reverse and circled back and away. We were about a hundred yards away when the Fiat's driver's door opened and a leather-jacketed youth tumbled out, raised himself on one knee and aimed a gun at us. From that distance they sounded like caps in a toy gun. He missed.

"Jesus Christ," I said.

"People swore to me when I came here I wouldn't see any action. They swore."

"I've lived here thirty bloody years and I still haven't seen any action. You're just lucky."

"What do you suppose that was all about?"

"God knows. Charity week."

We were driving back down the way we had come. Parker indicated left as we approached the shopping centre again.

"This doesn't seem like a sensible time to think about doing the shopping, Parker. They may still be after us."

"We should call the police, or the army, or whatever goddamn militia you have that deals with this sort of thing."

"In cases like this we call the Boys' Brigade. They can handle anything as long as you don't fuck with their lamps."

92

Parker stopped the car and said: "What?"

I shook my head. I was blabbering.

"I don't think it would be a good idea to call the police."

"Why?" He stared into my face. "We've just been shot at. We could be dead." His eyes narrowed suddenly. "You think they were the police?"

I shook my head. "They were Protestant paramilitaries."

"Protestant? How can you tell?"

"Two ways, really. One: they fucked up. Proddies have a habit of fucking up operations like this. They outnumber the IRA ten to one but couldn't organize a piss-up in a brewery. Correction. They usually do organize a piss-up in a brewery before they try anything and that's why they fuck it up."

"And two?"

"The skinhead who shot at us. He had FTP written on his head."

"FTP. Tattooed? What's it mean?"

"No, just written. Like with a felt pen. It stands for Fuck the Pope. It's a dead giveaway. Actually, they're improving. Usually they can't spell FTP."

Parker lit a cigarette. It was the first time I'd seen him smoke. His hands weren't shaking. He offered me one. I turned it down. Mine were.

"But why on earth shoot at us? What did we do to them? They couldn't have mistaken us for Alliance workers, could they? Maybe that's it. A political attack leading into the election."

I said nothing.

"Why not call the police, Starkey?"

I closed my eyes. Rubbed my brow. Scratched my nose. I had no idea why they attacked us. But it wasn't a case of mistaken identity, of that I was sure. It was me they were after and in some way it was connected to what had happened to me over the last few days. Paranoid. Paranoid. Paranoid.

Parker asked again: "Why not call the police, Starkey?"

I turned to face him. "It's a short story," I said.

We sat there in the car park and I told him everything that

93

had happened to me over the past few days. He went through most of a packet of cigarettes as I went over it again and again. Confessional. It wasn't a case of getting it out of my system. It would always be in my system. But it was a relief to tell someone.

When I had finished Parker rolled his window down and spat. "I hate cigarettes," he said. Exhaust fumes smelt refreshing.

"That's quite a story," he said.

"I wish it was a story. But it's fact."

"I can see why you might not want to call the police. Still, you don't know that they were after you. They could have thought we worked for the Alliance. That's the obvious conclusion."

"They could."

"But we still can't call the police."

"No."

"So what then? Are you going to go on the run? You seem pretty certain that they'll be after you."

"I don't know. I've never been in this situation before." And I laughed. "Stupid, isn't it?"

"Of course you could be a double killer."

"I could."

"And there's no reason why I should believe you."

"Nothing besides the close, trusting relationship we've built up over our years of working together."

"Apart from that."

"You could always make a citizen's arrest."

"There's that."

"And it would make a good story for your paper. Whatever you do, it will make a good story for your paper."

"It will."

"Of course it would make a better story if you could track down the real killers."

"There's that."

We sat in silence. The car park was beginning to empty as darkness descended. It was a little before 10 P.M. Parker switched the car radio on and we listened to "Alternative Ulster" by Stiff Little Fingers until the news came on. There was little extra information. Two police officers had been bitten by Patch as they entered the upstairs bedroom where the bodies were found. The cold-blooded killer had apparently eaten a meal in the house after the killings. David McGarry was in critical condition in a private hospital. There was an emotionally charged interview with Brinn in which he promised that whoever was responsible would be found and that "this act of mindless depravity only strengthens my resolve to bring a lasting peace to this Province."

Parker said: "I'm going to have to think about this. I honestly don't know what I should do."

"I didn't do it. I didn't kill Margaret. Her mum — it couldn't be helped. It was just a crazy accident."

"I don't think you did it, Starkey. It would just have been an awful lot simpler if you had."

"Sorry."

"That's okay. It says a lot for marital fidelity."

"It does. And I need a drink."

"We could go to a bar."

We went to a bar and had a drink. Neither of us enjoyed it. I was sure everyone was looking at me.

"You're a well-known columnist. Maybe they recognize you."

"No. They can tell. I know they can tell."

"Look on the bright side. You can write about it after it's all over. Don't you feel a column coming?"

"Last time I said that in a bar I nearly got arrested."

"I wouldn't mention getting arrested. Bad luck."

The bar was filling up now as last orders approached. I left Parker to order another drink and went and found a phone. I called Patricia. Joe answered.

"Hi, Dan. Yeah, sure, she's here."

Oh, God, here we go. Patricia, did you kill my girlfriend? Is that how to approach it, or skirt round the issue to see if she gives anything away?

"Stick her on, would you?"

"Sure. Oh, hold on. Trish? Trish! Hold on, she's just away to answer the front door. Just be a moment."

95

Joe set the phone down and I could hear him padding off. And then in the distance, a hundred miles distant, I heard a high-pitched scream, a shattering of glass and a gunshot and someone in a weak, weak voice saying, "Patricia, Patricia . . . Patricia?" and that someone was me.

12

Parker booked me into a guesthouse in South Belfast. It had seen better days, but then so had I. Three floors and an all-enveloping smell of boiled cabbage. Twelve pounds a night, breakfast included, in advance. The breakfast wasn't in advance. If it proves anything it proves I retained my sense of humour. I'd little else left. Parker said he'd find out what he could and get back to me as soon as possible. I don't know what he expected to find out when I was the one that knew the city backwards. I wasn't much help. I was having trouble thinking straight. I was thinking curved.

I lay back on the bed and stared at the ceiling. A lot of people must have done that in that depressing room, lonely, miserable people. A ceiling which had once been cream was stained yellow with nicotine. When I moved, the bed squeaked. It wasn't the sort of establishment where the beds enjoyed a lot of nocturnal movement; the only thrashings that kept the neighbours awake were nightmare-fuelled.

I was booked in under the name of Paul Cook. He was the drummer in the Sex Pistols. I owed Parker twelve pounds for the room and another hundred pounds for the telephone I smashed to pieces in the bar in Bangor, plus my grateful thanks for getting me out of there before being beaten to a pulp by a couple of bouncers with an overprotective attitude to newfangled equipment . . .

97

There was a small black and white television in one corner of the room. The reception was poor. There was a brief interview with Margaret's next-door neighbour. Only the back of her head was shown out of fear for her safety. She recalled her sleep being disturbed by a man screaming, "You f'n' move and I'll kill you." She'd thought about calling the police but had fallen back asleep while thinking about it. A police inspector reiterated that a major manhunt was under way and the killer or killers would be apprehended, but said that he couldn't reveal if any specific lines of inquiry were being followed for operational reasons. They repeated the interview with Brinn I had heard on the radio earlier, and added to it condemnations from the other legitimate political parties of any importance, the Unionists, the Social Democrats and the Conservatives. Government restrictions stopped them broadcasting the actual voice of a Sinn Fein councillor, but his words were read out by the newsreader. He denounced the killings as sectarian but blamed them on the continued British presence in Ulster. The reporter, in a concise piece of supposition, suggested that it was an attempt by the paramilitaries to disrupt the elections.

No one mentioned my wife. It was early days for that yet. Patricia was dead. That much was obvious. Possibly her father. Possibly her mother. Parker had gotten enough sense out of me to find out exactly where her parents lived and had stopped at the first phone box we could find after escaping from the bar and phoned the police. He had spoken to them in a truly appalling Irish accent. They would be staking out the house now, fearful of an ambush. When they went in they would probably find it smashed up. There might be a body, or two, or three, but they wouldn't approach them until they had made sure they weren't booby-trapped.

I drifted off into a sweat-drenched sleep. Some time during the night I found myself walking along a dirt track in the deep south of the U.S. There was a huge black man painting the front of a small cottage a heavenly shade of blue. As I got closer I realized that it was Parker. When I reached his rickety garden gate he climbed down from the ladder and stood back to admire his work.

98

I was about to apologize to him for my earlier unintentional comments about his receding hairline when I noticed that he had missed a spot or two of paint up in the top right-hand corner of the cottage.

"Bit of a bald spot there," I said.

And before the full import of what I'd said dawned on me he drew a Samurai sword from within his overalls and lopped off my head with a single swipe.

I woke up in a yellowy room. The sun had penetrated the thin lace curtains and had combined with the ceiling to imbue it with a sick, jaundiced glow. I sat at the edge of the bed. I was still fully clothed. I looked at my hands. There was an almost imperceptible shake. I made tight fists of them, squeezing until my muscles ached and my fingernails had bitten into my palms. Then I said a prayer. It went: God bless Patricia. God bless Margaret. After a pause I added: God bless Parker.

It was 12:30. I had slept through breakfast. But there was no hunger, not even the welcoming rumble of a hangover, just a numbness like someone had removed my stomach during the night but the anaesthetic hadn't yet worn off.

There were no in-room facilities. There was a bathroom at the end of the corridor. As I approached it the door opened and a young man about my age emerged. His hair was shaggy from drying it without the benefit of a comb; he'd used henna on it, and that and his sharp features made him look fox-wily . . . He was wearing a deep-blue suit; the top button of his white shirt was buttoned but he held a thin, crumpled-looking pink tie in his hand.

He looked up and apologized for nearly colliding with me, went to walk on and then turned back.

"Uh, mate, you wouldn't know how to tie a tie, would you?"

He held the tie up to me.

I shook my head. "Sorry, mate, I can just about manage my shoes."

He shook his head and laughed. "I've been at this for half an hour. I've tried everything, but it's determined not to sit right. I nearly bloody hung myself at the last attempt. Sure you can do nothing for me?"

"I'll give it a go if you want, but I warn you your head may come off in the process."

He put the tie around his neck and handed me both ends of it. He smelt clean and fresh and his eyes shone.

"What's the big occasion then?" I asked. He didn't look comfortable in the suit. It was contradictory clothing: old but seldom worn or new but out of fashion. The sort of suit a man would buy based on something he had spotted while trying to find the problem page in a three-year-old women's magazine in a dentist's surgery he was visiting to have an abscess drained.

"Meeting the wife for lunch. We split up about six weeks ago. She's had me living in this fuckin' dump ever since. I'm hoping we'll get back together." Realizing perhaps that he had somehow compromised his manly pride, he added with a conspiratorial wink, "I'm not that worried about her, but I really miss the record collection."

I finished the tie as best I could. He thanked me profusely and walked off with something that looked like a contortionist's gay octopus friend knotted about his neck.

I showered and shaved and then returned to my room and spent the afternoon looking out at the traffic buzzing along the Malone Road. It had the reputation of being one of Northern Ireland's richest areas, but most of the real money had long since fled to the country, or fled the country itself for that matter. Most of the money and all of the brains were located in England now. I had palpably shown over the past few days that I had neither and was stuck here for good. That small yellow room, given a set of bars, could be my prison cell. Home for eternity. Maybe I would be okay. I'd been there for hours already and I wasn't feeling claustrophobic at all.

During the afternoon the guesthouse owner made polite inquiries about my plans, as I was two hours past the checking-out time. I paid her for another night and she thanked me profusely and said she hoped my recuperation from the car crash would be without mishap. I began to feel that I'd been playing the car crash

100

thing up a little too much. She said what a nice black man Parker was just before leaving the room.

Parker, the nice black man, had still not returned by teatime so I made my way downstairs to the dining room. There were three tables, each with four seats. My friend with the pink tie but now without the pink tie was sitting by himself at a table by the window and I sat down opposite him, taking care to sit with my elbow propping my head inward, away from any curious passers-by.

"All right? How's it going?" he asked.

"Not bad, thanks. How about you? How'd your lunch go?"

He'd lost the suit as well. He wore a pair of black jeans and a black pullover with a little yacht motif over his left nipple. He shrugged. "Okay, I suppose." He looked a bit down in the mouth.

"But you're still here."

"Yeah, well, you take these things slowly, you know?"

"Yeah."

"It was quite nice really. There was no arguing, no cursing, no violence. The last time that happened she didn't turn up."

"Sounds hopeful, anyway," I said.

He made a bit of a face. "I wouldn't go that far. She's seein' another fella . . ."

"Oh, I'm sorry, I . . ."

"Never worry about it. It doesn't bother me. I follow this philosophy where I don't allow anger or jealousy to cloud my thought processes. I picked it up in the East."

"What, like in India or Nepal or something?"

"Nah, East Belfast. It's called the philosophy of who gives a fuck?" He said it straight-faced, but I could tell he was suppressing a cackle. I wondered what he would make of my marital troubles.

The guesthouse owner shuffled over and handed me a threadbare menu which told me what I was having rather than giving me a choice.

I ordered pork chops after a suitable minute of rumination. My friend ordered his. Rather perplexingly there was no boiled cabbage available, yet its aura hung over the dining room like a shroud.

"Paul Cook," I said, reaching across to shake his hand.

"Lenny Morrison. Local?" he asked.

"Ish."

"You look like you've had a hard time."

"Aye, the bruises are starting to go down, thank God. Car crash."

"Jesus. You go through the window or something?"

"Nah, I was in the back seat. Headbutted the guy in front of me when we crashed."

"Tough. You working?"

"On and off. Mechanic. In a garage. When they need me."

"So I'll know who to bring the wagon to in the future?"

"Any time. What about you?"

"Civil servant. Same as most everyone else in this bloody country." He laughed and then leant back from the table as his food was set down. As I moved back to allow the woman to set mine down I glanced across at the couple on my right. They looked to be in their sixties but may not have spoken since their thirties. They had the bluff red faces of country folk, he with ex-asperated wrinkles round his eyes that told of his annoyance at having to come up to the city to complete some farming transaction, she with the close-cut but still jagged white hair you get in a hill-farming community that has still not succumbed to the blue rinse. She was studying a knitting pattern set at the side of her plate, her meal half finished. He had cleared his plate and was intently studying an inside page of that evening's *Belfast Telegraph*, holding it up so that his wife could not see him. I was so intent on studying my neighbours that it was some moments before my eyes focused on the front page of the newspaper, and in particular on the picture of my wife. The headline read: MURDER SUSPECT MISSING AFTER GUN BATTLE.

A shiver ran through me. Footsteps on the grave. I leant over to read the story but as I did the man pulled the front page back towards him and stared at me. I sat back and gave him a little grin. He folded the paper so that it made a neat square he could set down beside his plate. I felt like reaching over and ripping it away from him.

102

"Friendly soul, isn't he?" Lenny said quietly.

"Probably just looking at the pictures," I replied, just a little too loud. The farmer's face went slightly redder and I could see he was staring a little too intently at the paper to be really taking anything in. His wife's eyes flicked up at him, darted across to me and a slight smirk appeared on her lips; she went back to studying her knitting pattern.

"I have a paper upstairs if you want one," Lenny said.

We finished our meal and he took me up to his room. There were newspapers and magazines scattered everywhere and his clothes were strewn about the room.

"Sorry about the mess. Pauline used to look after everything. I never was house trained."

I sat down on the edge of his bed while he rummaged down the other side, against the wall, finally emerging with a crumpled version of that evening's paper.

He handed it to me and said: "Doing anything tonight? You don't fancy going out for a drink? This place is driving me up the walls."

I would have loved a drink. A lot of drink. I shook my head. "Sorry, mate, love to, but I'm waiting for someone. Another time, eh?"

I took the paper back to my room and smoothed the front page out on my bed.

The photo of Patricia had been taken from her parents' house and dated back to the days before we were married. Young, free, single and alive, nothing she could put a claim on that day. She looked very pretty. Beneath the broadsheet's fold there was a much smaller picture of me. It appeared to be a poor reproduction of the picture used to head my column in the *Evening News;* doubtless the *News* would have printed the original. Still, it could have been worse: my face didn't cover more than a single column, black and white and my nose had to be seen in three dimensions to be unappreciated. A caption beneath it read simply: *Police are also seeking journalist Daniel Starkey.*

The news about Patricia had obviously just broken. With an exclusive tagged over it, it said that Patricia Starkey, who was being sought by police in connection with the McGarry double murder, had been abducted by person or persons unknown following a gun battle in Portstewart. Her parents were being treated for shock but were otherwise uninjured. She was described as a twenty-eight-year-old civil servant who had no known connection with paramilitary organizations nor a previous criminal record. "She is the wife of Dan Starkey, a reporter and columnist on another Belfast newspaper whom police also wish to question." There were a number of quotes from neighbours in Portstewart who had heard shots being fired and seen Patricia dragged screaming into a car, but nothing from her parents. There was no police substantiation on why they wanted to question her. Nothing, yet, about a love triangle. God, how they would have loved a love triangle. You never got love triangles in Northern Ireland, just endlessly repetitive murders which were written up to formula by bored reporters. Maybe if I'd worked at it I could have come up with a love rhombohedron. This reporter suggested that the abduction could be connected to a long-running feud between Protestant terror groups which had plagued the northwest of the Province over the past year. It recalled, helpfully, that previous abductions had resulted in the hooded corpses of the abductees being found several days later.

The bulk of the rest of the story concentrated on the double murder itself, the *Telegraph* having been well beaten to that one by the morning papers, and speculation on why it might have happened. It had clearly been written by a different reporter before the news about Patricia broke. In the absence of any evidence to the contrary the blame was laid clearly at the feet of the paramilitaries, although as the McGarrys were an Alliance family and were clearly neither Loyalist nor Republican, neither grouping was singled out as guilty. It was padded out with more of the usual condemnations from all shades of political and religious opinion. An opinion column on page three castigated the terrorists for carrying out such dastardly murders in a deliberate attempt to cause the maximum amount of heartbreak and upset in the days before the elections.

I lay back on the bed and took several deep breaths; they were hard to come by; it felt like there was an acorn lodged in my windpipe.

A number of things were clear from the story. Patricia was alive when she was abducted. The police had been closing in on her and were also after me. Nobody had any idea what any of it meant, but they thought it might have something to do with the elections. I agreed. I had no idea what it meant either.

The phone beside my bed rang suddenly, like they do, jolting me out of my thoughts.

A young girl's voice.

"Mr. Cook?"

"What?"

"Mr. Cook?"

"Oh. Yeah."

"This is Janice from downstairs."

"Downstairs?"

"The manageress. Janice. There's a Mr. Al Jolson down here asking for you. Is it okay to send him up?"

13

Parker didn't look anything like Al Jolson. For a start, Al Jolson was white.

Parker was far from white, although when he entered the room there was a desperate hint of paleness about him.

"Do you have any idea how difficult it is to lose people in this city when you're my colour?" he asked. He sat on the bed, pushing the newspaper onto the floor. Little beads of sweat stood out on his brow and he was making a concerted effort to take shallow breaths which were barely enough to sustain life. He took three or four major breaths, held the last, then exhaled slowly. "Four hours ago I left the hotel to come here and I've been dodging shadows ever since."

I sat on the windowsill with my back to the Malone Road. There was a quiet hum of traffic behind me. "You're not getting paranoid, Parker, are you?"

"Even . . ."

"Don't say it."

"I know I was followed, Starkey. You're big news."

"Patricia?"

"Sorry. Nothing."

"Oh, well," I said. And dryly: "No news is good news."

"So they say."

Parker didn't actually have to do any legwork of his own to find out what was going on. They'd queued at his door.

Neville Maxwell was the first to get to him. He was all flustered. He insisted that Parker make no mention in any of his stories that he had been accompanied to the meeting with Brinn by me. Parker nodded without promising anything.

"He seemed very jumpy. Too jumpy."

"He doesn't like bad PR."

"No. It was more than that. Jumpy."

"You've never met the man, Parker. He could always be like that."

"You have — is he?"

"Well — no. But I don't know him that well."

"When I told him about being shot at he said something very curious."

"Like?"

"'There's something very curious going on.'"

"That is curious."

"I'm serious."

"I know."

"Sometimes I can't tell when you're being serious."

"I know. It's curious."

"When he said, 'There's something very curious going on,' he didn't say it to me, it was an aside really, to himself. People who talk to themselves worry me. Either way, he wouldn't elaborate on it."

"He asked you where I was, of course."

"Of course. I said you'd run off after the gunfire and I'd no idea where you were."

"And he believed you?"

"He didn't seem concerned. He said you'd be picked up one way or another. Oh yeah — he said he hoped it would be by the police. That mean anything to you?"

"I presume he means the same people who got Patricia might be after me."

"That's what I reckoned. He recommended that I leave the country. He said things would probably get worse before they got better."

"I don't think they can get much worse."

107

"I don't think he particularly meant for you. He implied that I was in some danger myself."

"So you're taking him up on his recommendation?"

"What do you think?"

"I don't know. That's why I'm asking."

"I think he's trying to scare me off so I won't write about the lunch with Brinn or look any further into this thing."

"So you're staying."

"I can't go back with a half-written story, Starkey."

"Good."

"Then I had the Royal Ulster Constabulary come visit. They interviewed me for about an hour and a half. They were perfectly pleasant."

"That's always a bit worrying."

"I know. They made it quite plain that they thought I knew where you were. The senior officer, a captain, I think, or what is it, a detective inspector? He warned me that I could be kept in custody for up to seven days and then be charged with withholding information. The other guy kind of spoiled the threat by saying that of course as an American citizen they wouldn't do that to me. The captain gave him a withering look."

Parker began rummaging in his inside jacket pocket. He produced a crumpled piece of paper and handed it to me. "Then I had a reporter, said he worked with you. Mike Magee mean anything to you? Gave me this number and said it was important that you call him."

"Important for me or for him?"

"A bit of both, I suspect. He seemed genuine enough."

"I hate genuine. It's so false. Magee works with me on the *News*. But he also does some stuff for Maxwell."

"So then I got followed."

"Maxwell, police and Magee, or representatives of such?"

Parker shrugged. "Magee I spotted. Police, I think, out of uniform."

"Difficult to miss."

"Like myself. And skinheads. Skinheads everywhere. I couldn't make up my mind whether they were following me because of this business or because I'm black. Or both, the way things are going."

"Don't worry about the skinheads. By and large they're not as dangerous as they look. You can spend your life crossing roads to avoid them, then some twit in a nice blazer with a college scarf round his neck flattens you. You've heard of lager louts? It's the Liebfraumilch louts you've to watch out for."

Parker looked up at me, squinting slightly as the dying sun's rays invaded the room around me through a late break in the clouds. "Why do I get the impression that you're thinking up bright comments for your column as you go along? You're not in a very funny situation, Starkey."

"It's the only thing that keeps me sane, Parker. And if it was happening to someone else, it would be very funny. In a tragic sort of way."

"It takes a remarkable man to keep smiling through this, Starkey."

I shrugged.

"Or a very sick one," he added.

Parker brought a number of things back with him. He had a copy of the *Evening News*. Its story was much the same as the *Telegraph*'s only it made even less of my involvement and there was no photo of me even though they had access to dozens. The editor, Big Frank, had not flinched in the past from making capital out of colleagues who got into trouble, so I could only hope that he had held off using my picture out of some kind of particular loyalty to me or perhaps in the hope that I would reveal all to him when the time was right. Either way it gave me a little extra time — the police would doubtless have a photo, and if they had one the terrorists would have one, but at least I didn't have to worry yet about some idiot trying to make a citizen's arrest.

He also brought a change of clothes, washing materials, and three six-packs of Harp. For himself he had brought half a dozen bottles of Rolling Rock. We sat and drank.

He said: "You can't stay here forever."

"I know. Just tonight. Tomorrow I start finding out what's going on."

"And how do you do that?"

"I was thinking about it this afternoon. The one clue we have to go on is that last thing Margaret said to me. Divorce Jack. We've got to find out who Jack is."

"You think it's that important?"

"It was the last thing she said on this planet. It has to be."

"It could be gibberish. You don't know what goes through a person's mind when they're just about to die."

"It has to be important. What else have we got?"

"If only she'd said 'Klatu barada nikto' we could have blamed it on aliens and been done with it."

"*The Day the Earth Stood Still?*"

"The same. Then I'd really have a story."

"This isn't getting us anywhere."

"I know. So how do we find out about Jack?"

"I'll phone Magee tonight. But you go and meet him. I'll tell him it's too dangerous for me to come out of hiding. If he's assigned to the murders then he'll have done some work on Margaret's background; see if there's a Jack in there somewhere, without letting on that you're that interested. I'll take a dander round her university, see if I can track down any of her friends."

"Isn't it too dangerous to go out, Starkey?"

"I'm going to have to do something about my appearance."

I stood up from the windowsill and crossed to a cracked mirror set in the gloomy alcove above the dressing table. I was still bruised about the face, but the swelling had gone down considerably. I reached up and pulled my hair tight back against my skull. "You think I'd look good as a skinhead, Parker?"

"Well, you wouldn't look any worse."

"Thanks. Margaret once said I reminded her of James Stewart."

Parker looked incredulously at me. "I suppose you do. If you're mad."

"I'll need some denims. Jacket and trousers. Old. You can get me some in the morning from a charity shop, okay?"

110

"Okay."

"And no flares on the trousers. I'm not wearing flares."

"You're a murderer on the run. You can't afford to be fashion conscious."

"I can and I will. I'm not wearing flares for the same reason I won't get a curly perm in my hair."

"Which is?"

"I'd look like a spastic."

I borrowed some scissors from downstairs and went into the shared bathroom to cut my hair. It's impossible to give yourself a proper skinhead without a set of shears, but I gave it a good go. When I had finished my hair was short and tufty and I looked as if I was suffering from radiation sickness. But at least I looked a little bit less like the Dan Starkey everyone knew and loved.

As I was leaving Lenny was coming up the corridor. He said: "Jesus, I'd see a barber about your head, mate. Did you fall and break your hair or something?"

"Very funny."

He had a towel in his hand. He said: "You finished in here? Going for my weekly bath."

"Sure. Go ahead. Did you not go out?"

"Aye, I did, but you know what Belfast's like during the week. Dead as a doornail."

I smiled and let him pass. I lingered outside my room until he locked the bathroom door and then walked down the corridor to see if he'd left his door unlocked. I tried the handle. The door opened and I peered in. The room was in darkness. I switched the light on and went in. I was pleased to see that he'd tidied it up a bit. Boredom had never yet driven me to tidiness, but each to his own. I found what I was looking for on the floor beside his bed: a bottle of henna for my hair. The final touch. His suit was on a hanger behind the door. I checked the pockets and found his wallet. I pulled out his driving licence and studied the photograph; it was fuzzy and indistinct and could have been anyone. I stuck the licence in my pocket and put the wallet back. He only had ten pounds in it, which I left, so that he could buy himself a new bottle of henna.

Later, when I'd reoccupied the bathroom and dyed what was left of my hair, Parker gave me a once-over. "You've managed to dye part of your skin as well," he said. He reached across and rubbed some colour from below my ear. Then he examined his fingers, rubbing the dye between them. "You looked like you were wearing makeup, Starkey. Terrorist face powder. Or Khmer Rouge." He smiled broadly.

"We'll make a writer out of you yet, Al," I said and went to admire myself in the mirror.

"You look like a punker."

"A punker? You mean a punk, I take it."

"Whatever. A sick punk."

"I don't care if I look like Winnie the Pooh, just as long as I don't look like Dan Starkey."

"You look like a punk version of Dan Starkey. But you might get away with it if they don't look too closely."

After he was gone I prayed for Patricia and asked God to lead me to Jack. He didn't reply, but then He was probably busy moving in mysterious ways. Up there, He was probably having a good giggle.

14

There is no experience quite like walking the streets as a fugitive. Fear claws at your heart like a circus tiger claws at its trainer, closer, closer each time, until one day, in an unguarded moment, it strikes home. How to be alert, yet natural. Assume everyone is your enemy, and friend. Everyone recognizes you but nobody knows you. A friendly smile is a knowing smile. A blank expression is a mask of fear. The pump of a horn is a signal. The screech of brakes an ambush.

In fact, all eyes were upon me, because I looked so bloody ridiculous. Parker hadn't done too bad a job with the denims. Although the trousers clearly weren't flares they were somewhat less than straight: bell-bottoms was the term they were afflicted with in their heyday. He found them in a nearly-new shop on the Sandy Row, and knowing that part of the city well, I could easily believe that they were. Fashion and thuggery have never gone hand in hand. My hair had not benefited further from a fitful night's sleep. It looked like toffee poured into an icicle mould, brittle and unwieldy. The bruising on my face, all but invisible in the yellowed light of my room, was more noticeable, but ignored, as most everyone was too busy looking at my jaggedy hair. My skin was pale and chalky and my eyes red from an alcohol sleep. They wouldn't have sold me glue in a do-it-yourself shop.

I didn't check out. I just walked out. Parker, off to meet

Magee, had a good laugh at me and disappeared with my decent clothes.

Although it was before eleven the sun was blazing down as I took my first tentative steps along the Malone Road. It was the first time it had really felt like summer: car windows were down; T-shirts were on; summer frocks were being taken out of mothballs on the Sandy Row. By the seaside the last candyfloss seller in Ireland would be rubbing his hands. His day had come. It was the sort of day when anyone would feel good to be alive. Depressing, really, under the circumstances.

The McGarry murders had dropped to second place on the morning news: eight British soldiers had been killed when a lorry full of explosives exploded while passing a foot patrol in South Armagh; the driver, whose wife was held hostage while he was forced to drive his lorry past them, was blown to bits. It was the biggest single army loss for a couple of years and the news bulletin was extended to cover it. The McGarry murder story was little more than a rehash of the night before. Margaret and her mum were to be buried the next day. Elsewhere overnight there had been rioting in West Belfast following the arrest of two Sinn Fein party workers out canvassing and three Loyalist bombers had escaped following a firebomb attack on a Dublin shopping centre because the Garda still refused to carry guns. The elections were nine days away. The Government had sanctioned an unprecedented weekend election to allow absolutely everyone the opportunity to vote at least once. Brinn was still well ahead in the opinion polls. His position, if anything, had been strengthened by the McGarry murders.

The further I walked, the more confident I became. Keith Moon on my heart began to ease off. People were looking at me slantily, glancing at my hair, my bruising, but being careful not to catch my eye; when they walked on most bore little smirks on their faces that said: ha, the fallacy of youth, but there was no hint of recognition, no flicker of fear. I walked past Queen's University, looking dowdy in the sun, its old red-brick walls smudged black by pollution, its lawns neglected by students now that the exams were finished, only the strawberries of graduation ahead.

114

I stepped into a taxi at the bottom of Great Victoria Street feeling pretty proud of myself. I had passed two police foot patrols and neither had given me so much as a second glance.

I shut the door and the Belle of Belfast City turned to me and said: "What the fuck do you want?"

I went to open the door again, my heart in my mouth, but when I looked at her there was no hint of recognition in her eyes; it wasn't even anger; it was just her way.

"I want to go up to Jordanstown."

"You got money?"

"Yeah."

"Let's see it."

I showed her a fiver. She started the engine, looked back. "I've been ripped off by too many of you bastards."

"Not me," I said as she swung out into oncoming traffic. A roar of horns.

"Fuck off out of it, ya Fenian bastard!" she wailed out of her window.

It wasn't difficult to track Margaret's friends down. A list of the geology department's end of term results was pinned to a notice board in the quiet main foyer of the university. She'd passed, which was slim compensation for being dead. I noted down the names and crossed to the Students' Union where I was referred to an accommodation officer who was already working on the next term's housing shortage.

He was podgy. He had calculated that a black polo neck and black jeans with a two-day stubble would make him look cool but he had missed by a mile, although I was nobody to pass comment. He was maybe twenty-six and he had that relaxed air of somebody prepared to be an eternal student. I knocked on the table he was working at, his head down, double chins exposed. He looked up with a pained expression, mouthing a calculation. He said, "Hold on," went to write something down, then added, "Oh fuck," and put his pen down.

"Hi, John," I said.

"Hi." No recognition.

"Like the hair?"

He looked at the mess on my head and a smirk crept on to his face. He nodded. "It's different," he said. "I'm sorry . . . I . . . ?"

"Sorry . . . nobody's recognizing me like this . . . it's my summer look . . . Phil . . . Phil Cameron . . . You helped me with that grant down in the Holy Land last year. Remember, the ceiling?"

He thought for a moment, nodding at the same time. "Yeah, sure, yeah. What can I do for ya, Phil?"

He motioned me into a plastic seat before him and I sat, leaning in towards him. I looked briefly behind me and then said in a low voice, "It's terrible about Margaret, isn't it?"

He leant forward, hooked already into my conspiratorial tone.

"Jesus, I know. Desperate. A great wee girl she was."

"I've been walkin' around in a daze. How could anyone do that?"

"It's a madhouse this place. Total bloody madhouse."

I sat back a fraction. "Anyway, that's why I'm here."

He moved back a little himself, then forward again as if I was about to divulge some great secret.

"You know the funeral's tomorrow?"

"Yeah. I can't go. Wish I could." It was a can't go which was a could go, but won't go.

"No need, John. You know, she's gone now. It's only a ceremony, you know. But I thought it would be nice, you know, to get a wreath together and send it. As a mark of respect."

He nodded morbidly, his chins resting now on his folded hands. "Yeah, just right. I think the university's sending one though. I hear most of the staff are going."

"Oh, I know that. I've been in touch with them. But I thought it would be nice to send a special one, you know, from her special friends, her classmates."

"Yeah, sure, of course. Good thinking."

"I'm sure they'd all like to contribute, John. The only thing is we've broken up for summer now and I didn't take any home

116

addresses of the rest of the class. It's not the sort of thing you plan for really, is it?"

"God, no."

"So I was talking to her tutor, and he suggested you'd probably have the addresses here."

"Yeah . . . yeah, we do . . . although, like, it's not really my place to give them out . . ."

"I appreciate that, John. Do you want to check with her tutor? He said it'd be okay . . . it's just the urgency of it with the funeral tomorrow. It's a pity you can't go."

He looked thoughtful for a moment.

"I have all the names here I think . . ."

I handed him a sheet of paper on to which I'd hastily copied the names from the exam results. "Only a dozen or so," I said.

He scanned the sheet. He nodded his head again, blew air out of his cheeks. "Why the hell not," he said finally and pushed himself back from the table, propelling himself across the room on the casters of his chair to a battered filing cabinet.

Ten minutes later I had all the addresses I needed, and a five-pound contribution towards the wreath.

He was very helpful, our John. I said: "You couldn't do me a favour, could you?"

An exasperated look. I smiled cheekily. "Only a wee un. There's no way I'm going to get round all these people today if I'm hoofin' it. Any chance of borrowing a phone for ten minutes, so I can call them? And a bit of privacy to make the calls? I'm sure the university wouldn't object, under the circumstances."

Five minutes later he had me installed in a small office on the first floor of the Students' Union. It said Entertainments Officer on the door and there was something inscribed in Gaelic beneath it that had been partially scrawled over.

There were sixteen names on the sheet and I spent ten minutes with a telephone book and Directory Enquiries matching them to numbers. The first three I called weren't in. The fourth was a girl called Stephanie Murphy.

"Miss Murphy?"

117

"Yes?"

"Sorry to trouble you, Miss Murphy, this is Detective Inspector Boyle. I'm calling from the Royal Ulster Constabulary headquarters in Belfast."

"Yes?" Her voice had the harsh Newry edge and there was a slight falter in her voice as she replied.

"I understand you were a classmate of Margaret McBride? That is, Margaret McGarry?"

"Yes, yes, I was. I . . . I didn't know her that well though."

"We're following up several lines of inquiry into the murders, Miss Murphy, and we're trying to trace someone who may or may not be able to assist us."

"I didn't really hang about with her much."

"Were you aware of someone she may have known called Jack?"

"Jack?" There was silence for a moment. "No. No one called Jack. In fact I don't think I know anyone anywhere called Jack."

"You're sure?"

"There might have been one in primary school . . ."

"No, I mean, no friends of Miss McGarry."

"None I knew of. Like I say, I didn't really hang about with her."

I thanked her and tried another two or three; they were all in but not much help. The last one referred me to a girl called Colette Stewart who wasn't on my list but she said that she was Margaret's best friend at the college. She even furnished me with a number.

Colette answered the phone herself. She had a light Scottish brogue. I introduced myself again. She immediately burst into tears and I couldn't get any sense out of her for a few minutes. Finally she calmed down sufficiently to apologize.

"Nonsense," I said, "it's quite natural. I'm told you were one of Margaret's closest friends."

"Yeah. Yeah. We were very close."

"Are you aware of her having any enemies at college?"

"Margaret? Everyone loved her."

118

"Somebody didn't." I let that sit on her for a moment. "What about outside of college, you hang about with her outside of school?"

"Yeah, of course, all the time. Except the last month or so with the exams coming up, I'd to spend a lot of time at home studying. I'm not a natural brain like Margaret . . . was . . . I had to work at it; it always came so effortlessly to her."

"What about boyfriends?"

She let out a throaty chuckle. "Yeah, we'd . . . she'd lots of boys on the go . . . she was a very popular girl."

"Anybody in particular?"

"Not since I've known her. Never more than a couple of weeks. Said she wanted her freedom. It was always her that ended things, if you see what I mean. Nobody dropped Margaret. I had an idea that she was going out with someone last week. She sort of dropped hints on the phone, but she wouldn't say. That usually meant they were married. She kept those ones quiet. I think it gave her a bit of a kick, you know? Intrigue."

"Are you aware of anyone she would know quite well called Jack?"

"Jack? No . . . in fact yeah, yeah, Jack."

I could feel Moonie at my heart again.

"Jack who, Colette?"

"I couldn't honestly tell you. I didn't really know him, he was an old friend of hers from way back. I think they were quite close. From her pre-student days, a good bit older as well. Seriously weird individual Jack is."

"Weird in what way?"

"I don't mean dangerous or anything, Inspector. Jack is . . . well, sure you've probably heard of him yourself. He's a comedian, literally. Semi-professional, I think — you know Giblet O'Gibber? Does a turn in the Abercorn every Friday? That's why the name threw me. Margaret always referred to him as Gib, you know, his stage name. He doesn't use Jack much himself, only when he's signing on, I think. Maybe I shouldn't say that."

119

"That's okay. No one else needs to know that."

I'd heard of him okay. I'd always steered clear of going to see him because I didn't like meeting people who were funnier than me.

"Mad as a brush, Inspector. Margaret knew him from the old days. She once told me he was quite a normal guy till one day he locked himself in a room with a copy of Disney's *Fantasia* and three hundred magic mushrooms. He was never quite the same after that."

"You don't happen to know where he lives?"

"Sorry. No idea. Inspector, you don't think he . . . ?"

"We don't think anything at the moment, Colette. We just want to talk to him."

I thanked her and asked her not to talk to anyone about our conversation in the interests of the investigation.

At the end she said: "Inspector?"

"Yes, Colette?"

"If you find whoever did it — killed her and her mother — will you kill him?"

"I will arrest him."

"Kill him."

She put the phone down.

15

I didn't need to wait long to meet Giblet O'Gibber. A small ad in that night's edition of the *Evening News* said he was performing at the Dolphin Hotel, one of the new buildings that had sprung up along Great Victoria Street during the property boom of the mid-eighties. The Dolphin liked to think it had an exclusive clientele, but what it really had was a moneyed clientele, and that was something entirely different. East Belfast gangsters in flashy suits and droopy moustaches crowded the bar, shouting bad-natured insults at each other, while their counterparts from the west of the city preferred to relax in round-table packs near the stage where they could cover each other's backs. Not that they needed to worry. Nobody ever went armed to the Dolphin. Any violence that broke out was settled with fists or pint glasses and forgotten by the next morning, but it rarely did. Even gangsters have to relax sometimes.

Relaxation was the last thing on my mind when I arrived. I'd met with Parker in the Botanic Gardens earlier and his news had not been good. Mike Magee had told him the word out on the street, both sides of the street and right up the dotted line in the middle, was that there was a pile of money waiting for anyone who could get me. He said that the word had come from the very highest echelons on both sides of the paramilitary divide: it had filtered down in code through the complex cell structure of the IRA, while the philistines of terror in the UVF and UDA had merely gossiped it around their minions. Like it or not there was an admirable sophistication and military proficiency about the IRA, as long as you always remembered that they were murdering bastards. Magee said nobody on the ground actually knew why I was suddenly so popular: it was generally accepted that a blow against the Alliance was a good thing for both Loyalist and Republican paramilitaries, who had everything to lose in a peaceful Northern Ireland, so why pursue the perpetrator?

Walking into the Dolphin was entering the hornet's nest. One thing was on my side: it was the last place they'd be looking for me. On the other hand Magee's informer, who hung out with either set of gangsters depending on where the money was, was able to show him a print of the original photograph of me used in the masthead of my *Evening News* column, which he said was being widely circulated by both sides. Somebody had stolen the negative from the *Evening News* he said, which gave the terror boys a clear advantage over the police and army, who were still apparently making do with the old grainy likeness which had disgraced the front of the *Telegraph* the day before.

A bouncer on the door refused at first to let me in because the Dolphin observed a no denims rule. He was a big voluntarily bald-headed guy and serious about his job. I hung around outside for half an hour, trying to make small talk with him and look miserable — it wasn't a great effort — until he finally took pity on me and allowed me in as long as I left my denim jacket behind the bar. He also suggested I do something with my hair, but it was beyond rescue. Once inside I realized my re-evaluation was more to do with the fact that the lounge bar was half empty than the bouncer's good nature.

I sat at the bar with a pint and a trio of chattering women. I'd a good view of the stage, a small, circular, makeshift effort on which a vocalist and his backing track were performing a range of country-and-western classics. He had a broad Belfast accent which his singing failed to mask and which rendered the songs into unintentional comedy. I was the only one laughing, possibly because I was the only one listening. Around ten the place began to fill up: confident-looking gents used to having their own way crowded in with their obliging wives. As they drank, the men took their jackets off and rolled up their sleeves, displaying fleshy tattoos as if they were entered in an art competition. Some did look as if they'd been laboured over, complex multi-coloured interpretations of the defence of Ulster, but most looked like they'd been hastily pricked in a drunken stupor by the artistic equivalent of the backstreet abortionist. Their women drank Cointreau and brown and cackled at each other for no apparent reason.

The singer and his machine finished to desultory applause. I ordered another drink and as I paid for it I saw a familiar face coming towards me in the bar-length mirror. The characteristic swoop of black hair sweatily layered across his forehead, the full-moon eyes, the smiling leer. Billy "Dainty" McCoubrey. He'd been a leading member of the Shankill Tartan during the early seventies. The Tartan gangs, so named because they originally wore tartan scarves in memory of three young soldiers in the Royal Highland Fusiliers shot dead in Belfast, specialized in intimidating and beating up Catholics for no reason other than the fact that they enjoyed it. It seemed funny that barely a couple of years later wearing a tartan scarf would signify you were a follower of the teeny pop group, the Bay City Rollers, rather than a mindless thug. The Tartan gangs may have had a life span as long as most teeny pop groups, but McCoubrey himself had long since carved out — often literally — a solo career for himself. Most of the protection money along the Shankill Road ended up in his pocket eventually. I'd interviewed him a couple of times for the paper. He was one of those large men who come automatically muscled, a man who'd never taken a day's exercise in his life yet could still crush bouncers for breakfast. He was wearing a leather sports jacket and an open-necked, blue-striped shirt. He nodded at me as he set his money down on the bar.

"How're ya doin'?" he asked.

"Fine, thanks. How's you?"

"Doin' rightly."

I turned and walked the length of the bar with my pint and found an empty table in the shadows to the right of the stage. When I looked up again McCoubrey was chatting with a group of three or four other similarly attired but much smaller men at the bar. He caught my eye, held my gaze for a moment and then returned it to his friends. He recognized the face, but couldn't place it.

I sat so that I could half watch him and half watch the stage. As I sipped nervously at my drink the lights dimmed and I was relieved to find myself at an even gloomier station. A ripple of applause ran round the room as a thin, medium-built man in a crumpled white suit took to the stage. Jack, aka Giblet O'Gibber. He'd a strange face: one that looked as if according to the blueprints it should have turned out to be absolutely beautiful but somewhere along the way it had been inadvertently stretched; his chin was long and pointy, leading away from a wide mouth that displayed too many teeth. A comedian's face.

He tapped the microphone and gave the audience a toothy grin, or he might have just been opening his mouth.

"Evening," he said and the audience burst out laughing; a brightness sparked in his eyes as he realized he wouldn't have to work too hard. "Evening," he said again and the laughter continued.

He put his hand to his brow and peered mockingly out into the crowd. He shook his head. "Aren't the bouncers bastards in here? Eh? No denims allowed? Eh? Where the fuck do they think this is, the fuckin' Savoy Hotel? I was coming in tonight and they weren't going to let me in 'cause I was wearing fucking Denim aftershave! And my mate Dennis had to argue with them for half an hour before they would let him in!" The crowd was in hysterics already; big molten guffaws exploded from the back at the bar and travelled towards the stage, picking up lighter, higher-pitched giggles on the way. McCoubrey was enjoying himself. Giblet milked the laughter for nearly thirty seconds then added: "Fuckin' bouncers," and set them off again.

Giblet hushed them after a little with a raised hand. "Any gangsters in tonight?"

Laughter again, but slightly hesitant.

"Well?"

"Too right, mate!" McCoubrey's booming voice, joined immediately by throaty chuckles from his companions.

"Too fuckin' right!" That time from the Republican tables over to the left.

Everyone was laughing again.

"Sorry to hear that three IRA men died earlier today. Their car left the road and hit a tree. The UVF said they planted it." Laughter, strongest from the Republican side, joined by the Loyalists as soon as they'd worked out that it wasn't an insult.

Sharp. Quickfire. Giblet was better than I'd expected. He was obviously getting off on the adrenaline of performing before such an unorthodox crowd, people who would have him blown away for a word against their organization when they were on duty. After half an hour he called a halt and he left the stage to rapturous applause. The lights went up. Last orders were being called at the bar. McCoubrey was still standing there with his friends. I stood up and followed Giblet out of a small side door.

I followed him at twenty paces up a badly lit corridor; he pushed open a fire door and emerged into the open air behind the hotel. He walked along the back of the building until he came to a fire escape and climbed up to the first floor where he opened another fire door and disappeared. I nipped up behind him and caught a glimpse of him at the end of a corridor, entering a bedroom. He closed the door behind him without looking round. I knocked on the door. He took a minute to answer. He'd stripped down to a white T-shirt and boxer shorts. His suit, damp with sweat, was in a heap on the floor. He had a drink in his hand.

He said: "What?"

"Nice show."

He screwed his face up into a snarl. "Fuck off."

He went to slam the door, but I put my foot in it and as he opened his mouth to protest I stuck my fist into it. He fell to the ground. I stood there in the doorway for a second, half in shock that he'd fallen over so easily — in my sporting days I wouldn't have been picked for the pixieweight boxing squad — and half in

125

surprise at my own violence. Then I stepped into the room and closed the door behind me.

His gum was split and he was already dripping blood on to his white T-shirt. He pushed himself up on to one elbow. He'd held on to his alcohol like a professional.

"What the fuck was that for?"

"Shut up, Jack."

"Go on then. Hit me again."

"What?"

"Hit me again. While I'm down. You're not going to shut me up till you kill me."

"What are you talkin' about, Jack?"

"I tell whatever jokes I want."

"I'm not worried about your jokes, Jack."

"Well, what the fuck do you want coming in here and whacking me for then, you big bastard?"

I knelt beside him. He cowered back. I suppose I did look a bit threatening.

"I just want to ask you a couple of questions."

"What, like Trivial Pursuit?"

"You're not being paid to be funny now, Jack."

He snarled again, the blood around his exposed teeth making him look like a Rottweiler at a children's party.

"Why did you kill Margaret McGarry?"

I thought the direct approach was best. His eyes widened, face blanched, white on red.

"What the fuck are you talkin' about?"

"I'm just askin', Jack. Why kill her?"

"You're mad, mate. I don't know what you're on, but I wouldn't mind some of it."

I hit him again, on the side of the nose. His head rocketed back and banged off the carpet with a spark of static. Unconscious.

I got a cup of water and threw it over him, then another. I got a towel from the bathroom and wiped the blood from his face. There wasn't much I could do about the red T-shirt. He came

126

round slowly. I lifted him under his arms until he was resting against the foot of the bed and kneeled beside him again.

"When's the last time you saw Margaret, Jack?"

He spat up a mouthful of blood on to the floor then wiped a thin, freckled arm across his mouth, wincing as he caught the split gum.

"I haven't seen her for weeks."

"When's the last time you spoke to her?"

"Couple of days before she . . . you know."

He was compliant now, the stage confidence and alcohol knocked out of him.

"Anything wrong with her then?"

"Seemed happy enough. New man in her life. That bastard Starkey. I see him, I'll kill him."

I grabbed him by the hair and slapped him across the face. "Listen, you stupid bastard, I am Starkey. The last thing she said in this life was about you and I want to know why."

His punch came out of the blue, a cool right that struck the top of my nose and threw me back on to the carpet. He was on top of me in an instant, raining down blows with angry abandon. I jerked my head left and right, my arms above me. In his frenzy he wasn't taking time to place his shots and the half of them ended up pounding the carpet. I worked a knee free and brought it up forcefully between his legs. He let out a high-pitched yelp and toppled off me. In a second I had him pinned to the floor.

"You murdering bastard," he squeezed out between gritted teeth.

I placed the palm of my hand against his face and pressed his head into the floor. "Are you going to answer my question or am I going to have to kill you as well?"

His body went limp beneath me. He nodded his head. I removed my hand.

"Why'd you have to kill her, man? She never did anyone any harm. Kill someone, kill her dad. What'd she ever do?"

"I didn't kill her, Jack."

He looked unconvinced. He sniffed up a mixture of blood

and snot and tears. "What did she say, at the end?" he asked quietly.

" 'Divorce Jack.' "

" 'Divorce Jack'? Divorce? What a thing to say. We were never married. We never even kissed. We were friends."

"So what did she mean?"

He shook his head. "How do I know? 'Divorce Jack'? I don't know. If you hadn't've killed her you might've found out."

I lifted my hand to dab a spot of blood from my own nose and I could feel him tensing again for a blow.

"I've already been through this once, you bastard. You can't beat out of me what I don't know, okay? You want me to make something up? Okay, just ask."

"Been through it with who?"

He smiled sarcastically. "If I knew where it was I'd tell you, okay? It doesn't mean a fuckin' thing to me."

There was a sudden woodpecker rapping at the door. I replaced my hand over Jack's mouth.

The voice was unmistakable.

"Come on, Gib, open up, let's go through it again. This time no comfy chair."

Billy Dainty McCoubrey was making a backstage visit.

128

16

As McCoubrey entered, I left. Giblet O'Gibber clamped himself to my left foot as I pulled up the bedroom window and screamed at the door as it opened.

McCoubrey's bulk was almost bigger than the doorway. He stood for a moment, transfixed by the scene inside the room, and then came lumbering towards us. I stuck my right foot in Giblet's face and he fell away. I launched myself out the window into the darkness, my eyes closed and my arms wrapped round my head for protection.

It was only a couple of seconds, but it was a long couple of seconds, stretched like elastic in my mind, waiting for the snap. I expected pavement and pain; I got a soft metal bounce off the top of a Lada and a second, softer landing in a flowerbed recently piled high with fresh-smelling compost. I lay in stunned repose amongst the scarlet geraniums, looking up at McCoubrey staring down at me, framed in the window, his size somehow reduced as if he was on television. He was shouting something but my ears were ringing from the impact. Then he was gone, replaced briefly by Giblet, who shouted something as well. Then there was only the window and the bedroom light, repelling the human insects instead of attracting them.

I pulled myself up into a sitting position. I thought of McCoubrey and his friends and where their guns might be: the car park, and where I was: the car park. I raised myself cautiously. I'd landed both times on my left hip. It didn't feel broken, but it wasn't very receptive to having weight put on it. I hobbled along the edge of the flowerbeds which lined the car park and then along the side of the hotel towards the exit. Most of the cars were gone now, the evening's entertainment over. There were maybe only a dozen residents' vehicles left, haphazardly spread through fifty parking spaces. Useless as cover.

As I reached the exit the front doors of the hotel crashed open. McCoubrey and two cronies scanned the car park. McCoubrey saw me first, pointed, and his two colleagues started after me. He called them back and directed them towards a blue Volvo off to the left. Guns, of course.

I hurried as best I could along the side street, then halted at its junction with Great Victoria Street, stood for a moment blinking at the sudden exposure to neon. The Europa Hotel, with Parker, was just across the road, but it was the last place I needed to go. It would be out of the frying pan into the inferno. I looked behind me. A hundred yards back two figures were emerging from the darkness of the car park, moving at speed. As they entered the light I caught a glint of metal from one; it could have been a gun or a plate in his head, but there was no time to find out. I turned to my left. The sidewalk was thick with drunks being turned out of a disco. Three policemen shadowed them as they moved towards me, guns slung low at their sides like Western marshals. I began limping towards them, twisting and turning to avoid the barges of the dancers as they swaggered home. My pursuers rounded the corner, stopped for a moment, then one let out a shout as he spotted me. Another flash of metal. Definitely a gun. The drunks were talking at the tops of their voices, but the cocking of a gun has its own kind of deathly volume and I ducked instinctively. A girl screamed beside me, in fear not pain, and the crowd scattered as the first shot cracked past my ear. I dived to the ground. A second shot pinged off a flagstone to my right; three more whistled round my head, but from the other direction as the cops reacted to an apparent attack on them.

Cars, best equipped to speed from the scene, pulled up,

stopped as if an inanimate object would make less of a target, would render some kind of natural camouflage. I rolled from the sidewalk on to the road and came to a halt beside a small red Mini. All Minis are small, but this one looked tiny, withered by age and rust, sitting too low on its wheels; if it hadn't been stopped there in shock it might have come to a halt there of its own accord, exhausted. I put my hand on the passenger door. I looked back, saw McCoubrey's men retreating back round the corner towards the hotel, both now with guns drawn and shooting at the police. The police were lodged in the doorway of a hamburger shop, taking turns to pop their heads out and fire. Nobody appeared to have been hit.

The car door was unlocked. I pulled it open. A nun sat dwarfed behind the wheel, resplendent in brown and cream.

I said, "In God's name help me."

She gave me a look that was more Armalite than Carmelite and said: "Fuck off."

There was a sudden crack and a bolt of pain shot up my leg; I fell back from the car clutching at a hole in my jeans. I grabbed hold of the car door as I fell and swung myself up before I touched the ground. I tumbled into the passenger seat.

"Drive," I said. I held my hand up to the nun. It was soaked in blood.

"Jesus Christ," she said and threw it into first. "What did I do to deserve this?"

She swung the car to the left, squeezing it out between an ancient Anglia and a Jag that remained mesmerized by the gun battle. The police had emerged from their doorway and were carefully making their way towards the corner of the street; one turned to watch the Mini move off, but only for a moment, distracted by the roar of the car's faulty exhaust.

In a moment we were out of Great Victoria Street and moving past the university. Three police Land Rovers with blue lights flashing raced past us. In the half-light of the Mini my hand looked black and felt sticky, my fingers clamped together like they were webbed.

131

"Which hospital?"

"I've never heard a nun say fuck before."

"I'm not a fucking nun. Now which hospital or do you want to get out here?"

She pulled the car over into a closed petrol station on the Stranmillis Road and flicked the interior light on. Her face was small and sharp, pale, young-looking, innocent as you would expect a nun to be but with a flash of humour about the mouth that put the lie to her profession. Nuns have nothing to laugh about, they're too busy being bitter.

"What do you mean you're not a nun?"

"What I say, now what do you want?"

I shook my head. "I can't go to hospital."

"Why not? I'd think it was preferable to bleeding to death."

"I can't go to hospital."

She tutted. Shook her head. "Go on," she said, "tell me you're a terrorist. Tell me you're a fuckin' terrorist."

"I'm not. Honestly. I'm not."

She looked less than satisfied. She shook her head again and pulled her hat off and tossed it into the back of the car. (I have no idea what the proper term for a nun's headdress is. Possibly a Godpiece.) Her hair was jet black and cropped short. She was very pretty, but also looked like the footballer, Nigel Clough. This is not as horrible as it sounds. Nigel has a very feminine face.

I was starting to feel cold. You see people getting shot in the movies all the time and you see them start to shiver. It was like getting instant flu with toothache and somebody ripping the scab off a major wound thrown in for good measure.

I coughed. My throat had gone dry and I could feel Keith Moon back at my heart. Shock. I was in shock. I could feel the blood still oozing down my leg.

"My name is Dan Starkey. I am wanted for two murders I did not commit, I am being chased by the IRA, the UVF, the police and the army, my wife has been kidnapped and I have just given rather a good comedian a severe thrashing and I have been shot in the leg for my trouble and may be bleeding to death."

132

"So you've had a bad day, what do you want me to do about it?"

But the nun, God bless her, started the car again.

I was asleep for days. I do not remember fainting in the car, I do not remember being half carried half dragged into her house or being put to bed. I have no recollection of screaming nightmares or a nurse treating a wound to my right leg. I have a vague recollection of dreaming about The Clash re-forming and Sugar Ray Leonard coming out of retirement at age forty to reclaim the welterweight title, but those were night-time constants anyway.

Her name was Lee Cooper. Her parents had a warped sense of humour. And her friends called her Jean.

She was not a nun but a trainee nurse moonlighting as a singing nun-o-gram, stripping down from habit to suspenders and basque for thirty pounds a go. When I was feeling better and she was feeding me soup in her spare room, sun streaming in in thin shafts of brightness through a grimy skylight, I asked her why she'd taken pity on me.

"I was feeling really pissed off, it was a relief to meet someone worse off than myself."

"What pissed you off?"

"I'd been booked in to appear at a retirement party. Nobody told me it was a fuckin' priest's retirement."

"Red face?"

"Red arse, he couldn't keep his hands off me. It was disgusting."

I set the empty dish on the floor and turned to her, sitting on the bedcovers beside me. She was wearing a thin white jersey with a round neck.

"You're mad you know. I could be a killer. All you have to do is read the papers, Lee."

She shrugged. "I'm going to be a nurse. They teach you not to neglect anyone who's been hurt. I had to respect the fact that you didn't want to go to hospital. I don't need to know anything about you in order to cure you. It's like defendants in a trial have a right to a solicitor, guilty or not. I'm giving you your chance."

"But back here, in your house, for days on end? That's not a chance. That's harbouring a fugitive."

She shook her head slightly and a little smile jumped on to her lips. "Anyone who looks as much like a fugitive as you do couldn't possibly be a fugitive. You're so guilty-looking you must be innocent."

"Thanks. It doesn't worry you that I might have killed two women?"

"Of course it worries me."

"And?"

"And nothing. I'll take the chance."

"Thanks."

"And it's not every day I get an honest-to-God celebrity into my bed. I used to read your column, you know? Only reason I bought the paper. It was very funny. Anyone who can write that well doesn't need to kill anyone."

"Can I have that in writing? I'll present it at the trial."

"You never thought of writing something other than journalism? You could write a good book, I'll bet."

"I wrote a book once. *Born on the Twelfth of July* it was called. It was about a policeman who was so badly affected by the Troubles that he spent the rest of his life confined to a public house. The publisher sent it back. Said she didn't accept manuscripts written in crayon. I think she was trying to tell me something."

She shook her head and stood up. "I can't tell when you're being serious. You start off all right, then go off into a tangent."

"That's what they all say. Maybe I'll write a book about this. What do you think, will it have a happy ending?"

She smiled. "I hope so."

I pulled back the cover from the bed and examined the bandage on my leg. There was still a dull throbbing, but nothing I couldn't put up with.

"What do you reckon? Will I live?"

"Well, that won't kill you. I imagine there are quite a lot of other things that might." She leant over me and lightly smoothed the cotton dressing. "No — it wasn't much of a wound. But you lost a lot of blood. I mean, you didn't lose it; I know exactly where it is, it's dried all over the seat of my car, but it's not of much use to you there. Sure if I'd taken you to hospital I'd never have gotten you to pay for the cleaning, so it's just as well I hung on to you."

"Just as well."

One thing, I missed the funeral. The double funeral. It rained. Lee brought me a newspaper. The front page was dominated by Brinn and Agnes in tears at the cemetery. There was a small photo of Margaret inset.

Lee said: "She was very pretty."

"Yeah. She was."

Looking over my shoulder, she asked: "Which one's her dad?"

He wasn't there, of course. The report said that he was still seriously ill in a private hospital. The minister at the funeral had appealed for an end to the violence and for peaceful elections, as ministers had for twenty-five years of funerals. In the afternoon paratroopers shot dead three joy-riders in West Belfast and Loyalist gunmen walked into a city-centre pub, singled out two Catholics and blew their heads off. God's megaphone was busted. On an inside page there was a slightly better photo of me. It was taken from a holiday snap. No word of Patricia. Not even a bloody mention. Neither was there anything on Giblet O'Gibber or the gun battle in Great Victoria Street. Small incidents like that didn't warrant the space. Where my column used to be there was one by Mike Magee, headed *Where is Dan Starkey?*

Lee asked: "Do you miss your wife?"

"Yeah. A lot. I try not to think about her too much. If I think about things too much I'll have a nervous breakdown, and then I won't be much use to anyone."

"And how are you going to be of use to anyone, unless they catch you?"

135

I shrugged. "If I knew that I'd be halfway there, Lee. Right now all I know is I'm popular for all the wrong reasons."

Out there, somewhere, Patricia: alive but a prisoner of someone, or dead. But they would surely have found the body.

"What would you do, Lee, in my situation? What would you do?"

She thought about it for a moment, her brow scrunched up. She was young, free, single, everything in the world going for her, just like Margaret, except she was alive. She was a bizarre mix of Florence Nightingale and Nigel Clough, an innocent in a violent world whose only vice was dressing like a nun for cash.

"I'd lie back in bed," she said finally, "pull the covers up over me and wait until I woke up from the nightmare."

"You think that would work?"

"No," she said.

17

In her nun's habit, Lee said: "Did you hear the IRA have shot
two Mormons in Derry?"

She stood by the mirror, straightening her Godpiece, morbid
music glooming the room from the clock radio by the bed. She
liked to listen to classical music; it not only offended my punk
sensibilities, you also couldn't tap your foot to it the way you
could to Dr. Feelgood.

I snapped the radio off and walked over to her, warily testing
the weight on my injured leg.

"Philistine," she said wearily.

The bandage felt tight against the side of my jeans, but there
was no real pain and even the dull throb disappeared after a
couple of drinks. Not only had Lee sewn my leg, but she had also
repaired my trousers in such a way that they were no longer bell-
bottoms. She was such a marvel doing all this for me that I didn't
dare ask why she was taking the trouble. If she hadn't been a
foul-mouthed atheist I would have thanked God for Christian
charity.

"They've started shooting Mormons? That's getting a bit serious, isn't it?"

She had a wicked smile on her face. "Apparently they were
mistaken for plainclothes police — you know the cropped hair
and superior smiles — and taken out by a sniper as they were

going from door to door in one of those yuppie new housing developments. Not before time. They were a pain in the hole."

"The Osmonds won't be happy. The Provos have bitten off more than they can chew now. Once the Mormons weigh in, the IRA'll soon be on the run. A war of attrition."

Lee had work to do and I had Parker to meet. Lee did the phoning. Less suspicious. They'd be watching him for sure. He suggested meeting in a restaurant on the outskirts of town. He said it was important.

While I was out for the count Lee had cut the toffee chunks out of my hair. But still I hardly recognized myself in the mirror: I'd lost weight and I'd the paleness you only get in the terminal stages of hangover. The short hair made my face look skull-like, the pouches beneath my eyes sagged like fridge-black bananas.

"I don't look much like James Stewart now."

She fixed her gaze on my reflection. "Did you ever?"

"Once. A long time ago."

She stepped out of the room, her bare feet padding on the polished wooden floor hidden by the robe so that she appeared to be gliding, and disappeared into the bathroom. I sat on the side of the bed and carefully lifted my injured leg on to the quilt to tie my shoelace.

When I looked up she was standing in the doorway. That same wicked smile was on her lips and her eyes were bright and challenging. She said: "Divorce Jack."

It was like a punch to the stomach. Eyes wide, scared, I peered into the darkened shadows of the hallway behind her to see if the vastness of her garb was hiding the enemy. She was alone.

I had not gone into much detail about the death of Margaret. I had certainly not told her Margaret's dying words. I raised myself slowly to my feet; my legs felt weak, but not from injury, from fear. As I looked at her, as I got closer, her smile faded. Expressions of puzzlement then apprehension chased each other across her face. When I was so close that I could see my face reflected in her eyes I knew what she was thinking. She was harbouring a killer.

I grabbed her by the shoulders, squeezing them tightly, then pulled her towards me and past me and tossed her on to the bed. She let out a little yelp of pain, like a dog unjustly sent to its basket, and kicked in the process.

She landed on her stomach but immediately rolled on to her back, drawing her knees up as a man would to defend his groin. I pivoted to the left on my good leg and her knees followed my movement, then I sharply dived to her right, pinning her down before she could move them back; I let out my own little yelp as I felt the stitches in my leg rip.

I grabbed her wrists and put my full weight on her habit.

"Who're you working for, Lee?"

My voice sounded hollow.

She shook her head in confusion, furrows on her brow bunched like pasta strips.

I pressed her harder into the bed, but the fear in her eyes stopped me from hitting her. Why taunt me, then act scared? I pressed down harder.

She screeched: "Will you fuck off me?"

She pulled to left, to right, but couldn't move me.

"Who're you working for?"

"I'm working for the fucking health service, who do you think? I'm a nurse." She pulled again. "What's got into you, Dan? Please. Please get off me." There were tears in her eyes. They began rolling down her face. I tightened my grip. "Please don't hurt me."

"Why did you say that?"

"I am a nurse, Dan. That's who I work for. Please, Dan . . . just leave . . . I've helped you all I . . ."

"Not that. What you said before?"

"When?"

"Just there. In the doorway."

"I didn't say anything. I didn't mean anything. I just said about the radio . . ."

"What about it?"

"There was a tune on the radio you said was crap. I'd been trying to remember who it was and it just came to me in the toilet . . ."

139

"What are you talking about, Lee?"

"The radio. You turned it off. I was trying to remember who the composer was and it just came to me. They used it on that bread advertisement on TV."

The tears had stopped now. I relaxed my grip slightly. Her body remained taut.

"You said 'Divorce Jack,' Lee. The last words Margaret ever said to me. That's what you said."

Another rush of tears. She freed her hands effortlessly and clasped them, small and cool, in mine.

"Dan, I'm sorry, I'm sorry. I didn't say that. I said 'Dvořák.' The composer. The composer, Dan. Dvořák. I just wanted to say who wrote that music, that he wasn't crap."

And it was like coming back to life, or reaching heaven and discovering the meaning of everything. Suddenly all became clear.

Dvořák. Pronounced by a slurring dying woman as "Divorce Jack." The tape she had haphazardly tossed to me as an unwanted gift, a tape from her father the politician. And that was what they were after: not me, not Margaret, the tape. Whatever it contained was worth killing for. In fact, whatever was on the tape was very important, because you didn't need a reason to kill people, not here.

The tape I had sold to a second-hand shop just as thoughtlessly as Margaret had given it away to me.

I collapsed on top of Lee, felt her arms go round my neck.

"I'm so sorry," I cried, my face in her neck.

I felt the tautness leave her body, warmth coursing through her just as I had been sparked back to life by her revelation. We lay there until her legs went numb and I'd no more tears to shed.

It was getting dark by the time we set out. A fine summer's evening. Red sky at night, shepherd's delight. Swallows curved past us, twittering at the moon, as we walked to the Mini. I felt calm, relaxed, as sure of myself as I had been since the whole bloody mess had evolved from a stolen kiss. The world was still after me, Patricia was still missing, I was still a killer on the run, and I had a disturbing tendency to burst into tears, but I wasn't going to let little things like that get me down. In a second-hand bookstall in Bangor there was a cassette tape which, for whatever reason, was extremely important to a lot of people. In the morning I would get it and for the first time I would have at least some say in my own destiny. And then they would probably kill me, but at least I'd have had my say.

Lee had missed her first appointment but had two others to fulfil, one on the outskirts of Holywood, which was handy enough for my rendezvous with Parker at Ricci's Parlour in Sydenham.

We drove in silence, skipping the hardline Loyalist stronghold of the lower Holywood Road by cruising along the dual carriageway towards Bangor and then doubling back at the Sydenham bypass. Less chance of a police or army checkpoint.

Ricci's was barely a hundred yards from the Chinese restaurant where I'd met with Neville Maxwell. A neon swan sign dominated the window. Lee stopped the car, but I cautioned her against turning the engine off; it wasn't an area you were ever likely to see many nuns; the locals were more likely to throw boulders first and ask questions later.

"I wasn't born yesterday," she said.

"I'm sorry. I keep thinking of you as a nun. Sheltered and virginal."

"You'd be surprised."

"I would?"

"That's as much as you hear."

"Och, go on . . ."

"Fuck off."

Which said it all really. We sat in silence. I could feel the throb in my leg again. The tear in the stitches hadn't been too bad; I'd lost some more blood, but not enough to keep me in bed.

She said: "Do you want me to come back later and pick you up?"

"Are you serious?"

141

"Yeah."

"Do you not think you've done enough? Jesus, Lee, you could be put away for this."

"So?"

"You do have the innocence of a nun. You don't have to invite all this shit upon yourself. There's no point. You've done everything I could possibly have asked of you."

"I'm just trying to be polite, Dan, I don't really mean it."

Poker face, then a little blushing smirk as she realized she hadn't fully pulled it off.

"Nuns can't lie, Lee. When they do they explode. It's a fact."

"No, I mean it. I mean, I've looked after you this far, so I'm already guilty. A few extra days aren't going to make things any worse for me, are they?"

I brushed at the seat between my legs. Crumbs of dried blood.

She shrugged. "I will if you want me to. I'd like to help."

"I know you do. Listen, if I need help, I'll call you. I know where you are."

"Don't call us, we'll call you."

"I'm sorry if it sounds thankless, but it's better that way. I'm responsible for enough people being in the shit without getting anyone else involved. I mean, look at Giblet O'Gibber. I punched his lights in for nothing. Jesus, I nearly gave you a beating, Lee."

"You've the world on your shoulders, Dan. I'm just offering you a shoulder pad, y'know, to lean on?"

I put my hand on her shoulder. I leant over and kissed her lightly on the lips.

When we parted there were two elderly ladies staring at us and shaking their heads in unison.

We burst into giggles.

"I think you've just reinforced a few old wives' tales about nuns." Lee laughed. "Another time, another place, we could have taken it a bit further. Really given them something to talk about."

"Who knows?"

She placed her hand on my leg. "Look after yourself, Dan. Look after that leg. Find your wife."

142

I squeezed her hand and got out of the car. I closed the door and tapped the roof and she ground it into first gear and drove off.

The two women were still standing watching. One, a bag of chips in her hand, said: "You're disgusting."

"Fuck off," I said and crossed the road to Ricci's.

"Fuck off yourself, cuntface," she replied. It was a nice area.

Parker was sitting alone at a table for four at the back of the restaurant. He had a half-finished glass of lager before him and he was studying a large menu the front cover of which was a repro-duction of an American dollar bill, albeit with George Washing-ton biting into a pizza. He closed the menu and set it to one side as I sat down opposite him.

"Well?" I said.

"As well as can be expected under the circumstances." His face was sullen, charcoal grey as if his pigment was fading with-out the benefit of strong sunlight, his voice dull.

"Well, you're full of the joys of spring, Mr. Parker. Cheer up, sunshine, things are starting to look up."

"Are they?"

He didn't look convinced. A figure appeared at my elbow. Without looking up I said: "A pint of Harp and a vodka chaser, mate, please."

The figure pulled the seat beside me back and sat down. His hair was cropped short and prematurely grey. Piercing blue eyes and a strong square chin. He put out a hand towards me and I took it after a moment's hesitation.

"You'll be Starkey then?"

He shook my hand warmly. I glanced at Parker, who pursed his lips apologetically. At the table opposite, two men turned to watch us; one pulled the side of his black Harrington jacket back to reveal the butt of a pistol.

He was still shaking my hand. He looked familiar.

"The name's Coogan, Pat Coogan. Perhaps you've heard of me."

"Cow Pat Coogan?"

He nodded.

143

I looked across at Parker. He said: "I'm sorry, Starkey. I had no choice."

Coogan said: "Shall we order?"

I nodded.

He said: "I understand you killed my girlfriend."

"I'm not very hungry," I said.

18

A waiter in a white jacket and crimson bow tie handed out two extra menus. He was tall and emaciated with thin silver hair. One eye was wide and glassy, as if it was propped open by an invisible monocle, the other narrowed and speculative. His voice was Belfast, with maybe three weeks in Florida and a couple of months in London.

"Gentlemen, we offer a wide-ranging menu of international cuisine. Tonight I would particularly recommend a breaded escalope of turbot, which is prepared in a mixture of white bread and brioche crumbs, and served with a sorrel cream."

He stood expectantly for a moment and then moved across to the table opposite and repeated the spiel.

I set my menu down and said to Coogan: "I thought you were in prison."

"I was. I've been released, for good behaviour."

"Does this constitute good behaviour?"

"What, eating dinner?"

"You know what I mean." I nodded across to his companions.

"With a reputation like mine, you don't think I need some protection?"

"I thought you usually offered protection."

"Me? Never. Not my line. I wouldn't harm a fly."

"You two know each other?" Parker asked.

"I know of Mr. Starkey from what he writes in the paper. You read everything there is in prison."

"And I know Mr. Coogan from writing about him in the paper."

Parker, his visage more composed now, clasped his hands before him, elbows on table. "Which leaves me the only person not knowing exactly who you are. This afternoon was illuminating, but in a different way."

Coogan nodded, raised an eye to one of the men at the other table, and accepted a sheet of white paper from him. He handed it across to Parker.

"This is my CV. I had it prepared when I left prison. It saves a lot of time explaining how nasty I am."

Parker ran his eye down the sheet.

"That's novel," I said.

"That's poetry, mate," Coogan corrected.

"The poetry of crime?"

Coogan shrugged. "To each his own. If I could produce a newspaper maybe I would. As it was I didn't get much past potato printing."

"You still IRA?"

Coogan glanced across to his friends. They smirked back. His face remained serious.

"Still? You think the 'Ra wear suits like this?"

He had a prison pallor, a jawline heavy with stubble. So different from the youthful picture I'd seen of him in Margaret's bedroom, taken before he'd turned to crime and carved out a niche for himself as Cow Pat Coogan, before he'd made Margaret pregnant and split up with her over an abortion. Had he loved her at all, or too much or not enough? Had the split with Margaret pushed him round the corner into crime, or had he already been shaped by Belfast's bitter streets? I'd known once, I'd written about him, but the details escaped me now. Life stories pondered over in courts merged in repetition after a while until you could look back and identify only one common denominator, a jelled identity of misshapen lives, depraved by politics, gunfire, bigotry, repression and poverty, with God in a supervisory capacity.

146

The waiter reappeared at our table.

"May I take your order, gentlemen?"

Coogan looked up at him, silently contemplating. The waiter gazed back, odd eyes holding Coogan's for an extended moment before looking away. It unsettled him, not being able to outstare a customer.

Coogan said: "I'd like a jam sandwich, please."

"I'm sorry?"

"A jam sandwich. Raspberry if possible."

"I'm afraid that's not on the menu, sir." He reached down and opened Coogan's menu for him, adding haughtily: "You are unlikely to find that on any menu in any restaurant in this city, sir."

"You have bread?"

"Of course."

"You have butter?"

"I see what you're getting at, sir, but . . ."

"You have jam?"

"For certain desserts, perhaps, sir, but my point is . . ."

A gun at his earhole shut him up. One of Coogan's companions, the one who'd earlier flashed a pistol at me, stood up and offered the waiter some advice.

"You make a fuckin' jam sandwich, mate, or we'll do a fuckin' Lord Mountbatten on ye. They'll find your fucking head and shoulders on the beach."

The waiter blanched, nodded.

"Thank you, Frankie," Coogan said, and Frankie sat, still glowering at the waiter as he replaced the gun. A courting couple seated behind Frankie, just entering their first course, glanced nervously back. Frankie's head, thick like a bulldog's, slanted towards them and they quickly looked away.

The waiter, his voice shaky, said: "Will that be all?"

"Fish fingers," Coogan said, closing the menu, "to go. For all of us."

The waiter was about to burst into tears. He had my sympathy on that. He nodded sharply, completed writing the order and retreated to the sanctuary of the kitchen. Coogan guffawed.

147

"What's going on?" Parker asked.

Coogan smiled at him. "Gun law," he said, simply. His blue-black suit was a fashionably cut Adolfo Dominguez but it sagged a little at the shoulders, like it had been made to old measurements. A white shirt, grey silk tie.

Parker handed me the CV. It was a litany of law breaking, dominated by a string of close-printed armed robberies he'd been found not guilty of, together with a string of offences he'd been questioned about but never charged with. Under a list of leisure pursuits it read, "the cinema, theatre, and amassing a fortune by whatever means possible because I like to live well."

"Anyway," Coogan said, "to get back to murder."

I spread my hands, palm upward.

"What can I say? I'm not guilty."

"Most everyone seems to think you are. In fact most everyone wants you dead."

I shrugged.

Parker said: "I don't think he did it."

"When I want your opinion, I'll let you know. Didn't this afternoon teach you anything?"

Parker sat back.

"What happened this afternoon?"

Parker shook his head.

"We got bored waiting for you to call," said Coogan, "so we had a game of Irish roulette. I won't go into it in detail, but it involves a petrol bomb and an ability to blow out matches very quickly. You didn't enjoy it very much, did you?"

Parker shook his head again, his eyes lingering for a defiant second on Coogan's face before darting away.

"I should tell you now, Parker, that those bottles were filled with urine. It was just Frankie's idea of a wee joke. He has a wicked sense of humour, our Frankie. He has never really warmed to Americans since they turned down his application for a visa. It seems an armful of convictions for violent assault doesn't help your chances. He wanted to go to Disneyworld."

Frankie smiled and nodded from across the way.

"It was a fun afternoon," Parker said humourlessly, his eyes

148

fixed now on the courting couple who were explaining to a different waiter that they had changed their minds about a main course.

I lifted Parker's glass and drained it. My mouth was dry. "So what are you going to do, kill me?"

"Possibly. I wouldn't mind knowing where the tape is first, though."

"He's looking for a tape," Parker said.

"A tape?"

Coogan smiled wanly. "Now let's not play stupid bastards. We all know about the tape, you hand it over now and we'll see what we can do for you that doesn't involve lead."

"That's kind of you."

"Don't get fucking smart with me, Starkey. Right now you're a flatliner and I'm God. Only I can bring you back to life. Give me the tape and that's a start."

"I thought you were concerned about Margaret."

"I am concerned about Margaret."

"But this tape is more important?"

"For the moment."

"What's on it that's so great?"

Coogan sat back in his seat. "This is getting tedious, Starkey." Abruptly he stood, his seat toppling backwards. It cracked off the polished hardwood floor. None of the other customers looked round. He nodded to Frankie and his companion and the pair stood up. "We'll go somewhere they can't hear you scream, Starkey. Pain is a marvellous memory stimulant."

"Pain is bad enough, but the prospect of pain can be just as bad. Travelling towards pain can be worse than pain itself."

"Starkey, that is the most goddamn stupid thing I think I've ever heard."

"I was just trying to reassure you about what's to come."

"Starkey, they're not going to torture me. I don't know where the tape is. I didn't even know about the goddamn tape until today. You're the one they're gonna torture, so don't get philosophical about pain with me, save it for yourself."

"Will you two stop bickering?"

149

Frankie leant back from the front passenger seat. He had locked us securely into the back of a small van which had GERRY BLACK'S GARDENING SUPPLIES untidily painted on the side. In case we felt like trying to escape, his mate, whom he introduced as Mad Dog, sat opposite us with a gun pointed between us. Coogan drove, incongruous behind the wheel of the trades- man's van in his smart suit. We drove through the city centre and turned towards the west of the city. The roads were quiet. Nine times out of ten driving that late at night in the west you would be stopped by the police. Luck had not been running my way; right then the police would have seemed like the ultimate good luck.

"When we get close to where we're going," Coogan said from the front, "I'm afraid we'll have to blindfold you. We have to keep certain secrets, y'know?"

"I don't see why you're taking me," Parker ventured. "I don't know anything."

"You'll see."

It was a disquieting answer. Parker slumped forward. "This is ridiculous. I should have turned you in to the police in the first place, Starkey."

"Think of the story, Parker."

"Fuck the story, Starkey."

Mad Dog leant across and tapped Parker on the knee. "If he doesn't talk, we put the blindfold on, take you to a secluded spot and shoot you in the back of the head."

Parker looked up. "Why put a blindfold on if you're shoot- ing me in the back of the head?"

Mad Dog smiled crookedly. "I wear the blindfold. Some- times it takes nine or ten shots. But it's a good laugh."

Frankie, his mouth half-full of sandwich, looked back again. "Pay no attention to him. You'll be okay as long as you cooper- ate." He started picking at a raspberry seed jammed between his front teeth. "Good sammies, Pat. Just what the doctor ordered."

"A doctor ordered these?" asked Mad Dog. "They brought us a doctor's food? What sorta fuckin' place is that?"

"Maddie," said Coogan, mock scolding, "shut up."

We pulled into a side street off the Falls Road. Mad Dog put his gun away while he put blindfolds on us: not real blindfolds, but musty-smelling balaclava helmets, back to front. The barrel of Frankie's pistol peeked at us from the rim of his seat. The last thing I saw before the lights went out was a little wink from Frankie.

Coogan started the engine again and we drove for another ten minutes. Then the van drew to a halt and a door opened on the driver's side; I felt the slight tilt of the vehicle as Coogan got out and a muffled knock on a door. It opened with a slight creak and I heard hushed voices.

"What's going on?" Parker whispered.

"Fuck up," Mad Dog whispered back and followed it up with a dull thump which I presumed by the way Parker wheezed was the sound of metallic gun barrel on fleshy knee.

The door to the van was pulled to again and Coogan climbed back in. "The fuckers are down the road, we'll have to go the long way round."

We started off again and it was another ten minutes before we pulled to a stop. The engine was killed and the back of the van opened up. I heard the hum of a street lamp and a child crying somewhere way above me. Mad Dog pushed us forward and Frankie guided us down from outside. My feet splashed through a puddle and I smelt urine.

Our feet moved from gravel to smooth cement and then a tiled floor. Then a hiss as an elevator door opened. We began moving upward. I counted twelve tings on the bell and then we stopped.

Twenty feet along a corridor with the same smooth floor, and still the smell of urine. A door opened, closed. My mask came off.

We were in a small, average-looking lounge. There was a poor reproduction of the *Mona Lisa* on one wall, a black and white television tuned to Channel 4 in one corner, a mustard-coloured three-piece suite afflicted with a series of cigarette burns along another wall. A smell of vinegar.

Frankie had me by the arm, his grasp tight; his pistol was in his other hand, hanging down by his side. Coogan stood by a large window which opened out on to a balcony. He pulled the window inwards and stepped out until he was framed against the blacker-than-night colossus of the Cave Hill. So much for security — twelve floors up and with the Cave Hill behind him, it could only be Hillside Apartments, the tallest and ugliest public housing in Belfast. A breeding ground for rats and terrorists. Parker was by his side, still with his balaclava on, and held tightly by Mad Dog.

"I don't believe in messing about, Starkey."

"I know."

Coogan nodded to Mad Dog, who helped Parker up on to the balcony wall. Parker obligingly stepped up, but his body suddenly shuddered as he felt the cool breeze.

"What's going on? What are you doing?"

There was a frightened edge to his voice. He moved an exploratory foot six inches forward, felt the open space before him and arched back from the edge. Mad Dog held him firmly in place.

"You stay where you are, Parker, and you'll be okay. As long as Starkey here cooperates you'll have nothing to worry about and a good story to write in the morning. Take it easy."

He turned to me. "His life in your hands, Starkey. I'm going to make this very easy for you. We are twelve storeys up here. I am going to count to three. At the count of three, if you haven't told me where the tape is, Parker learns to fly. Okay?"

I nodded.

He said: "One."

"Starkey, tell him where the fuckin' tape is!"

I had no choice.

"Two."

No choice at all.

"Starkey?"

"Okay, okay . . ."

Coogan pushed him. Parker gave a sharp little yell, and disappeared over the edge.

I surged forward, screaming, but Frankie cracked me behind the knees and I collapsed to the floor.

Coogan peered after Parker then turned from the window, grinning. "Fastest reader I ever knew," he said, "twelve storeys in six seconds."

19

Frankie grabbed my jacket collar and pulled me to my feet. "Don't curse at the boss, fella," he growled. He jabbed a fist into my kidneys and my legs gave way again, but he held me up.

Mad Dog, bent out over the balcony, turned his head back towards Coogan and shouted: "Flat as a pancake, Pat."

The shrill whistle of the wind over the Cave Hill all but drowned out Coogan's reply. He shook his head lightly and turned to usher Mad Dog back into the flat. He closed the balcony doors. "Have him removed," he said quietly. Mad Dog nodded curtly and left the room; he winked at me as he walked past.

Coogan stood with his back to the balcony, watching me intently for a moment before advancing.

"There was no need for that," I said.

"No, there wasn't." He nodded sagely, his hands clasped before him. He held my eyes for a long moment and then looked down. "Here's the church," he said, holding his hands up to my face. He raised his index fingers until they joined at the tip. "And here's the steeple." He finished it with a flourish, turning his hands inside out, his thumbs spreading to reveal the six thin cigar-like fingers remaining, wildly cavorting within. "Open the doors, and there's all the stupid bloody people."

"You're talking nonsense, Coogan."

He wiggled his six fingers again. "All these stupid people, all talk no action." He separated his hands again, the fleshy church palm upward and still. Slowly he curled them into two tight fists. "The only thing they understand really. You were too slow, Starkey."

"You said you would count to three."

"I say a lot of things, I mean very few of them. You were fuckin' me around, you paid the price."

"I was ready to tell you."

"It's not a case of when you're ready, Starkey. Understand that and you'll get on a lot better."

"He didn't deserve that!"

"Who deserves anything? The kid who gets bombed? The guy that gets run over? Yeah, sure, Parker didn't deserve the flying lesson. Tough. That's the way it works. He's a casualty of war, a means to an end. It was a mistake of his to assume he would get some sort of special treatment because he was an American. His death is your fault, you got him involved in all this."

"Don't try blaming me, Coogan, you sick bastard."

Frankie punched me in the kidneys again and this time let me flop on to the ground.

"Is this not the pot calling the kettle black, Starkey?" Coogan was above me, leering down. "I didn't murder Margaret and her mother, did I? A little assist off a wall hardly compares to that, does it? He was only a fuckin' Yank."

I pulled myself up on to my knees.

"You can stick your fuckin' tape up your hole, Coogan." Rage as bile. I was sick on the carpet.

"Jesus," Coogan said, turning away, "I can't stand people being sick."

"He can fuckin' well clean it up," Frankie moaned. "You can be bloody sure I'm not."

"Someone has to."

"Let Mad Dog do it, Pat. Sure he'll probably eat it anyway."

"Jesus," Coogan winced, "do you have to?"

"Or let the bitch do it."

"Sure isn't the bitch going to learn to fly too?"

155

Frankie smiled. "Oh, yeah. I forgot."

Coogan got over his squeamishness. He smiled at me. "I don't think that tape would fit up my hole, Starkey." He bent down beside me. "But I know whose it might."

He nodded to Frankie. Frankie turned and disappeared down a darkened corridor to the right of the door. A door opened and I heard him rasp: "Up you get, sweetie."

There was a derisive snort and a flurry of curses.

Frankie appeared in the corridor again. Smiled at me and moved to one side to make way for a woman in a shapeless pink dressing gown. I raised myself to a kneeling position.

"Well, look what the cat's dragged in," she said.

"Hello, Spaghetti Legs," I said.

Patricia looked tired, her skin wan but for the dark rings under her eyes. Her lips were pale and chapped. She held a cigarette in her left hand, the butt clasped between her index and second finger, the fiery tip pointing into her palm as if she were trying to hide it.

I stood up, cautiously.

"Spaghetti Legs?" Coogan asked, incredulous.

"It's a pet name, okay?" I volunteered.

"Some pet."

"You okay, Patricia?"

"Do you care?"

"Of course I care!"

"Spaghetti Legs?" He stood with a half-grin on his face, staring at Patricia. He left it for a moment then added, "Can't say I noticed. I don't think we even had the light on." Another moment, then: "Did we, darling?"

"Away and fuck yourself."

Patricia kept her eyes on me. Cool. Penetrating. Guilty.

And in that moment I knew how she must have felt when she found me with Margaret: the icy pain of betrayal solidifying in the pit of my stomach.

I started to cross to her but changed mid-step and planted the best punch I have ever thrown on Coogan's nose. He wheeled away with a yelp and I collapsed to the ground as Frankie cracked my head from behind with his pistol. I saw stars and flaming chariots and big frothy pints of beer and then was consumed by a spinning darkness.

When I dream, I often dream of my father and of making him sandwiches. In the last week of his life, shrunken by cancer, he asked me to make him a ham sandwich. Glazed by alcohol, I made him a whole plateful but he sent me and the food away, angry at the waste. It seems a trivial thing to dream about, time and again. I once explained the dream to Patricia after which she took to hugging her pillow every night out of a fear that I might consume it while trying to compensate in my dreams for the waste of bread and ham.

When I woke my mouth was dry and my head was sore. I was lying uncomfortably on top of an unmade double bed. Patricia lay beside me, watching me, propped up on one elbow. Her dressing gown hung open. I rubbed the back of my head, examined the flakes of dried blood on my hand.

Straight to the point. "You slept with him, didn't you?"

She shrugged. "You look like shite."

"You're no oil painting yourself."

"Thanks."

"You did, didn't you?"

"There wasn't much sleeping involved."

"Oh, that's lovely."

"Shits in glass houses shouldn't throw stones."

"Shits can't throw stones. Shits throw potatoes."

She shrugged again. "All's fair in love and war."

I sat up. The room was windowless and smelt of sweat. Mine. I felt dizzy.

"Did you kill her?"

She looked hard at me, a deep gaze that penetrated my soul and seemed to suck away the dizziness. "Of course I didn't bloody kill her, what do you think I am?"

I shook my head. "I don't know."

157

I stood up. My joints cracked.

She lay back on the bed, her eyes on the ceiling. "It wasn't him either. Coogan."

"What was that? Pillow talk?"

"Don't be stupid."

"I can't believe you screwed someone who kidnapped you. Jesus, fuck."

"It happened. I was at a pretty low ebb, Dan. He cheered me up."

"What, by kidnapping you? Jesus. I don't believe I'm hearing this. I could understand if it was rape, for God's sake, but this?"

"What do you mean, you could understand if it was rape? You would have preferred it to be rape?"

"Yes! Jesus, I don't know."

"It doesn't matter any more, Dan."

"Of course it matters."

"It matters as much as you sleeping with her."

"It's a different thing entirely, Patricia! Jesus, okay, okay, it wasn't right, and God knows I've — she's paid for it. But screwing someone who kidnaps you. Jesus."

"It happened to Patty Hearst."

"You're not fucking Patty Hearst. You haven't got any fucking money for a start."

"It never crossed your mind that I might be doing it for revenge? To get even?"

"Grilling my Sex Pistols record was even enough."

"Not in my book."

"What, are there rules laid down now or something? Screwing your kidnapper! Jesus."

"Well, it worked, didn't it?"

"You're presuming a lot, aren't you? How the hell did you know I would end up here? That I would ever find out?"

"I knew. He knew. He's very good at what he does. Apparently."

"What's that, part of his charm then? This isn't the movies, Patricia. He's not Robin Hood. He's not some Disney loveable rogue, some Border Squirrel. He's just pushed a really good man off the balcony out there. He's just killed him. Don't you understand?"

"I understand. It's not nice. But it's part of what he does to survive."

"It had nothing to do with survival. It was pure bloody murder for the sake of it."

"It's what he does."

"And you screwed him."

"Okay! I screwed him!" She flared up out of the bed and swung for me, but I arched back away from the slap and she fell back on her side again on the bed. She buried her head in the pillows and began to cry. Big whooping groans shuddered through her body. I stood and watched her. Finally her breathing returned to normal and she turned a damp cheek towards me. "It's over now," she said quietly.

"What do you mean?"

"I mean, it's over. With him. We aren't sleeping together any more. Not for a few days."

"You mean you slept with him more than once?"

She nodded.

She dabbed at her eyes with the crumpled top sheet. "But it's over."

And I started laughing, big comic-strip chortles which shook my body as much as her tears had rattled hers and which forced a puzzled half-smile on to her lips which faded and then returned with every moment my laughter continued.

"What is it, Dan?" she pleaded nervously.

"He dropped you, didn't he? Isn't that it? You screwed your kidnapper and fell for him and he's used you and dropped you."

The smile slipped from her face. "It's not funny."

"I think it's one of the funniest things I've ever heard, Patricia. The revenge that caved in on itself. You must feel pretty bloody dirty."

She pulled herself up, folded her arms on her bended knees and rested her chin on them. She pushed a strand of hair from her forehead. She tutted. "We're a couple of stupid bastards, aren't we, Dan?"

I sat beside her and put my hand on her head. Her hair was rough and dry but not as comical as mine. "Always have been, Patricia, always will be."

When the door opened and Coogan and Frankie came in I was sitting at the top of the bed with my arm around Patricia. She was nestled into the crook of my arm, her tear-stained cheek against my shirt.

"Och, isn't that lovely," Coogan said.

He had a strip of pink Elastoplast across the bridge of his nose.

"I like the nose, Coogan. You could get a job as a stunt man on the remake of Pinocchio."

He gave me a tight, thin smile. "You're very funny, Starkey. We'll see how funny you are when the little woman goes flying in a few moments."

Frankie had his gun out and was pointing it at us. I felt Patricia tense against me. She probably felt me tensing against her.

I tried hard to act cool and calm and collected. I said: "Uh."

Frankie motioned with his gun for us to get up. We got up and followed them into the lounge again.

"I'm glad to see you've kissed and made up," Coogan said, "although I wouldn't rate her much as a kisser."

"It doesn't worry me, no-willy."

He gave me a childish little grin. "Sticks and stones will break my bones . . . no, in fact, they'll break your bones, smart-arse."

Mad Dog was standing grinning by the door. He pushed himself off it with his shoulders and in passing by me grabbed Patricia suddenly out from under my arm. She gave a little scream and I went to go after her but Frankie pressed his pistol into my scalp and said: "Stay."

The balcony window was open again. Mad Dog led her across the room and helped her up on to the step. The fresh rush of Antrim air enveloped the room and she seemed to luxuriate

160

in the breeze for a moment before turning frightened eyes towards me.

"So," Coogan said, "about this tape . . ."

"What happens to us?"

Coogan shrugged. "I'll let you go."

"You think I believe that?"

"What difference does it make? You'll have to trust me."

"I wouldn't trust you as far as I could throw you. And I'd like to throw you, believe you me."

"Oh, Starkey," he groaned with mock exasperation, "gimme a break, will ya? Look, I enjoy these little shows as much as you do. The only thing is no one I love is going to go over the edge. Just some little bit of skirt. Now tell me about the tape and take your chance or we'll let her fly and then find some other way of getting it out of you."

"What do you think, Patricia?"

She looked coolly towards Coogan. "I'll join your gang if you let him go. I'll work with you. I'll sleep with you. All of you."

Coogan laughed. "Oh, please, be serious."

He turned to me. "Well?"

Patricia stood with her back to the void, her gown billowing in the wind.

"Okay, here we go, same as before. One . . ."

"It's in a shop," I snapped.

"Where?"

"In Bangor. Outside Bangor. On the way out. A big shopping centre. There's stalls just inside the entrance, a mini-market place. There's a second-hand bookstall. It also sells tapes. I traded in the tape for some change for the phone. I didn't know what was on it. I still don't know what's bloody on it. That's all I know."

Coogan smiled. "And that's all I need. Now . . ."

"You let her . . ."

His eyes narrowed and flashed towards me. "Sucker," he said.

161

20

The knock on the door couldn't have been better timed. The sharp rap came in the instant before Coogan's sucker slur was converted into the push from Mad Dog that would have sent Patricia looping out into the darkness. Everything but the billowing pink dressing gown seemed to go into slow motion in those seconds: Coogan's glow of triumph at another killing flickered like a dying candle flame; Mad Dog's eyes wide with shock at the sudden removal of his pleasure; Patricia's flushed cheeks, her mouth open to scream but silent; Frankie's resolute stare into my eyes faltered, darted to the door; my own stony heart suddenly pumping at the slight hope of reprieve.

Coogan arched his eyes at Frankie who pushed me sideways on to a settee. He signalled at Mad Dog who pulled Patricia in from the balcony to sit beside me. Frankie went and stood behind the door, his pistol still drawn. Coogan sat opposite us in an armchair. Mad Dog walked to the door.

"It can't be anything," he said. "Davie's down there, he would have let us know."

"Get rid of whoever it is then. It's getting late."

Mad Dog opened the door a fraction and said: "What?"

A small voice, thick with Ireland, said: "I'm collectin' for the black babies."

"Not tonight, thanks," Mad Dog said, closing the door. He

162

turned and grinned at Coogan. "Fuckin' penguins at this time of night. They never give up."

Coogan stood up. Frankie sauntered over to him. "Back out then?"

Coogan nodded.

The door went again.

Mad Dog pulled it open. "Look . . ."

"Now, you're the only one on the whole floor hasn't given . . ."

"I said . . ."

". . . a penny . . ."

". . . not tonight, sister . . ."

"Will you shut that door?" Coogan shouted, turning towards the balcony again.

"Sure come on in then, sister, if you put it like that."

"What?" Coogan roared, twisting back.

Mad Dog backed into the room. Frankie turned towards the door and watched with mouth gaping as the nun walked calmly into the room, a small revolver pushed out in front of her.

"Jesus, things are getting heavy when they start arming the nuns," Coogan said.

The nun pointed her gun at Frankie's own weapon, resting forgotten in the palm of his hand. "Out the window," she said.

Frankie looked quickly at Coogan, who shrugged, and then threw it behind him, out into the night air the way Patricia would have gone a minute before.

"You too," she said, pointing at Mad Dog, who slowly withdrew his pistol from inside his jacket and sent it after Frankie's.

"What about you?"

Coogan opened his jacket. His white shirt gleamed, but there was no weapon. "I don't believe in violence," he said.

I stood up and walked over to him and kicked him very hard between the legs. With a screech he collapsed in on himself, shrinking on to the carpet.

"Neither do I," I said.

I turned to the nun, still holding her weapon resolutely on Coogan's comrades without arms.

"Lee, this is ridiculous."

She shrugged and smiled. "I couldn't help myself."

Patricia rose beside me. "Could you please tell me what's going on?"

"Do you think we could get out of here first?"

"I want to know who she is, Dan!"

"Patricia, for fuck's sake, look where we are. Can you wait just a little while until we get somewhere safe? Jesus wept."

Mad Dog and Frankie lay face down on the floor while I walked Coogan to the balcony. He knew what was coming.

"You make me fly and you're a dead man, Starkey."

"I can live with that."

"I'm serious."

"So am I."

I helped him up on to the perimeter wall. The breeze was refreshing. Coogan shivered. I held him by the arm. He looked tentatively over the edge.

"You'll regret this."

"Not as much as you."

"You're not going to let him do this, are you?" he appealed to Lee. Her face remained impassive, but she angled the pistol towards him, offering him the alternative.

He turned to Patricia and began to say something and then thought better of it.

"So," I said, "about this tape . . ."

"What about it?" he snapped quickly, peering out over the edge again.

"Well, for a start, what's so bloody important about it?"

He snorted. "You mean you never listened to it?"

"I didn't need to. I had no idea there was anything besides some crappy music on it. So?"

Coogan shook his head. "I don't know."

"Okay. So I'll count to three. And my hearing isn't the best. One."

"Okay, okay . . ."

"Two . . ."

"I don't know exactly what was on it . . . !" he spat. He took a deep breath. "All I know is that McGarry was hawking it around; he was looking for like a hundred grand for it. He said it was dynamite. Of course no one was going to pay him for it, it's not the way things work round here, but everyone was keen to have a listen."

"You must have had some idea what was on it."

"Well, yeah, sure, I mean it has to have something on Brinn, doesn't it? And we've all got a vested interest in anything that'll keep him off the throne."

"So all this . . . death is just so as yous can get a bit of dirt on Brinn?"

"I would have hoped it would be something a bit more substantial than a bit of dirt."

"And nobody would pay McGarry?"

"No. He soon realized he was on a hiding to nothing. When he was put under a bit of pressure he started to panic; easiest thing would have been to destroy the tape, but he's a greedy man and couldn't bring himself to do it. So he put it somewhere he didn't think anyone would look, but somewhere he could have easy access to it. With Margaret. It was a stupid bloody idea, but sometimes you do stupid things when you're in a jam."

"But you found out, and you killed Margaret."

"Aw no, not that one. You can't pin that one on me. I have some standards. I loved her once, you know." There was an odd touch of emotion in his voice for a moment, but it soon disappeared, like a match on ice. "I have a fair idea it was McCoubrey and his gang that done her. And one day I'll do him."

"You reckon you'll be around that long?"

I gave him a little shove, but still held on to him.

"Jesus!" He steadied himself on the parapet. "Can I buy my way out of this?"

"No."

"What will get me out of it?"

"An ability to fly."

165

He held my eyes for a moment, a strong, leader's stare, bereft of the mental unbalance I had expected. "Did you love her? Margaret?" he asked.

"She should be alive."

"Did you love her?"

"That's none of your business, Coogan."

"All I'm saying is that if I'm gone . . . it's up to you to get whoever killed her. McCoubrey."

"Whatever you say, Coogan . . ."

I stepped back to give my push a little extra weight.

"Dan!" Patricia shouted from behind me and I stopped, my hand clamped on Coogan's sleeve. I turned to her. She was standing by the kitchen door, the collar of her dressing gown pulled tight around her throat. "Don't."

"What?"

"Don't push him, Dan," she said quietly, her eyes avoiding mine.

"After what he did to you?"

"It wasn't rape, Dan."

"It was in my book."

"Dan, let him down."

"He killed Parker. You never met Parker. He was a good man and he pushed him right out this bloody window. Coogan's no sort of a man at all, why shouldn't he go the same way?"

"It makes you as bad as him, Dan. And you're not."

I thought about that for a second. "Is that some sort of a compliment?"

"Dan, you're in enough trouble already. Don't make it worse."

"You mean it can get worse?"

Was she being humane or showing loyalty to him? Before I could think it through, Lee joined in. "She's right, Dan. It will only make things worse. They're not going to give you a medal for killing him. Murder is murder. Just because he puts his head in the fire doesn't mean you have to."

"I'd love to put his head in the fire."

"You know what I mean."

166

Nothing would have given me greater pleasure than to push him over the edge. In fact, a lot of things would have given me greater pleasure. Margaret alive. Her mother alive. Parker back. An end to my persecution. A decent haircut. But Coogan had killed Parker, and was as responsible for Margaret and her mother as any other gangster in the city, so why shouldn't he die? Those who live by the sword die by the sword. The pen is mightier than the sword. A bird in the hand is worth two in the bush.

And in the end the reason he didn't die, despite that burning horror at what had happened to Parker, was because even with him up there, just needing the slightest of shoves to go to hell, the merest push, I couldn't do it.

We tied them up with a roll of electrician's tape we found in the kitchen. Flats like that always have rolls of tape for tying people up.

"You have clothes to get into?" I asked Patricia.

She shook her head. "I don't know where they are. We had to leave the last place in a hurry."

"And he didn't even think to get you any new ones? What a callous lover."

"Don't start."

"Sorry."

I took a carton of milk from the fridge, smelt it and put it back. The fridge was well stocked but it had the pungent smell of good food that had spent too much time in its own company.

"I take it this isn't the Coogan family residence?"

Patricia shook her head. "We've only been here a night or two. We arrived and the family moved out. I think they're downstairs somewhere."

The outside of the fridge was decorated with little plastic stickers like you get once in a while in a Cornflakes box. There was Mickey Mouse and Donald, Goofy and Pluto, and beside them a little tricolour and a colour photo of a Gaelic footballer.

I walked back into the lounge. Lee stood over the three of them, helpless now, her gun still trained on them. "You okay?"

167

She grinned. "Best fun I've ever had." She nodded back into the kitchen. "Still getting divorced?" she asked quietly.

I shrugged. "We have these ups and downs," I said.

"Just an average sort of night then."

"You know, more or less. Bit quiet."

Patricia moved into the doorway. "You two getting on all right?"

"Fine," I said.

Lee kept her eyes on Coogan and Co.

"You must tell me how you met."

Before we left I got Lee to phone the police and tell them where they could find several known terrorists. I said to Coogan, tied as he lay, awkwardly shielding his groin, "I hope I've interfered with your capacity to have children, because frankly we could do without any more of you." As he was opening his mouth to reply I stuck a very dangerous-looking sock in it.

On the way out we passed someone who may or may not have been Davie, Coogan's guard. There wasn't much he could do. We made a curious trio, tripping out into the breezy night: the glue-head in denims, the lady in the pink dressing gown and the nun with the pistol.

21

We drove in silence, or at least as close to silence as we could get in Lee's collapsing Mini. The streetlights of Belfast were harsh against the greyness of the advancing summer dawn; a dew-tinged chill permeated the car, but there was no gathering together for warmth. Lee drove, her Godpiece sitting flat on the passenger seat. I sat in the back, separated from Patricia by a radio-cassette speaker that lay face up between us; a tangle of wires falling from its back to the floor disappeared under Lee's feet. She was playing a tape by Van Morrison. It was slow and mournful and suited our speed and our mood. Patricia stared resolutely out the side window, lost in thought.

Maybe she was thinking of Cow Pat Coogan, tied up, whom she had saved from a death I did not have the capacity to bring about. The great Cow Pat Coogan, the legend, so nearly brought to a sticky end by a trio as unlikely as us. What was the secret of his legend, good public relations? Here was a rebel more famous for his love of money than for revolutionary zeal, a bandit more suited to a bad Western than a contemporary civil war. A bank robber better suited to "We ride muchachos" than the Gaelic promise "Our day will come." A man with sufficient charm to seduce Patricia even though it was within a few hours of kidnapping her. A man who had thrown Parker from the balcony without remorse.

I had few illusions about him being captured by the police. For a start there was an accomplice watching out for him somewhere in the flats. He would sooner or later check in with Coogan. And the police weren't about to storm in to capture him. They would treat Lee's call with extreme caution. They had been caught in too many ambushes in the past. It would be the old waiting game. They would wait for daylight at least. At best Coogan might be pinned down in the flats for a few hours.

As we entered the centre of Belfast, Lee said: "Well?"

"Mmmm?" Patricia answered, lazily.

"Where to?"

"The old question," I said.

"Seems like old times."

"What old times are you thinking about, exactly?" Patricia demanded, focused now.

"You know, you're getting awfully paranoid in your old age," I said.

She was about to reply, but stopped as I put my finger to my lips. "Let me explain," I said quietly.

And I told her about Lee. She listened in silence, occasionally glancing forward and catching Lee's nervous looks into the mirror.

"Which is where Lee comes in," I concluded. Lee didn't take her cue. "I said, this is where Lee comes in."

She darted a look back at me. "Sorry," she said, "I can't take my eyes off those posters."

I had half noticed them on the way in, little white cardboard rectangles hung from lampposts all the way down into the centre. In the grey of dawn I hadn't properly made out who they depicted, but now as the day broke properly I could make out Brinn's long bent noses, hundreds of them, everywhere. "I keep thinking about that tape, what might be on it. I was going to vote for him, y'know?"

"Innocent until proven guilty," I said.

"Yeah," Lee replied, half-heartedly.

"You were going to tell us how you managed to turn up and save us," I said.

"No, you were going to tell me where I'm supposed to be going."

I sat back and thought for a moment. "We need somewhere where no one is going to look for us, somewhere safe but comfortable, where we have access to good health care and fine food."

"You're not talking about my house, by any chance?"

"Now that you mention it . . ."

Lee shook her head, but it wasn't a refusal, it was mock exasperation at the predicaments she kept volunteering herself for.

Patricia leant forward, placing her hand on the back of the driver's seat. "I should thank you for looking after my husband," she said, and then added after a moment, "I don't know what you see in him." She gave a shy half-grin, looking at Lee, but it was meant for me.

We sped through the empty streets, devoid even of soldiers and drunks, towards Lee's. When we got there Patricia went up and had a bath and I dozed on the settee while Lee made breakfast. Patricia borrowed a T-shirt and a short skirt that was just a little too small for her. She put on some makeup. She still looked tired. Lee got out of her nun's habit and into her nurse's outfit. "I've been up all night and now I've to go to work. Life's a bitch."

"You can't take it off?"

"I've exams coming up. They'd have my guts for garters."

We all sat to have breakfast. She'd scrambled eggs. They disappeared very quickly.

"So? Our heroine, how come?" I asked finally.

She sat back and laughed. "Madness, I suppose."

"Thank God for the mad," I said.

"I don't know, maybe the few days you were here made me a bit, you know . . ." She glanced nervously at Patricia. ". . . protective of you."

"Yeah, sometimes you do just want to smother him with kindness," Patricia said, pushing a crust of toast around her plate with a fork, "but mostly you just want to smother him. I don't know how you put up with him." There was little or no malice in it.

"Anyway, I gave him a lift down to the restaurant, went off

and did my thing, and swung past there on the way back, just to see if I could be any use. I hung around for a while and saw you coming out. It didn't look like you were with friends, so I followed you up to the flats. I hung around out there for a while and I'd more or less worked out what floor you were on from the lift — at night you can follow it up the centre of the building — and I sat around some more gnashing my teeth wondering whether I should go home until I saw that guy come off the balcony and then I knew what I had to do."

"You don't do things by half measure, do you?"

She shrugged.

"And the gun?"

She reached over to the armchair behind the breakfast table where she had left her weapon and picked it up. She pushed it into my face and pulled the trigger. It clicked.

"Fake," she said. "Not only am I a nun-o-gram, but I do a mean Highway Patrol woman."

My legs were shaking under the table and my heart was drumming: I had stared death in the face again and won.

"I thought it might have been," I said.

Lee was going to work. She shouted cheerio from the front door. I got up from the table and went after her. Patricia watched me.

"It seems silly for you to go to work after last night," I said.

"I'm a nurse. It's what I always wanted to be. Saving lives, y'know? Look on last night as an extension of the National Health Service."

I smiled. "You're very blasé about it all."

She looked so sweet. "I think it's called shock. I'm sure mopping up some oul' bastard's shite will bring me down to earth."

She opened the door and stepped out; I hovered in the hallway, nervous of the daylight and recognition. "You don't mind Patricia staying here for a while, do you? There's nowhere else really, till this is over."

She shook her head. "No. Not really." And after a moment's thought: "She doesn't like me very much, does she?"

"She doesn't like anyone very much right now."

172

"So," Patricia said, as nonchalantly as if the night before had been nothing more exacting than a nurses' disco, "that's two women on the go in the last few days. One of them dead, unfortunately."

"Purely platonic."

"Which one?"

"Lee. Both, now."

"Yeah."

She sipped on a cup of coffee. It had been bright for some time and the chill of the dawn had given way to a light summer heat which gave the kitchen a nice musty flavour.

"Trust is a wonderful thing, isn't it?" she said.

"What're you saying?"

"You know, how it used to be. It used to be I didn't have to worry. Maybe I should have. Maybe I was too naïve."

"I don't want to get into all of this right now, Patricia."

"I was too naïve."

"You weren't. You were right, it's how it should be. I fucked up. I'm sorry. You've had your revenge. Can we close the subject?"

"As easy as that?"

"As easy as that."

"No screaming match, no three-day sulks?"

"No. I've a tape to retrieve, I can't afford to sit around talking shite for days. I mean, face it, no matter if we talk till we're blue in the face we're not going to change anything. I can't persuade you to love me, and I can't persuade you to trust me. You either will or you won't. Okay?"

She sipped her coffee again.."Okay," she said quietly.

"Okay," I said.

I got up and went out to look for Lee's phone. I had expected Patricia to go for the screaming match with an option on the sulking. It was a pleasant surprise. Maybe she'd changed. Maybe I'd changed. Maybe it was the new haircut.

The phone was in the front lounge, partially hidden by an album cover. The Pogues. I phoned Mouse.

"YES?"

"That's not a very pleasant greeting, Mouse."

For the first time in my life I heard him speak quietly. "Dan?"

"Y'know, Mouse, if this line is bugged, speaking quieter isn't going to fool them."

"JESUS, DAN, OF COURSE IT'S NOT BUGGED. HOW THE HELL ARE YOU ANYWAY, DANNY BOY?"

Last time he'd called me Danny Boy was at a party when we were eighteen and I'd attempted to punch his lights out for it; he had given me a hiding, but he'd never called me it again. Bugged. Electrical wizard that he was, he could tell a bug at a hundred yards. Clever and quick Mouse.

"I need a car. See you at the monkey puzzle in twenty minutes."

I put the phone down.

Patricia was standing in the doorway when I turned from the phone.

"How's Mouse?"

"House Mouse? Where?"

"Ha-ha."

"Yeah, well. He sounds okay. Wasn't exactly an in-depth conversation. He's getting me a car. I'm going to Bangor." I looked at my watch. It was 8:15. "To see a man about a tape."

"By yourself?"

"By myself."

"I should come with you."

"You should not. You should wait here for Lee to come home and sit around and watch TV and not let yourself get into more trouble."

"A man's gotta do what a man's gotta do."

"Something like that."

"And you've done so well so far, I'd just be a hindrance."

"Mmmm."

"You mean just because you've managed to flop from one frying pan into another for the past week or so, barely escaping by the skin of your teeth, murdering by accident, beating people up by accident, getting shot, having friends killed and wives kidnapped, you think I might in some way cramp your style."

"Put like that, yeah."

She was silent for a moment, then nodded slowly. "I suppose you're right. A lot has happened. I have a lot of thinking to do."

"Besides," I said, "it will probably simplify the thinking if I get killed."

"There's that," she said.

Patricia turned and started to make her way up the stairs. "I didn't realize how tired I was," she said. "I'll take a rest and then maybe do that thinking."

"Okay."

I watched her move her weary limbs methodically up, step by step. She was near the top when I said: "What was he like?"

"Who?"

"Coogan. What was he like?"

She turned and sat on one of the pinky-grey carpeted steps. Her brow furrowed and her eyes looked kind of lost for a moment, as if she was maybe looking for some lost feeling of ecstasy. "He was . . . strange. Very sure of himself . . . charismatic . . . is that the word? I don't mean, like, he spoke in tongues . . ." She giggled, then lost them again. "Revenge is a funny thing, Dan, isn't it? It burns you up, and then once you have it, you think, Jesus, what have I done?"

I looked up into her eyes and said: "I haven't had any revenge yet."

"What would you do to me?"

"Not on you. On him. You stopped me. I don't need to get any revenge on you. I deserved it."

"Don't come all holier than thou, Dan, it doesn't suit you."

"I'm serious."

"Yeah." She stood up and stepped on to the landing. "Goodnight."

"Patricia!" I called after her.

She stopped and stood with one hand on the banister.

"What was he like in bed?"

175

"Ah," she said, nodding her head slightly, "so that's what you're after. It isn't me you're thinking of at all, it's your fuckin' male ego . . ."

"I just need . . ."

"Come back alive, Dan, and we'll talk about it, okay?"

She spun quickly away from the stairs and strode determinedly into the room I had first woken up in after being shot. I made a move to go after her and then stopped. Maybe she had a point.

22

I waited in the bushes on the edge of the Botanic Gardens for Mouse to arrive. It had turned into a beautiful morning: a cloudless sky as smooth as linoleum; the sun, low, but already promising intensity, hung on the tree line as if resting before the big push up to noon. There were other men waiting in the bushes as well, dirty, unshaven characters with the shallow complexion you get on men who have spent too much time standing in undergrowth, but they didn't come near me. I tried my best not to feel slighted, but it was tough.

Mouse wasn't followed, unless the police had employed a troop of Brownies. He sauntered into the park and made his way towards the monkey puzzle tree. The fact that it wasn't really a monkey puzzle tree would have further confused anyone listening in to our brief telephone conversation. We had grown up in this park as underage drinkers, always meeting in the shadow of the great five-armed tree which dominated the south side of the park. Mouse had called it the monkey puzzle because in those early days he was more interested in botany than designing missiles and had recognized it in a book. Actually, he got it completely wrong, but by the time we found out it was too late to change its name.

I stepped out of the bushes as the Brownies were passing. Their commandant moved to the side of her pack to protect them and gave me a withering look. I smiled sheepishly at her. She barked at the children to hurry along. I still wasn't looking my best.

Mouse stopped by the monkey puzzle and knelt down to tie his shoe. I was no expert, but it looked like a pretty ham-fisted attempt at surreptitious surveillance to me. His lace wasn't even undone and he just kind of played with it for a bit while he eyed up the surrounding bushes. He saw me coming towards him but looked away. It was a moment before his eyes came back for a closer inspection.

He was about to speak but I put a finger to my lips and said quietly: "Mouse, for once in your life, try not to shout, eh?"

He shrugged impassively. "OKAY."

"Lower," I said.

He nodded.

"That's fine," I said.

It was good to see him. He was wearing a black sweatshirt and a pair of fading black jeans. He was unshaven and his glasses were dirty. His sandy hair looked, as ever, windswept. But he was clean: an outsider to the whole sordid business. I hadn't seen that much of him since he'd married and I'd met Patricia. Weekends and parties mostly, but we went back. There are things that happen between males when they're growing up that bond them for life. I had once seen him try to commit suicide by putting his head in the fridge.

"Well, how's it goin'?" he asked quietly; well, quietly for him. The Brownies could probably have picked it up if they'd been interested. He stood up and shook my hand. For a moment it threw me off my guard.

"Just wonderful, Mouse," I mumbled.

"No need to be sarky."

"Would you love me if I was any other way?"

"I wouldn't love you at all, Starkey."

"Well, now that's settled, what about the car?"

He twisted his head more or less in the direction of Botanic Avenue. "Down there. I went and hired one. A green one." He knew I knew nothing about makes of cars. "It's an automatic and takes unleaded petrol. There's half a tank in it and three vouchers towards a glass tumbler with George Best's head on it. You need another four. I put two names on the insurance document, my own and a fairly illegible D. Stark. We have third-party fire and theft insurance."

"I'm glad we have both."

"You have a licence?"

I nodded. I still had Lennie's from the guesthouse.

"You want to tell me what's going on, Dan?"

"No."

"You want to tell me where you're going?"

"No."

He was embarrassed. He looked at his shoes. Fading purple brothel creepers. Other people looked at his shoes, they got embarrassed. "Dan," he said, "you didn't do everything they say you did, did you?"

I looked mock hurt. "Hey, Mouse, it's me. Dan Starkey, ace reporter who couldn't kick his way out of a paper bag. What do you think I am?"

He didn't look convinced. "What about Patricia?"

"Patricia's fine. She was kidnapped by some people, but I got her back. She's staying with a friend."

"Dan, I know all your friends."

"Mouse, I'm sure the police do as well by now. I can't go to them, yet, for obvious reasons. She's with a new friend, if you like, but she's okay. I'm sorry I can't really tell you more. It wouldn't be safe."

"I wouldn't tell, Dan," he said, suddenly sounding like the eleven-year-old I had first met in this park. In this park where I had met Margaret such a short while before.

I nudged his arm and we started walking slowly along the paved path that skirted the central green. It made it look less like a gay encounter. More like an honest heart-to-heart between a bohemian lecturer from Queen's and a born-again thug. "I know you wouldn't, Mouse. But what you don't know can't hurt you." Clichés aren't clichés for nothing. "I take it the police have been to see you."

"Sure. A couple of reporters. Then a few hoods in suits. The wife chased them away."

"Good on her. What about the bug?"

"She's feelin' a lot better."

"In the phone, Mouse."

"I know. I was only joking."

"Is this a time for humour?"

"Probably."

"Okay. The phone."

"Standard bug."

"Police?"

"That would be illegal."

"Police?"

"Can't tell."

"Whoever it is, they're not likely to have heard anything, are they? I mean, you don't know anything."

"They've heard plenty."

"Meaning?"

"I compiled a five-minute audio tape of excerpts from *The Godfather* and played it to a random number in New York. I got a Chinese guy who seemed quite happy to listen in. Whoever was taping will be confused for a little while at least."

"Glad to see you're making yourself useful, Mouse." I stopped and took hold of his arm and gave him the look that said, wise up. "Listen. Don't do anything really stupid, you know? A lot of people have gotten killed over this."

"But not by you?"

"I've told you."

"You haven't told me anything, Dan. I'd like to help. I'd like to know what the fuck is going on."

I started him walking again. "Mouse — look, it's just so fuckin' complicated. Look — you know that film, who was it, Cary Grant was in it, you know, *North by Northwest,* where the guy is chased all over the place by bad guys and the cops alike, right? And no one will believe him and everyone keeps betraying him. Right?"

"Right."

"Well, this is kind of the same, but instead of suave, sophisticated Cary Grant you have a fuckin' eejit like me runnin' around, okay?"

"Okay."

"Okay."

"A bit like *The Thirty-Nine Steps* too."

"Yeah. Sure."

"Or *The Terminator.*"

"I think we'll leave it with *The Thirty-Nine Steps,* Mouse."

"Here," he said suddenly, stopping and thrusting the keys into my hand. His skin felt clammy. "I wouldn't be going down through the centre of town, Dan. Traffic's startin' to jam up."

"More bomb scares?"

"Nah, sure today's Brinn's big peace rally. They're sealin' off round the City Hall."

"I hadn't heard about it."

"Ach, he's turnin' more American every time I hear him. He calls it a peace rally, but it's an Alliance rally. If we had a decent hall in the city the Provos hadn't blown up he'd hold a fuckin' convention. But still, miss the centre, security's liable to be tight."

"I expect it'll be aimed at people heading into the city. I'm heading out."

"Oh yeah?"

"And that's as much as you hear."

"You used to tell me everything."

"I used not to be wanted for murder, Mouse."

He said quietly: "No, I suppose not. Look, all the gang, they've been askin' for you. You know we're there, if you need us. Not out of any misplaced sense of loyalty, you understand, but just 'cause we're pissed off with the cops coming round and questioning us and searching our houses. Okay?"

"Of course. They cause much damage?"

"Ach, not that much. Sure we were planning a new kitchen anyway, this way the bastards have to buy us a new one."

"Tell them I'm okay."

"Okay apart from your clothes, eh?"

"Yeah, well, horses for courses, y'know? I fit in better dressed like this."

"God, I wouldn't like to meet who you're dealin' with."

I grinned. "You wouldn't."

181

"Gerry, y'know, had a theory that you're enjoying all this. That you're savin' it all up for a column or two in the paper."

"I've never put myself out for a story yet, Mouse, you know that. Tell Gerry he can stick his theory up his hole. And the wife's okay?"

"Fine. You know what she's like."

I nodded. "Still pullin' the strings . . ."

"Yeah, well, I'm kinda used to it." He smiled suddenly. "She's not really talkin' to me at the moment 'cause I wouldn't take her to see Peter Ustinov in the Opera House. I mean, I don't mind him, but the only tickets left were £26.50 each. Y'know? I wouldn't pay £26.50 for the second coming of Jesus Christ, 'cause y'know fine well there'd be some cow in a fur coat in the row in front sayin', 'Of course I saw it the first time . . .' So I'm gettin' the silent treatment."

Small talk. I loved it. I wanted back to it. But things would never be small again.

It was time to go. I stopped him by a park bench occupied by a solitary wino. His brown trench coat appeared to be colour-coordinated with his beige paper drink bag and deep ruddy face.

I put my hand out to Mouse. "Thanks, Mouse. It was good of you."

"That's what friends are for, mate."

It had a kind of sad finality to it. He turned and loped off towards Queen's Physical Education Centre on the other side of the park. I watched him for a moment and then turned towards the car.

As I turned, the wino said: "Fuckin' poofs."

I winked and blew him a kiss.

I tried the key in three green cars before I found the right one. I hadn't driven an automatic in a long time, but it's the sort of driving even an imbecile can pick up in a couple of minutes.

Traffic was nearly all in the opposite direction, and heavy. Maybe they'd declared a holiday for the peace rally. Last time there'd been this many people on the move for peace we'd gotten a Nobel Prize for our efforts. It didn't bring peace but it bought a powerful lot of sausage rolls for meaningful interdenominational coffee mornings. Ah, journalistic cynicism.

BBC Radio Ulster was giving the rally the full treatment, live broadcast 'n' all. Up the Shankill Road they were giving it the full treatment as well. A carload of peaceniks up from Dublin strayed off course, stopped and asked for directions. They were dragged out and badly beaten. There was too much security about the city for the IRA to try anything much that day, but that didn't stop them lobbing a few mortars at army bases near the border and taking over a small village near Crossmaglen for a few hours in the pre-dawn, just to prove that they could.

It was a twenty-minute drive to Bangor. I wasn't mentioned once on the news, which was a relief. Towards the end of the report the newsreader said that a body believed to be that of an American reporter had been found in the north of the city. Cause of death had not yet been established. I thought it would have been fucking obvious. Still, it was early days. A dead American was big news and there'd be reporters swarming all over it soon enough, once Brinn got his peace rally out of the way. Brinn and peace. McGarry and his tape. Margaret and me. Patricia and Coogan. And all for the want of a little overtime and too much alcohol.

23

Remember me?"

"No."

"Sure you do. I sold you a tape a while back."

"Sorry, mate, no idea."

He wasn't really interested. There were plenty of tapes. A lot of Irish country and western. The Monkees' greatest hits. The New Seekers. But no classical cassettes at all.

"It was a classical tape. You know, the music from all those advertisements on TV."

"Sorry," he said. He was concentrating on his newspaper. He hadn't looked at me yet.

"It's important."

He looked up. "Sorry."

"Really important."

Maybe he was impressed by my hair. He said, languidly, "It's not my stall, mate. I buy at a standard price and sell at a standard price. It's not exactly collector's corner, y'know? I hardly look at the things."

I took a twenty-pound note from my pocket. Lee had lent it to me. "Would you look at one of these?" I asked.

He folded his paper up. "Now that I would."

"I was asking about a tape. Classical stuff."

"You know what was on the cover?" He was leaning over towards me now, almost sniffing the money. He had a shrewy face and he read the *Sun*. "I don't pay much attention really to the singers, y'know? But I usually remember the covers."

I could barely remember it. It hadn't been important, then. I shrugged. "I don't know. I suppose it was an old oil painting. Something Nordic maybe. With Vikings. They usually are."

"All sorta like Valeries and stuff, right?"

"Something like that. Yeah."

"Sure. I remember that."

"You know who you sold it to?"

He shrugged and nodded at the money. I handed it over.

He riffled through the tapes. "It's not here."

"I know that. I need to know who you sold it to."

"I . . . well, y'know, I've a lotta trouble with kids stealing things. Happens all the time. Thing is, I don't remember selling it. Could have been knocked off. I mean, kids don't listen to classical stuff, I know, but they could have done it just for badness, y'know?"

"This isn't very helpful . . ."

He shrugged.

"I thought maybe if someone was prepared to pay twenty pounds for a crappy tape, he might pay some more, eh?"

I tutted. "Listen," I said, "don't give me a hard time. It was me ma's favourite tape, right? I sold it by mistake and now I don't mind payin' to get it back rather than break her heart, so give us a break, eh?"

"For another tenner, I could put you in the right direction."

I looked at him hard. This intimidates few people.

I said: "Look, I can understand you wanting to earn some money, and, sure, I really want the tape. But I can't pay you any more. I've paid you twenty quid and I think you should play fair by me. We're coming up to the elections and we're all meant to be much nicer from here on in." I gave him a hopeful smile. He wasn't fooled by it. I tried another tack. "Or to put it another way, I will stay here all day and really annoy you. And if that doesn't work I'll start eating your books. That would be bad for business."

He looked at me. Expressionless. Save for a little tic in the left eye. Or his right, if you were him.

"Are you serious?"

"Partly."

He smiled the way a shrew might smile if it suddenly discovered quantum physics.

"Okay," he said.

"Okay," I said.

"Okay," he repeated. "If it's the one I'm thinking of, I didn't sell it. I took it with the rest of the stuff when I left day before last. It was my day off yesterday. That's when the boss does his day's graft, God love him. So he's the one would know."

"So you'll phone him?"

"I've got this place to mind."

"Sure the phone's only over there and there's no one else around. It would only take you a moment. I'll mind the stall if there's a rush." I looked over into his cash box. There were only a few coins and a fiver. "I'll promise not to make off with the bullion."

He shook his head slightly, but it wasn't a negative reaction. He chuckled to himself while he passed. "I don't know if he's in. He plays a lot of golf."

I reached into the cash box and picked up ten pence and chucked it to him. He dropped it. "For the phone."

The phone was about twenty yards away. It was early yet and the centre was still mostly empty. Those people on the move were on their way to work. Stocking shelves. Selling shirts. Weighing bananas. Slicing beef. What they would all give to be in my exciting shoes. Who was it said about the man with no legs, are there many in your shoes? Brinn? Brinn's wife? Where was she now? Standing on a sun-kissed platform beside her husband, waving to the tens of thousands pursuing peace and a new beginning. Except there weren't any new beginnings, just old beginnings dressed up.

I shuffled in behind the stall. His books were about as impressive as his tapes. Trashy romances mostly, a few dishevelled hardbacks with their library stickers ripped out, the complete

186

works of William Shakespeare in one volume of tiny print and a huddle of Cold War thrillers.

I sat down on his stool and took a sip of his coffee and glanced at the *Sun*. Purely for research purposes. I wasn't mentioned on the first three pages.

Somebody knocked on the stall, three knuckle raps on the wood, as if at a door.

I looked up. Two men. Early thirties maybe. Both well built but kind of thick round the waist. One wore a lumberjack jacket, zipped at the very bottom but open the rest of the way up, a white T-shirt and blue jeans. He had a blotchy, boozy face. Unkempt hair. The other wore a Cavalier moustache and shoulder-length hair; a knee-length leather coat hugged a bulging stomach. Neither looked like he could read.

"Yup?" I grunted.

"You sell tapes?" the rotund Cavalier asked. He was looking at the pile of tapes. It was one of those stupid questions.

I nodded at the stall. "Sure. What're you after?"

"You buy tapes as well?"

"Sure. What're you sellin'?"

"You bought any tapes in the last few days?"

"Maybe."

"Don't get smart with us, fucker."

Lumberjack turned to the Cavalier and said: "Take it easy." He turned to me. "Sorry. We're lookin' for a tape of ours that was sold by mistake. It's quite important to us."

"It's not ours," Cavalier corrected.

"But we think it was maybe sold to you. And we need it back."

"You know what it was called?"

"It wasn't ours."

"Not directly. But we do know it was sold in the last few days." Lumberjack ran his fingers down the side of the cassette cases. "You buy any of these recently?"

I looked at the tapes and I looked at Lumberjack and then I looked at the Cavalier. Coogan's men. It hadn't taken them long.

"I bought them all over the last few days. But I didn't notice

187

anything particularly valuable in there. They're all crap mostly. Depending on what you like, of course."

"Nah, it's not that kind of valuable. More of sentimental value, really." Cavalier ran a dirty fingernail up the side of the cassettes. "So it could be any of them, really."

"Unless I've sold it since."

"Have you sold any since?" Lumberjack asked.

I shook my head. "Not since, now that I think of it."

"So if it's here, it would need to be one of these, then."

I shrugged.

"We'd better take the fuckin' lot then," Cavalier suggested.

"Yeah," Lumberjack agreed.

"How much, the bunch?" Cavalier asked.

"The whole lot? That's say, a dozen tapes, a pound a throw. Say the dozen for a tenner, okay?"

Cavalier looked at his companion. "He could play them for us here, save us some money."

"Wise the scone, son, we don't even know what we're fuckin' lookin' for."

"I was only suggestin' . . ."

"You're always trying to cut fuckin' corners. That's yer problem."

I glanced across at the phone. He was talking, but watching the stall carefully. I winked over at him, but he was too far away to see, unlike the rotund Cavalier, who was plenty close enough and asked me what I was winking at.

"Nothing," I said.

He looked behind him but could see nothing besides shoppers. "You was winkin' at somethin'."

I chuckled at him. "It's an old trader's ploy. Wink at the customers. Encourages them to buy. Makes them think they're getting a bargain."

He stared into me.

"Which you are. Honest."

"Yeah?"

"Yeah. Fiver for a dozen tapes. Couldn't beat that anywhere."

188

He smiled. He fished out a crumpled fiver from his trouser pocket and handed it to me. He turned to the Lumberjack. "See me cut fuckin' corners, eh? Stick that in yer cakehole and eat it."

Lumberjack picked the tapes up awkwardly and walked off. "Yeah, yeah, motormouth, yeah, yeah."

The Cavalier held back for a moment. "Anyone else asking about tapes this mornin'?"

I shook my head. "Nobody ever much asks about them, mate. To tell you the truth, you're a godsend. We haven't sold that many all year."

"But you'll buy them back. The ones we don't want."

"Uh, well, I couldn't promise that."

He'd put the phone down and was coming across.

"Some of them anyway?"

"I'd have to see. They wouldn't be second-hand any more. They'd be third-hand."

"But we're only gonna play them once. Till we find what we're after."

"Sorry," I said, "that's the law."

"Ah, well," he said. He nodded his head a couple of times. "Sorry about the cursin', like," he added, then walked off.

He was kind of quaint that way. Quick to anger and just as quick to forget and forgive, like a child. Thick, but quaint. Like tartan paint.

I breathed out, a big gasper. I hadn't felt nervous at all in their presence, but their departure seemed to leave a vacuum, as if my confidence in handling them was a reflection only of their stupidity.

"What the fuck was that all about?" the stallholder asked, nostrils flared.

"Hey, take it easy. I just sold a load of crappy tapes for you. Be happy."

I put the fiver into his hands.

"For all of them? A fuckin' fiver?"

"A fuckin' fiver, yeah. They're not worth half of that, mate, and you know it."

189

"It's not a question of what they're fuckin' worth, it's a question of what I fuckin' sell them for, okay? A fuckin' fiver!"

"Twenty-five if you consider what I've already paid you. Now don't tell me you're not still in profit on that."

"That's hardly the point."

"Hey, listen, when's the last time you sold any of those tapes, eh? They're shite, and you know it."

"Well, I sold your tape for a start, you fuckin' bastard."

He had a point. "Exactly," I capitulated, "and here's the other tenner he gave me for the tapes."

I took it out of my back pocket. The last of Lee's paper money.

He burst into laughter. "You're a fuckin' chancer, mate."

"Ach, you gotta try, eh?"

"Sure."

"So?"

"So what?"

"So what about the tape?"

He took his place on the stool again. Sipped at the remains of his coffee for a moment. "Good news and bad news."

"Shoot."

"Right. The boss says he remembers selling a classical tape yesterday. Just at closing time. He was just packing the books up and the cash box was already away and he didn't want to be bothered selling it to the guy. But he was kind of insistent because he was keen on the tape and he wasn't often up this way."

"I don't suppose he got a name. On a cheque or something?"

"Cheques in this game? Sure. Visa and Access, mate. Nah, he didn't get a name. But he says the guy said he was going back down to Crossmaheart. Says he was wearing a collar, like, y'know. A priest. A priest from Crossmaheart. Your lucky day, mate, eh?"

Crossmaheart. He was smiling and I smiled back at him. Crossmaheart. In the heart of the Congo.

24

The first story I ever wrote for the *Evening News* began with the lines: "Of the twenty-three soldiers blown to smithereens in Crossmaheart on Saint Valentine's Day, three are still alive."

It took an irate schoolteacher to point out to our editor on the phone that soldiers blown to smithereens could not expect to enjoy the benefits of breathing, even if they were as resilient as paratroopers.

Crossmaheart lies about sixty miles south of Belfast. Years ago it consisted of a couple of white-cottaged streets and a handful of pubs, a village possessed of a quaint kind of poverty that looked well on a postcard. It was at the heart of a large but financially stricken farming community more famous for its rogues than agricultural produce. In the early seventies when the religious riots were tearing Belfast apart, the powers that be thought the solution to the problem might lie in shipping whole communities out to the country, getting them away from the maelstrom of hatred by providing them with cheap housing, grants and state-supported industry. Shangri-o-La. They chose Crossmaheart because despite the local population being predominantly Catholic, the borough council had a Protestant majority that could bulldoze through the planning restrictions with the minimum of fuss. And so they did.

The cottages are still there. Behind the cottages sprawl housing estates as wild and wicked as any in Belfast. They thought

191

that by transplanting the disaffected to a life of comparative luxury they would heal the divisions, promote harmony. They'd never have it so good. Instead it was like treating the bubonic plague by transferring the infected to previously clean cities. Within a few years the industry had collapsed, the new houses were wrecked and Crossmaheart, slap-bang in the middle of what has become known as Bandit Country, was casually referred to by the security forces as the Congo.

You don't wander into the Congo without knowing what you're about. They don't hang back, sizing you up. They come up to you and poke you in the eye and say, "What the fuck do you want?"

There's no such thing as silence in the Congo. It's such a high-risk area for the army that they no longer travel through, but skirt it in very large convoys. They've established a base on the outskirts of town to which they commute by helicopter, over three hundred flights a day, which makes it the busiest heliport in Europe. The buzz of choppers is a twenty-four-hour thing. They say the army knows everything that goes on in the town: electronic surveillance is so sophisticated that they can pinpoint trouble within three seconds of it breaking out; the only problem is that it takes them at least four hours to get to it. The word in Belfast has always been that they prefer to stay well out of the Congo. Seal in the trouble, let them fight it out themselves.

There's a big shopping centre on the edge of town, for the poor are nothing if not well off these days. But the heart of the town is still the Main Street. There are still small, family-owned shops with dull window displays made duller by thick metal security grilles. The international chains which have infested every other town in the North do not come here: there is no McDonald's, no KFC, no Pizza Hut. There is Victor's Chips and Bobby's Burgers and the Panda House Chinese Carry-out. There are two pubs, twenty yards between them but worlds apart. Jack Regan's and The Castle Arms. The ones that made the mistake of going into the wrong bar are buried on the outskirts of town; well, parts of them are.

I didn't make the mistake of going into either of them though I'd a thirst on me, sure enough. I went into the post office. A young fella with glasses and straw hair peered out from behind a meshed hatch and said: "Howdy, stranger."

I nodded. "Quiet in here," I said.

"Only day we're busy is when they come to cash their unemployment cheques. Then it's pandemonium."

I leant on the counter and peered through the mesh. It was like a prison visit. I presumed.

"So you reckon I'm a stranger in town?"

"I know you're a stranger in town."

"How?"

"That hair. I saw it in the *New Musical Express*. Or something like it. Hair like that hasn't reached Crossmaheart yet. We're still waiting for the second coming of flares."

"Well spotted."

He shrugged. "So what can I do for you? Sell you a stamp? Though we only have second class, to reflect the standard of our clientele."

"That's a damning indictment of your clientele."

"You haven't met them yet."

"You must make a lot of friends with that attitude."

"On the contrary."

We smiled at each other for a second. "I'm looking for a priest," I said.

"Confession?"

"No, I'll tell anyone."

"What?"

"That I'm looking for a priest."

"Tell me, when you're not looking for priests, do you spend all your time perfecting your repartee?"

"No, I'm just naturally gifted."

"Well, it's a pleasure to meet you. I'd shake your hand but it wouldn't fit under the mesh."

"My hand or your hand?"

"Neither. Though you usually find on cheque days that the barrel of a gun fits quite well under it."

193

"You have a lot of trouble like that?"

"Is the Pope a Catholic?" He laughed to himself. "Sorry," he apologized, "under the circumstances, that's rather inappropriate."

"Meaning what?"

"It is Father Flynn you're after, isn't it?"

I shrugged. "If he's the local priest. Yeah."

"Aye, then, I suppose he's the man you want."

"And what's inappropriate about it?"

"You've not met the man?"

"No."

"Well, then, it wouldn't be my place to say, really."

The door behind me opened. I stood back from the hatch. A young woman pushing a buggy with a dirty-faced toddler strapped into it.

"Morn', Janice," my friend said.

"Hiya, Billy." She looked at me for a moment, at my hair for a moment longer. "We got tourists?"

I smiled and shook my head. "Nah."

"He's lookin' for Father Flynn," Billy volunteered.

Janice nodded her head. "Whaddya want with that old bastard?"

"Business."

Janice had a fine-featured face, but her body looked clumpy inside a purple tracksuit. She nodded her head again, this time in a conspiratorial fashion towards Billy. "Well, you'll probably find him up the road then, takin' Mass."

"But not preaching to the masses," Billy added.

"Up what road?"

"The road outside," Billy said. "Just follow it up the hill for a couple of hundred yards. You'll come to the church, his house is just behind it."

I thanked him and left. I smiled at Janice, but she didn't smile back. I smiled at the kid and he didn't smile back either.

I stood for a moment outside the post office, contemplating. A helicopter flashed overhead, drowning the sounds of traffic

194

from the street, its camouflage conspicuous against the summer sky.

The priest was standing in a small garden at the front of a middle-sized bungalow. In fact you couldn't really call it a garden at all. It was a small rectangle of undulating concrete bordered by flowerbeds. Flynn stood erect, a long-handled brush clasped in his hands, but he was motionless, his eyes staring vacantly into the distance. He didn't even blink when I shut the car door.

I stood at the edge of the flowerbeds. I coughed lightly, but he paid no attention. I said: "Father Flynn?"

His head moved slowly towards me and he regarded me silently for a moment, until he suddenly shook his head as if shaking off a dream, and smiled at me. He was tall and thin and his hair was cropped short and grey; his skin was grey and tightly drawn over a beak-like nose.

"Sorry," he said, "miles away."

"Sorry to disturb you."

"Ach, never worry. Sure I'd spend all day in another world if I could and that wouldn't be good for me, would it?"

I shrugged and said: "Doing some gardening?"

"Nah, just tidying up."

I nodded at the concrete. At the hills and valleys and cracks and crannies, and weeds and moss, yet it had a black sheen that suggested it had only recently been laid. Unlike myself.

"That's interesting paving," I observed.

"Yes, it is a bit rough, isn't it?" He gave it a token sweep with his brush. "It's Gypsy paving. No one else in the town would do it for me. So I took the chance on the Gypsies and look what they did. I mean, they had a spirit level, I saw it, so I can only presume that at some point they drank it. Still, it's ecologically sound. They spread the layer so thin it allows the weeds to grow up through it. Somcone will be pleased with that."

"You should sue them. It's an awful job."

"I wouldn't like to. I don't think they did it deliberately. They're just inefficient. Like us all really."

195

"You should have gotten someone from the town. I'm sure there's plenty wouldn't mind earning a few pounds, and I'm sure they wouldn't have botched it quite so badly."

"Yes. You would think there would be, wouldn't you?" He moved the brush in an arc, moving loose gravel and chunks of tar around, not so much tidying as rearranging. "Anyway," he said after a moment, looking up, "did you just come to run the garden down, or is there something I can do for you?"

I blushed slightly and said: "Yes, of course. Sorry."

"You're not from round here, are you?"

"No. Belfast."

"Ah."

"I was wondering . . . uh . . ."

"Perhaps you would like to come into the church?"

"It's a . . ."

"A confession?"

"Uh, no . . ."

He seemed disappointed. "Oh, well . . . but perhaps a problem of a religious nature? I get so few these days."

"Uh, not exactly, no, Father."

"Well, there can't be many reasons to seek out a religious man other than religious reasons. Unless you've just come in a roundabout fashion to give me some abuse. If it's that I'd rather you just got on with it rather than messing about. Though I must say I'll be surprised if you come up with anything I haven't heard before. I believe antichrist was the last one I heard. Perhaps you could improve upon that one?"

There was something sad about his demeanour, the vacant way he pushed the brush about, the soft, clipped tones as he challenged me to abuse him. Being a priest in the Congo couldn't be a lot of fun.

"Are the Protestants giving you a hard time, Father?"

He looked round at me again. "Protestants? No, not at all. They don't talk to me. It's the Catholics."

I laughed, suddenly, involuntarily.

"There's nothing funny about it," he scolded, his voice sharper but still quiet.

"I'm sorry, Father. It just — sounded so strange."

He laughed himself then, but it was a hollow self-deprecatory laugh that failed to move the corners of his mouth towards a smile. "Yes, I suppose it does sound a bit strange if you're not from around here." He moved across to the wall of his bungalow and set the brush against it. "Sure come on inside for a cup of tea then, and you can tell me what you're after."

He pushed the front door open and led me through a bright hallway into a compact, modern kitchen. Spotlessly clean. He sat me down at the kitchen table and set about making some tea. I hate tea, but I wasn't about to ask him for Coke. I would have to grin and swallow it, though not at the same time.

He stood with his back against the sink as he waited for the kettle to boil.

"It's a long time since I had anyone in the house," he said.

"I thought priests' houses were the centre of the parish?"

"Oh, they're supposed to be, all right. Just not here."

I waited for him to continue, but his eyes were away again, lost in a dream.

"How come?" I asked.

He shook his head again, ridding the demons. "They didn't tell you down below?"

I shook my head.

"Well, I suppose there's little harm in you knowing." He did nothing for a moment, while the kettle came quickly to a high-pitched boil. He switched it off but made no effort to continue with the tea. He stood on the other side of the table, regarding me quizzically for a moment. Then he slowly removed his dog collar and set it on the table before him. He began to work at the buttons of his shirt, opening them one by one to reveal his bare chest beneath.

I shifted uncomfortably.

25

I tried to look everywhere but his chest. I looked into his eyes, but he was looking into mine so I turned away. I looked at the cupboards. At the fridge. At a calendar still depicting a winter scene. At a drip hanging desperately on to the end of the tap. My face burnt with embarrassment as he undid the last button and pulled the shirt out from the confinement of his trousers. You hear about priests.

"Well?" he asked.

"Uh."

"What do you think?"

"I'm, uh . . ."

The hair was thick on his chest, grey and vigorous as a Brillo Pad; I couldn't help but bring my gaze back to it, the way you can't help staring at an amputee's stump or a winestain birth mark.

"It's starting to fade a bit of course, but it's still pretty impressive, no?"

"Uh, oh . . . yeah, of course."

"The surgeons say it won't completely disappear. But I can live with that. That's what I say a lot of the while now, I can live with that. Sums it all up really."

"I . . ."

"It's the root of all my problems here, of course. But I can live with that."

He smiled at me. It was a nice, innocent, celibate kind of a smile that hacked away at my embarrassment. I clenched my teeth and focused my eyes on the fine curly filaments that made up the plantation on his chest. Through the grey, like a river trace of lava on a winter landscape, I discerned a thin red scar line.

"Somebody stabbed you? Somebody stabbed a priest?"

He laughed out loud. "Stabbed! Not at all!" He thumped his chest with a clenched fist and exclaimed proudly: "Self-inflicted!"

He was laughing quite steadily now. He turned and poured the boiling water into a teapot and added a teabag, returned to me, his shirt still hanging open and his face wide with a smile.

"Sorry, sorry," he laughed. "Self-inflicted! You think after all the troubles I've had here I took a knife to myself? Ha!"

"Nah, I . . ."

"Years of all the wrong foods, no exercise, worrying too much about nothing, that's the kind of self-inflicted I'm on about. Gets to the old ticker eventually. People like to think God looks after his own, don't they? In truth we look after ourselves." He thumped his chest again. "Yes, it gets to you. I was on the way out till the surgeons gave me a brand new heart. Can you believe that? You read about it happening all the time in England, but you don't expect them to extend the service to us Paddies, do you? I didn't even pray for it. I didn't dare. He has far too much on his plate as it is. But I suppose He was looking out for me, in his own way."

"A heart transplant? Jesus — sorry — but you're right, you don't come across many of them over here. Well done."

"Ach, it's not so strange if you think about it. Sure they're doing them every day across the water, they've got it down to such a fine art that they can nearly do it with their eyes closed. "

"And it took okay?"

"Well, I'm standing here, aren't I?"

I started to apologize again, but he cut me off. "I mean, you didn't see me before I had it, I didn't have the strength to stand. Could hardly breathe. They weren't sure I'd have the strength to go through the operation. Sure in the weeks before they found the right donor the whole church got together and gave me a party,

gave me gifts and made their speeches like I was going to die.
And I was ready for it. I had my suitcase all packed and I wasn't
one bit fussed whether I was going to heaven or hell or London, I
felt that bad. Then I went off and had it and spent a few weeks
convalescing across the water. I came back and it was as if they
were almost disappointed that I'd survived."

He poured tea into two big mugs and set them on the table.
He got a carton of low-fat milk from the fridge and poured a little
in both. He didn't offer me any sugar. I let mine sit. He sipped at
his, dainty sips of simple pleasure.

"How do you mean?"

"Ach, it was just wee things at first. Y'know, not so many
turning up for church. A fall-off in the various clubs. A few comments I just missed when I walked down the street. It didn't really
worry me, because I felt so good. So alive. You don't really appreciate life until you have intimate experience of death."

"Mmmm . . ."

"I tried to tell this to people . . . but they really weren't that
interested. The usual . . . nodding their heads and saying yes, Father, and then not paying a blind bit of attention. I think they actually preferred me when I was sick — and I hadn't been well for a
long time, so they were kind of used to me huffing and puffing
about. And suddenly there I was bouncing around like a five-year-
old, preaching love and understanding. Then they really turned on
me. Stopped coming to church. Turned me away from their doors.
All sorts of names. A priest, their priest, and they were cursing
me up and down! I couldn't believe it. And then one day the Cardinal came to see me. He took me into the church and sat me
down at the back and he sat beside me and turned to me and said
how pleased he was that I'd made such a splendid recovery, and
did I feel now was the right time for me to be moving on, to a new
challenge. I thanked him and said the challenge was greatest in
Crossmaheart because I'd lost the faith of the congregation and I
didn't know why. He took my hand and said, 'Frank, the people
are saying the English played a trick on you.' 'What kind of a
trick, Your Eminence?' I asked. 'They gave you a Protestant's
heart, Frank, and you haven't been the same since.' And I don't

think there's ever been such laughter in the house of God. We were rolling in the aisles. So here I am still in Crossmaheart with the Cardinal's blessing, trying to convince these stupid people that although I have a new heart — and it is a Protestant's heart, I checked — they can still trust me."

"You've not started . . . like . . . going round shouting Kick the Pope or Remember 1690 or anything, have you?"

"You'd've thought I had. I have an English Protestant heart. Sure they don't give a fig about Protestant and Catholic over there. But try as I might telling people . . ." He stopped, rubbed at his chin for a moment while he gazed thoughtfully at the wall behind me. "But . . . then again . . . maybe they have a wee point in that I have become a little more liberal. Less nationalistic maybe, more attuned to reconciliation if you like. It's not a word they say easily in this town. And definitely not one they can spell. It's like I was saying, because I've been given life, I can see the waste of deliberately taking it away."

He shook his head slowly and smiled wryly at me. "I feel like I've just been to confession," he said. "Forgive me. I think I just wanted to get it off my chest, if you'll excuse the pun."

I took a sip of the tea, to be polite. "It would make a great film."

"A film? Ha! A film? Imagine that! Who would you get to play me then? Charlton Heston?"

He slapped the table with that, spilling some of my tea. "I'm sorry, son, I'm getting carried away."

"Never worry."

"You came here for a reason and you've been listening to me rattling on like nobody's business."

I clasped my hands around the mug of tea and looked at it for a moment.

"Take your time," Flynn offered. Then he asked: "You're not well?"

"No. Not that."

"You're in trouble then? Is it sanctuary you're after? The church is always open to you, son, but I'm not sure the police look on it as sacrosanct."

He got up and poured himself another few mouthfuls of tea. I had enough. He replaced the pot and began to button his shirt again.

"Father, you were in Bangor the other day, weren't you? You bought a cassette tape."

"I was. I did."

"That's what I've come about. It was actually sold to you by mistake, Father. It was my tape. It shouldn't have been on sale."

"I see."

"And I'd like it back. I'll pay you for it. I . . . don't have any money here and now, but I'd send it to you. Honestly. Just I need it kinda quick, y'know."

He tucked his shirt back into his trousers and replaced the dog collar. He took his seat again. "And you came all the way down to Crossmaheart from Bangor just for this tape?"

"All the way from Belfast, Father."

"But it was only a wee cheap thing."

"But of great sentimental value."

"And the sound quality isn't very good."

"It doesn't matter, I . . ." And I stopped. "You've listened to it?"

"I have."

"All of it?"

"All of it."

"Oh."

His gaze was steady and confident, devoid of humour, but not malignant. "I've never been much of a one for classical music. I suppose like a lot of people I didn't get the right education. But I do like some of the more widely known pieces."

"Like they use on the TV."

"Exactly."

"So that tape was exactly what you were looking for."

"Exactly."

"But then again . . ."

". . . not quite."

"Mmmm."

202

"So what I have is a tape with a couple of drunks talking on it. Of no good to man nor beast and certainly not one I'd want to keep around the house, not for a man in my profession."

I smothered a sigh of relief. "Aye, Father, it was my mistake putting it into the wrong box, like, then my da just whipped it down to the shop to get some cash . . . just a couple of mates of mine slabbering over their pints . . . they lent it to me 'cause they said it was funny and I promised to give it back to them . . ."

Flynn took another sip of tea. He swirled the remainder of it round in the bottom of his mug for a moment, his eyes circling the rim as the thin brown liquid leapt optimistically towards freedom. He set the mug down and his head slanted up towards me again. "Unless of course you recognize one of the voices."

"Ah."

"So you're a drinking buddy of Mr. Brinn's then, are you?"

"Uh."

"The other voice I don't know, but our Mr. Brinn's voice — well, you do get used to hearing it all over the place, don't you? A bit slurred maybe. But the man himself."

"Well, yes."

"I must admit it was a bit of a surprise. I mean, there was me looking for a bit of light entertainment and I get something very heavy indeed."

"I haven't heard it myself, Father."

"You haven't?"

"No — I just need it."

"After hearing it I should think a lot of people need it. Mr. Brinn especially."

"Is it that bad?"

"Well, now, I don't know. I suppose it depends whether you're Brinn or not. He might describe it as, well, cataclysmic is a word that springs to mind."

"Oh dear."

"One of the good things about this new heart of mine," Flynn observed, rising from the table and motioning for me to follow

203

him, "is that it gives one an incurable — and incurable is a word I know all about, so maybe it's a bit of a misnomer — sense of optimism." He led me back out into the bright hall and then left into a study lined on two opposite sides by bookcases. Between them there were several cases of records and a box of cassette tapes and a fairly basic stereo system. Nothing on CD. There was a tan leather chaise longue and a single armchair of similar material. He directed me into the armchair and went to the box of cassettes.

"Well, it would," I ventured, eyeing the cassettes and wondering when to make my move. A quick grab? A shove and grab? A bloody good hiding and grab?

"Optimism, for a start, that this tape, damnable indictment that it is, might do some good. In the right hands."

"You haven't passed it . . ."

"No, no, it's still here. As a matter of fact I haven't even copied it and secured copies in various bank vaults, like I imagine one should in these situations. I'm only a local priest. How would I know whose the right hands were? The IRA, to destroy Brinn? Once, maybe, I would have. Before I had a change of heart. Brinn himself, to give him a chance to repent? The police, to give them the chance to show where their loyalties lie?"

He held a cassette box in his hands now. It looked like the one Margaret had tossed to me decades ago, but I couldn't be sure.

"I thought about it a great deal, and I prayed about it a great deal. And you see, I don't know if you're religious at all, but God doesn't, say, phone you back and advise you what to do. It just, I suppose, seeps into you, a feeling, an idea. My feeling was that I should just stay here with it and whoever came for the tape, I should give it to them. So here it is."

He held it out to me. I shook my head.

His brows furrowed for a moment.

"You don't want it?"

I wanted it all right. I needed it. I was in a hurry. "Play it, Father, would you?"

26

Afterwards he went to make more tea and opened a packet of Jaffa Cakes. Then he thought better of the tea and brought in a bottle of Bushmills and poured me a large glass.

"Of course, I don't drink it myself these days," he said, pouring himself a glass only slightly smaller. "I exist purely on a diet of farm-fresh vegetables and the barbed comments of my congregation."

We remained in his study. There were three framed photographs of children in school uniforms on top of the speakers. "Yours?" I asked, and followed it immediately with, "I'm sorry, what a ridiculous question."

Flynn laughed. "No, not mine, of course. Well, perhaps — high achievers in school. Oh dear, I do sound a bit like Mr. Chips, don't I? I suppose I do get a bit nostalgic for my flock."

He took the tape out of the stereo, put it back into its box and handed it to me. I put it into the inside pocket of my denim jacket.

"What will you do with it?" he asked.

I shrugged.

"Well," he said, "as far as I'm concerned, God wanted you to have it."

I pursed my lips, nodded. I ate a Jaffa Cake. I grew up in a house where my old da couldn't make his mind up whether to be a Jehovah's Witness or a Mormon and ended up with a foot in both doors. God was the second last person I asked advice off.

"Of course," he continued, a whiskey sheen on his lips, "I haven't asked you anything about yourself. I presume it's better that I don't know. I mean, you could be a blackmailer or a murderer yourself, a terrorist or a politician. Or just someone who wants to do some good."

I nodded again. I thought about how great it would be to be able to sit back and let God take care of everything. Sort out the murders. Sort out the tape. Sort out Brinn.

"Lost in thought?" Flynn asked.

Lost in space. God and honesty. Straight talk and shame the Devil. "Have you ever heard the expression, Father, I haven't a fuckin' notion what I'm doin'?"

Flynn sipped on his whiskey. He savoured the taste for a moment, then set the glass down. "Well, yes, I mean, you do down here, where no one really knows what they're doing. And that's okay. I can live with that. I might even feel it myself sometimes."

"Sure."

"But from where I see it . . . ," he began, then stopped and lapsed into one of his thoughtful poses. I poured myself another drink, topped his up, though he didn't seem to notice. It was exactly what I did and didn't need. His eyes cleared. "From where I see it, you have something very powerful in your possession. That is presuming it's authentic. You've told me nothing about its background."

"I think we'll have to go with it being real. Everything that has happened would be too sick if it wasn't."

"Everything . . . ?"

"Yeah."

Flynn waited for a moment, saw he wasn't getting anything, sighed lightly, and continued. "I believe they can do wonderful things with tapes these days. I mean they could make an authentic tape sound like a fake as well, couldn't they? However, taken as real, in the right hands, indeed, in almost anyone's hands, it could decide the future of this country. What you have to decide is whether Brinn's past crimes should stop him having his chance to put an end to this civil war."

"Right."

"I mean, look at most of the countries that have emerged from civil wars or revolution. Their leaders are often men who were once denounced as criminals. It's often an important part of their development, that they believe so passionately in something they're prepared to put their lives at risk. If they later denounce violence and do some genuine good, should they not be forgiven? I mean, an end to the violence would be nice, wouldn't it?"

"Brinn elected doesn't guarantee an end to the violence, Father."

"But he'll make a stab at it, if you'll forgive the expression. On the other hand, to withhold the tape from public scrutiny . . ."

I switched off. He wasn't telling me anything that hadn't already raced through my tiny mind. He had a dog collar and all that training and God and the Bible and he was about to bring his advice full circle because his God hadn't fully seeped his thoughts through to him yet.

After a while, I cut in. "What are you telling me to do, Father?" I asked flatly.

He drained his glass. "I believe you might say, I haven't a fuckin' notion."

He walked me to the door. He put out his hand and said: "Good luck."

"I hope you get your congregation back."

"It's all right. They're all papists anyway." He smiled brightly and clasped my hand. "Only joking. Don't pass it on."

I shook my head and walked to the car. He was still standing in the doorway as I drove off. He waved. I waved back.

I headed back into Crossmaheart and tried to think about what I was going to do. The tape was my protection, and my danger. Whoever had the tape had the power, but only if he knew how to use it. And why. And when. I could go to the paper, expose Brinn. I could go to the police, trade it for my freedom. I could destroy it, give peace a chance. I needed time to think. My head was buzzing. I couldn't get things straight. Who was right, who was wrong. I needed a drink; Flynn had got me started. A big drink. No.

The first thing I had to do was get the tape out of my possession. I could feel it glowing against my jacket. I knew well enough by then that I was an adventuring liability and to keep it about my person would be a silly mistake. At the very least security would be much tighter on the way back up to Belfast. If they didn't get me that way Cow Pat Coogan and his gang or Billy Mc-Coubrey and his outfit or any other of the myriad interested parties would find a way to get to it. God knows I'd left enough clues about where I was going for the tape.

Crossmaheart's main street was livelier now that the pubs were open. The pavement wasn't wide enough on either side to accommodate more than a single file of tables. They were all full. The outdoor clientele was exclusively male. I parked outside the post office and walked in quickly; I didn't give them the time to give me dirty looks. My friend was still behind the counter. He was about a third of the way through a battered paperback version of *Dr. Zhivago*.

"Do you have any padded envelopes?" I asked.

"That's not a very witty start," he replied.

"It's not meant to be."

"You're not in as playful a mood as you were before."

"You could say that."

"I did say that."

I looked at him.

"And now the steely look." He pushed his seat back and began to fuss around beneath the counter. "I hate these moody types," he said testily, his face hidden from view.

He produced a small padded envelope and asked for 80p. I counted out some change. I paid for the envelope and borrowed a pen from him. I put the tape in the envelope and asked him for a piece of paper. He ripped a page out of a spiral-bound notebook on the counter and I scribbled a note to Patricia. Then I sealed the envelope and addressed it to Lee. When I'd paid for the postage I'd 30p left. It wouldn't buy me much of a drink. I knew people who'd asked for 30p's worth of drink before.

"Do you want a receipt?"

"No."

"Sure?"

"Certain."

"Your meeting with the Prince of Darkness must have gone badly."

I nodded and turned to leave.

"Have a nice day, now," he said.

I turned at the door. He'd picked up his book again. "*Dr. Zhivago?*" I asked.

He looked up. "Yeah."

"Seen the movie?"

"Nah."

"You know he dies in the end?"

I closed the door behind me. It was thirsty weather. The sun, high in the sky now, gave the whitewashed main street a Mediterranean glow. The two men sitting on my bonnet looked like they were enjoying the sun. One had a goatee beard and long curly hair. He wore a denim jacket in better shape than my own. The other was a squat skinhead in DMs. The skinhead said, "You're about as difficult to find as a goat."

His companion looked at him for a moment, then at me. "I'd get in the car, mate, no need to cause a scene."

"You don't look much like traffic wardens," I said. Bravado masking knocking knees.

The skinhead tutted and said: "Wise up."

"He has a point," Goatee added. He held out his hand and I threw him the keys. He unlocked the passenger door and pulled the seat forward to let me into the back. He turned to the skinhead. "Seanie, away and see what he was doin' in there, would ye?"

"Will I hit him?"

"Who?"

"The fruit behind the wire."

"Please yourself."

"Cheers."

Seanie walked in an ape-like fashion, his curving arms hung low, his furry head bobbing Tysonesquely. Goatee climbed into the passenger seat, then turned and extended a hand to me. I shook it. "Malachy Burns. Pleased to meet you, Starkey." I nodded. "Mr. Coogan will be pleased to see you."

"I dare say."

I thought briefly about violence. There was only one of him and he didn't look that fit. With a bit of luck I could have taken him out and be off yomping across the fields or driving like fury. Before I could work myself into a combative state Seanie appeared at the door of the post office, my parcel in his hand. Burns leant over and opened the driver's door. Seanie handed the parcel in to him, then clambered in behind the steering wheel.

"That was some goin'," said Burns, turning the package over in his hands. He looked back at me. "This what I think it is?"

I shrugged.

"Any trouble?" he asked Seanie.

Seanie shook his head. "I just asked him for it and he handed it over."

"So you didn't hit him?"

"No, but I gave him a really mean look."

Seanie started the car. "This'll only take a minute," Burns said to me as we moved off along the main street. He turned to our driver. "I was meaning to ask, Seanie . . ."

"What?"

"Don't take it the wrong way, like."

"What?"

"I mean, as difficult to find as . . . a goat?"

"What of it?"

"A goat?"

"Yeah, a goat. What of it?"

"A goat?"

"You ever tried to find a goat?"

"Can't say I have."

"Right then, case proved. It's fuckin' difficult."

"Ah — I see. I see."

"You see what?"

"Nothing."

"You see what?"

"Nothing."

210

"You see fuckin' what?"

"I . . . I thought you were being sarcastic. About the goat."

Seanie turned his head from the road for the first time and fixed Burns with a bulldog stare. "I wasn't." He turned his eyes back to the road. Burns nodded.

The change from cottage quaint to breeze-block poverty was almost instantaneous. From the bright optimism of white to the grey of depression. The roads were glass-strewn, the paving as undulatorily impressive as Flynn's had been but with none of the care and attention. Tiny gardens grew wild. One in five houses was bricked up. Cars, wrecked or burnt-out, lay in dry rust. And everywhere the summer cackle of children. Seanie drove slowly, negotiating the potholes as if the car was his own pride and joy. Maybe it was, now.

We moved onwards and upwards in a meandering but loosely circular pattern. My hosts stopped occasionally, talked to men lazing in gardens or standing barechested on corners. As we stopped, children came running out and peered into the back of the car. I stared resolutely back, but they weren't intimidated. The half of them looked like miniatures of Seanie, all scalped heads and threats. The men were big on cursory glances, the children more demanding, shouting questions, their bravery hastened by our slow departure.

"Only a mo' now," Burns said after a while.

"You know that tape's worth a fortune?" I ventured.

Seanie looked back. "Wise up," he said.

"I'm serious."

The car thumped into a pothole, throwing the three of us forward, then back as Seanie roared out of it. "See what ye done?" he shouted.

"We know what it's worth," said Burns.

"So wise up."

It wasn't a very good effort at inspiring insurrection. We entered a cul-de-sac which was in conspicuously better condition than the rest of the estate. The road was smooth, gardens tidy. At the end stood a house which had once been similar to many others in the estate, an end-of-terrace dwelling. It had been enhanced at the side by a long extension which occupied most of a large garden. Pale-yellow stone cladding. A satellite dish. Big red car in the driveway. Smaller one sitting outside. It wasn't a palace, but compared to the rest of the estate it looked like the Hall of the Mountain King.

"Chez Cow Pat, as we say," Burns volunteered.

27

It's funny what attracts two people, isn't it?"

"I'm sorry?"

"Sexual chemistry is a curious business, Starkey, wouldn't you say? Beautiful to beautiful, beautiful to ugly, ugly to beautiful, ugly to ugly. You never can tell how people will end up, can you?"

Cow Pat Coogan sat in an armchair in a spacious lounge, his arms folded. I sat opposite him in an identical armchair. We were separated on one side by a sofa and on the other by a wide, ancient fireplace. The room was refreshingly cool. He still had a small plaster on his nose, but he was very much king in his castle. He oozed a confidence that fell short of charisma. Burns and Seanie lolled against the windowsill outside, their talk blurred by double glazing.

"I mean, me and Margaret, you and Margaret, me and your wife, you and your wife. We're so different, yet we have so much in common, wouldn't you say? I suppose to complete the circle you would really need to sleep with my wife."

We were alone in the room, yet there was another presence, dead, but alive. Margaret's self-portrait was framed above the fireplace, just as it had been in her own home. It dominated the room. The last time I'd seen it it had been sliced up, lying in her lounge. The smooth tear lines were just visible if you looked hard enough.

"But I wouldn't recommend sleeping with my wife, for health reasons, if you get my meaning."

"You mean she has some sort of embarrassing disease?"

Coogan smiled. "You're very cocky, Starkey, and I can't work out why. I wouldn't have said you had a lot to be so chirpy about. Perhaps you can tell me. I mean, don't get me wrong, but I'd say that having this tape, having the address your wife is at, and you, really put me in the driving seat, wouldn't you?"

I chose my answer as carefully as I always did in desperate situations. I shrugged.

"And I also have about a dozen other cassette tapes which you so thoughtfully supplied at a knock-down price. I thought that was quite clever, of course. Audacious even, given your circumstances and intellect. I suppose I should really have sent some better men to Bangor, but I was trying to cover a lot of bases at once. It isn't always the easiest thing to coordinate a lot of activity when you have the army on your tail. You tie a decent enough knot, Starkey, but not decent enough. And the dig in the balls was rather painful. But I'm afraid you have let yourself down a bit by coming to Crossmaheart. Entering the lion's den, rather."

"I didn't know you lived here."

"I don't live here," he replied disdainfully, "I own here. This was all ours before they built these fuckin' hideous estates. Country born and interbred, if you like. All our land, but they got it off us one way or another, paid us a fuckin' pittance for it. Still, the name mightn't be on the deeds any more, but it's still ours. Ours to play with. And it can be fun."

I could picture him out in the fields. The range. Stealing. "This is where you started your cattle rustling. Where the Cow Pat comes from."

"Oh, yes. Good country fun. Of course, there's not a lot of danger in stealing cattle, and you're never going to make your fortune from it, but it can be a bit of a laugh under the right circumstances."

"What, funnier than pushing someone off a balcony?"

"Ach, you're not still smartin' about that one, are you? It was business. He knew too much."

214

"He knew fuck all."

"He knew a lot more than he let on."

"He'd only been here a few days, for God's sake."

"True, but I imagine it doesn't take CIA agents that long to get acquainted with a place."

"What?" I spat sharply. My cheeks burnt. Pictured Parker, falling. I leant forward.

"Thought that might wake you up."

I sat back. Take it easy. "You are the ultimate bullshit man, Cow Pat."

"What an interesting run of words. But, no, your friend wasn't everything he said he was. Or, rather, he was everything he said he was, but a little more besides."

"I don't believe I'm hearing this."

"Well, that's up to you, of course. But y'know, a man can say quite a lot if you give him a really bad tickle. Especially with a pistol. It does wonders for the memory. Your friend Parker did a lot of talking. He really wasn't made of the stern stuff you expect to find in secret agents. God love them though, the Americans, they really haven't got anywhere proper to play now that they've lost the communists. It's all they're trained for. Everything else they do seems so ham-fisted, don't you think?"

"Whatever you say."

"Don't be like that, Starkey. You'll agree him being a CIA agent does put a different perspective on things."

"What, to a cattle rustler?"

"Now let's not be naïve. If you take it as fact, you see my point in killing him? Granted, you may not agree with the manner of his death, but you see the thinking behind it?"

"You people have never had much trouble justifying murder in the past. To yourself, that is. No one else believes you."

"Jesus, man, I'm not justifying anything, I . . ." He paused for a moment and glanced at Margaret. "You think I enjoy killing people?"

"Yes."

He shook his head. "Sometimes it has to be done. Simple as that."

215

"And you feel you have to look happy doing it just to impress people?"

He let out an exasperated sigh. He stood up and walked slowly to the fireplace. He put his hands on it and looked up into Margaret's face. "You recognize this?"

I nodded. He couldn't see me.

"Salvaged it from her house. Captures her well, don't you think?"

"I'm sure your wife appreciates it."

"As a work of art, yes. I can't say she's aware of its significance. I'm sure it wouldn't worry her, mind. She's an open-minded woman."

"I'm sure she is."

"Of course, she doesn't know about the abortion. Margaret told you about that, didn't she? Silly thing to break us up, really, but it seemed so important then. Her faith allowed that sort of thing, mine didn't. But it's a nice painting. She was a talented girl."

She was a talented girl. "It brings back unpleasant memories."

"Not pleasant ones as well?"

"They're kind of tied up with the unpleasant ones. Murder does that, Coogan."

"I suppose that one could argue that she was herself a killer, killing my baby."

"Somebody like you could, from the crackpot school of philosophy."

He opened his hands to me. "There you go, back to cockiness again. Y'know, if I didn't have a special use for you, you'd be under ground as well. Like everyone else, Starkey, you know too much. I imagine your wife knows too much as well. And as for that fucking nun, I don't know how much she knows but we'll have her for supper."

"It's a pity you don't enjoy killing."

"Business is business." His chin jutted forward, a movement childlike in its innocence. "I have a simple rule. Anyone who can complicate my life to such an extent that my freedom of movement is curtailed has to be dealt with. The extent of that dealing varies. For example, the British Army can interfere with my movement, but not as much as they like to think, and, besides, I can't very well eliminate them all — something the IRA doesn't appreciate yet — so they're not a target. On the other hand, those individuals who can be dealt with are. For example, those who have detailed knowledge of this tape, and could use it to upset my plans, and therefore my freedom, well, they can die. Simple, no?"

Simple, if deranged. A primary school battle plan. "So Father Flynn is next?"

"Flynn?" The innocence evaporated. His eyes narrowed. "I'd all but forgotten about him. Yes. Flynn. Something will have to be done about him as well. Such a pity really, he's been through so much."

I looked out of the window at the fading blue and thought about who else I could implicate by mistake. "Fuck Flynn, Coogan. Tell me about this special purpose you have for me. I'm dying to know."

He wasn't deflected. "Flynn, with that tape all that time, what did he do with it, I wonder, before he gave it to you?"

"He did nothing with it. Didn't even listen to it. Leave him alone."

Coogan turned from the fireplace and prowled along the carpet before me. He was wearing a pair of grey jeans and a white cap-sleeve T-shirt, altogether more unfashionable than the flash suit I'd first met him in, but much more natural for his surroundings. They fitted a lot better as well. He still didn't look like he'd been out in the sun much. His eyes were dark. Searching. Then they brightened.

"The list just keeps getting bigger, doesn't it, Starkey? Your wife, the nun, yourself, now Flynn. And you say you won't help me out with all those lives resting on you."

"You're talking in riddles, Coogan. You've already told me you're going to kill everyone involved with the tape. That's not much of an incentive to be helpful."

He clapped his hands together with a sharp crack that caused

Seanie and Burns to peer through the front window. "But that's the beauty of it, man. Your being helpful gives all those friends of yours longer on this earth. Longer for something to go wrong with my plans! It's a small possibility, but it's better than nothing, wouldn't you say?"

"I'd say it falls short of being generous."

"Do you want me to get a phone and you can call the lot of them and tell them they're going to die sometime today because you don't feel my offer is generous enough? I mean, be my guest. Tell your wife. Tell the nun." He stood before me, hands on hips, stared into me. "Tell Flynn. I haven't the heart to." It was a good pun, for a nut, but neither of us smiled. Perhaps he hadn't meant it.

Coogan walked me to the front door. Night had fallen. The cul-de-sac was brightly lit, but the estate falling away below was illuminated only by the pale glimmer of a crescent moon and the occasional unvandalized streetlight. Seanie started the hire car. Burns stood with one hand on the roof and one thrust into his trouser pocket.

"You could just drive off into the night," Coogan suggested. "It might, just, save your life. It wouldn't do any of the others much good."

He stood in the doorway. To anyone else we might have looked like neighbours saying goodnight. It was an unsettling thought. "What would you do," I asked, "in my situation?"

"Oh, I don't know, Starkey, it's not really my problem."

"But hypothetically."

"You haven't met my wife."

"Nor slept with her."

"Not much chance of that. No, I really think you should make your own mind up. Now, on your way, I'll expect to hear from you at some point during the night. Obviously the earlier the better. Good luck."

Seanie got out of the car, flicking on the lights as he did so. He held the door open for me. As I climbed in behind the wheel he said, "Drive carefully."

I wound the window down and shouted across to Coogan. "What if I get stopped on the way. By the police or army, or anyone?"

"You won't," he said.

"Why don't you just fuckin' phone him?" I asked.

"Because. Now get the fuck out of here."

I put the car into drive and moved slowly down the cul-de-sac. Then I stopped it and reversed back. Burns and Seanie stopped halfway up the drive and stood protectively in the garden as I approached. The man himself took a moment to reappear, but was in place by the time I'd found park and wound the window down again.

"You never gave me your number, Coogan," I called.

Coogan shook his head and turned back into the house. Seanie walked down the path and leant into the car. I moved back instinctively.

"It's in the book, Starkey," he hissed, "under C. For Cunt."

28

The first chance I had, when I was sure there was no one following, I stopped the car and phoned Lee's house. Directory Enquiries gave me the number. A man answered. I said: "Is that the taxi place?"

There was a slight pause and then he said gruffly: "Starkey?"

"Excuse me?"

"Is that you, Starkey?"

"I'm looking for a taxi, mate, I . . ."

"If that's you, Starkey, Cow Pat has a message for ya. Get on with the fuckin' job and stop fuckin' around."

"I'm just . . ."

"And if it's not, just fuck away off."

He rang off. I walked back to the car. I leant on the roof and looked up the road along the main thoroughfare of a village. It was about twenty miles from Crossmaheart. I missed its name. Bar-room beery chatter added body to the light breeze blowing in my face, vinegar and battered fish a slight odour. Teenagers lazed on corners. A summer's night. The election was in two days. Posters hung on every lamppost. Brinn's face. Mr. Popularity. If Coogan had my balls in his pocket, he had Brinn's in his mouth.

I drove on. I switched on the radio but it was too late for much in the way of news. For the first time in my life the idea of listening to rock music repelled me. I found a classical station. It wasn't exactly soothing. The music was slow and haunting, dark music suited to a night lit only by the moon and the occasional flash of a passing car. The commentator credited it to the Berlin Philharmonic and Dvořák.

A mile outside Bangor I came upon a police checkpoint. I thought, what a ridiculous time to be caught by the cops. I was upon it before I had a chance to even think about trying to get away. I dimmed the lights and waited to be arrested. When the tap on the window came I was calm and collected. I didn't have the energy to say you'll never take me alive, copper, never mind fulfil it. I smiled pleasantly and waited for the cuffs.

"Good evening, sir, can you tell me where you're going tonight?"

"Bangor."

"And could I take a look at your driving licence?"

I handed him the licence I had stolen from the guesthouse in Belfast. He shone a torch on it, then on me, then round the interior of the car.

"Where are you going in Bangor, sir?"

"To see Mr. Brinn. Of the Alliance."

He let that sink in for a moment. "Yes, sir, and I'm the god-father of soul."

He leant in the window. He had a thick black moustache and stubble-darkened skin. He stared into my face.

"Seriously," I said, quietly and with a slight nod of my head.

He gave me a little sarcastic smile. "We'll see," he said and stepped back from the car. He walked over to a grey police Land Rover and reached inside. He stood back with a small radio microphone in his hand and started talking. Another policeman waved forward the traffic which had started to build up behind me. As I looked out my side window the lights of a car passing on the other side of the road picked out the bright eyes of a soldier lying crouched in undergrowth. His rifle was pointed at me.

The policeman returned. He handed me the licence. "Very good, sir, that will be all."

I said thanks and started the car. I moved off slowly. He stepped back and said quietly, "Have a nice night now, Mr. Morrison," as I passed. The name was said with obvious sarcasm. Rumbled but free. How far did Coogan's arm stretch? And if it stretched that far, why did he have to bother messing around with little people like me?

The gates to Red Hall were closed. Floodlights illuminated the driveway. On my last visit, a little old woman in a wheelchair could have breached the security. Now two guards, armed, young, and alert, stood warily to each side of the stone pillars, staring out through the metal gates. I drove slowly up and flashed the lights, then stopped the car.

The gates swung inward. I moved forward with them and stopped the car again.

"You Starkey?"

I nodded.

"Any ID?"

I shook my head.

The one doing the talking was tall and lithe and looked like a policeman. His uniform was black to the RUC's bottle-green, but otherwise there was little difference. His comrade was more rotund, like a prison officer, and somehow more threatening. Both had pistols, holstered.

"Right car though," the prison officer observed. "Right numberplates."

"But no ID." The police officer rubbed his finger along the side of the passenger door, examined it, then wiped it on the door again. "You should always carry ID, Mr. Starkey."

"I have ID. But not mine."

"I suppose fugitives like yourself would have access to fake ID."

"It's not fake. It just isn't mine."

"Ah. You don't look like the kind of fella could give everyone the run-around for so long."

I shrugged. "Or a murderer," I suggested.

"Oh, you look like a killer okay. You don't need brains to be that. No, I can recognize a killer when I see one okay. I was just thinking that you don't look like the kind of fella would have the wherewithal to keep one step ahead of everyone all this time."

"Thanks."

"Don't mention it."

I started the engine again. "Okay if I go through?"

"If he wants to meet a killer, he wants to meet a killer, be my guest."

"You're not worried about letting a killer through?" I asked, revving the engine slightly.

"Worried? A bit. But Mr. Brinn knows what he's doing, I'm sure. See, that's what I like about the man, he's up front about everything. He gets on the phone to me and says, 'Bill, that reporter, Starkey, wanted for the McGarry murders, is coming to see me in the next hour or so. Let him through, would you?' And that's good enough for me. He didn't try to be mysterious or anything. Didn't try to pass you off as something else, y'know? Because I would have recognized you. He knows that. Clear?"

"Right on."

It was late, but a dozen or more cars were parked outside the hall. A rattle of masts emanated from the marina a few hundred yards beyond the garden wall.

The door opened before me. Alfie Stewart looked me up and down. Alfie had always been okay. "Times are bad when the party's security spokesman mans the door," I said.

"Don't be stupid, Starkey," he snapped and waved me in. He led me up the stairs, taking them three at a time. He was puffing slightly as he reached the top. I lagged behind, but still puffed. A sympathy puff.

"A lot of cars here this late," I said. "Crisis meeting?"

"The election's two days away, Starkey," he wheezed. "Of course we're meeting."

As I reached the top I stopped him as he gestured me forward towards the room where Parker and I had first met Brinn. Ah, Parker. If only he'd known then what was to befall him. And then I thought, Parker, CIA? Nah. No way. "You know what this is all about, Alfie?"

"Kinda."

"Kinda how much?"

"You should discuss it with Brinn."

"You know I didn't kill Margaret McGarry."

"I don't know that. I know you're here from Cow Pat Coogan, and that yous might have something on Brinn to make him want to deal. I know it all sounds pretty shoddy to me." He thrust his face into mine. "You've fallen an awful long way, Starkey. An awful long way. You're down beneath the bottom of the barrel, son." Alfie blew out his cheeks, turned on his heels and led me down the corridor to Brinn's almost familiar study. He told me to take a seat. "And try not to destroy anything," he warned. I smiled at him and he turned to leave.

"Hey, Alfie?" I said. "You knew about Brinn, didn't you? His past. You knew all about him."

He waved an admonishing finger at me. "It'll take a better shit than you or Cow Pat bloody Coogan to bring Brinn down, Starkey. He's a better man, a better politician than any of those fuckin' hellions out there, better by far."

"Yeah," I said to the door as he slammed it, "kinda."

"Ah, Mrs. Brinn. Nice to see you again."

Agnes put her head round the door and stared at me.

"Are you coming in?"

It had only been a few days since we had met, yet the additive-free face I had so admired had become rather haggard and her hair lay dank on her head. I was no oil painting myself, of course.

She wavered uncertainly in the doorway then slowly stepped forward. She closed the door behind her and leant against it. She kept staring. It was unsettling.

"Is he coming then?" I asked.

"He'll be along when he finishes his meeting."

I nodded. My seat by the window gave me a good view of the floodlit garden. I turned away from her to watch the progress of the guards as they patrolled the perimeter wall, their black uniforms brightened only by the pinprick glow of cigarettes.

224

"Why are you here?" she asked, her voice drink-dulled.

"To see the man."

"What about?"

I kept my eyes on the garden. "That's between me and the man."

She clicked a heel sharply against the door. I looked up at her. Her top lip was trembling. I'd never seen a top lip tremble before.

"Why won't anyone tell me anything?" She was on the verge of tears. I started to rise from my seat but she tensed up against the door and I lowered myself back down. "What's going on?"

I opened my palms to her. It was better than shrugging. "Too much," I volunteered.

"Why won't anyone tell me anything?" she repeated, running her hands through her hair, which can't have been pleasant. "Why are you here? He didn't tell me you were coming, you of all people. I mean, after what you did . . . he brings you here?"

"Agnes, I didn't do anything."

"He's been in foul form for days and he won't tell me a thing, and he used to tell me everything. Everything." The tears started to roll. She wiped at her eyes with the back of her hand. "It's like I don't know him at all. And he's got everything going for him."

Then all of her was trembling. I stood up and walked across to her and went to put my arms round her but she pushed me away. "It all started when you came here. Everything was going so fine till you came. It's like there's a curse on you. I don't know why he doesn't get the police and have done with you."

I crossed to the window again. There wasn't much I could say. Then she was beside me, looking out over the grounds, at a rabbit valiantly defying the floodlights. "It's not going to work, is it?" she asked. "After all we've achieved, it's all going to fall apart at the end, isn't it?"

"I don't know. It's not up to me. I'm only a messenger."

"The devil's advocate," she said.

"That's a drink made with eggs, isn't it? No wonder he's so evil, it tastes like shite."

She gave a sad little chuckle and said wearily, "In the middle of all this, you're writing." It wasn't writing. It was wit. It was an entirely different thing. I hadn't thought of writing for an eternity. "What will you write about it then, when it's over?" she asked.

I shook my head. "I never write something until I know how it ends."

The door opened. We both looked round. Brinn. The same pale face, but his eyes hooded now, menacing. "What are you doing in here, Agnes?"

She put her hand mockingly to her chest. "Me? Oh, you can see me, can you? What a surprise."

"Agnes . . ."

"Oh stop it, wouldja?"

She took off across the room. He moved to one side of the doorway and she stormed past without looking at him. Brinn gave her back a lingering gaze, then closed the door and turned to face me.

"Women," I said, to break the ice.

"Men," he said, "and what they do."

"Yeah," I said.

29

We sat opposite each other. The decaffeinated coffee table was between us, as before. A copy of the *Belfast Telegraph* sat upon it, with a colour photograph of the masses attending Brinn's peace rally staring up at me.

"Is that there for a reason?" I asked.

"It may be. I didn't put it there. Maybe Alfie was being cryptic."

"Yeah."

"Maybe he was just reading it in here. Maybe you're reading too much into it."

"As the great communicator I thought you might be trying to tell me something. Something about peace and love. No?"

"From me? If you know what I think you know, you won't be expecting that, will you?"

Slipping back into old habits, I shrugged.

"So let's talk," he said, "about the pleasures of home taping. They say it's killing music, but I wonder if they thought about it killing democracy?" His smile barely curled above his upper teeth and tugged only lightly at his cheeks. "Shoot," he said.

"Just the facts, then." I spread my ten fingers before him and began counting them off. I had no plans to get as far as ten. "As you know, I've been sent here by Cow Pat Coogan. He has possession of a tape in which you confess to the bombing of the

Paradise restaurant in 1974 in which eight people died. He would like to sell it back to you for £250,000, which, he says, isn't very much. Otherwise he will make it public."

Brinn shook his head slowly, but it wasn't a negative response as such, more an instinctive reaction. "And of course there's only the one copy," he said. He stared at me for several seconds. "£250,000 isn't very much, is it? He wouldn't dream of bleeding me dry from now till kingdom come, would he, or controlling the country through blackmail?"

"He gave me his word," I said. "Of course, he could have been lying. I imagine he isn't called Cow Pat for nothing."

"I imagine not." Brinn stood up and walked to the window. He shook his head again as he stared out over the floodlit gardens. "Tell me, Starkey, what's your role in all this? I've managed to keep out of the papers that I know you at all; I hoped that might be the worst of my problems. What was it, you decided the sword was mightier than the pen, or you just wanted to get rich quick? And why Cow Pat Coogan of all people?"

His voice was wispy, carried on the slightly musty air of the paperback-lined room like a chicken feather rising on a thin beam of sunlight in a slaughterhouse. It wasn't easy to feel sorry for him. I felt sorrier for myself.

"It's quite simple really," I said. I'd get to the tenth finger yet. "I was having an affair with Margaret McGarry. She gave me a tape. Somebody killed her. I got blamed. The tape was taken off me. Now they'll kill my wife if you don't deal. See? Simple. Your turn. The tape. It is authentic, isn't it?"

Brinn turned from the window, leant against it. "I haven't heard it, of course. But I have no reason to doubt its existence." He tilted his head up towards the ceiling, puffed out his cheeks and blew air. "These things do have a habit of coming back to haunt you, don't they?"

"I'll take your word for it."

"I mean, things you do when you're drunk."

"You were drunk when you bombed the . . ."

"No, no," he snapped, "when McGarry . . . betrayed me. Do

you ever wake up after you've been drinking and you just go, oh no, when you remember what you've done?"

"Always."

"That's what it was like. I'd been to a Party party, if you know what I mean. The campaign was just under way. I was with friends, so I was able to let my hair down a bit, first time for a long time. I just got drunk and a bit depressed over this and that. Maybe it was the bomb. It never really goes away, you understand? McGarry took me home. We had a long conversation. He was the first person I ever told about the bomb. Not even my wife."

"I gathered that."

"The more I think about it now the more I realize he steered the conversation towards violence, towards the bomb. Somehow he got to hear about it and took advantage of me when I was drunk to tape what amounts to a confession. The bastard. To think of all the help I'd . . ."

"Things like that always come out."

He shook his head. "You'd be surprised. The number of things I could tell you about . . . people. You'd be appalled. But I'm not like that . . . forgive and forget."

"Difficult for eight families to forget . . ."

"Jesus!" Brinn snapped. "Don't you think I know? How do you think I got into politics?" He returned to his seat, crossed his legs, rubbed his fingers over a lightly stubbled chin. His eyes glazed in memory. "I was only a youngster when it all happened. Easily led. I thought I was fighting for a just cause. They told me I was bombing a police dinner. I was bombing a police dinner, but the restaurant had double booked it and the police agreed to a change of venue at the last minute and I got to bomb the Cavalier King Charles Spaniel Club. You, and I mean you, might describe it as barking up the wrong tree."

"That's a sad comment on me."

"Yeah. It's all sad. You experience death like that, it changes you. It changed me. I worked hard. I got all this. I nearly got to be prime minister, didn't I?"

229

"Nearly," I agreed.

"But not now," he said.

I shrugged. "Things might work out okay."

"Don't be stupid, Starkey. This is all the Unionists have been waiting for. If this gets out, voters would rather slip tongues with lepers than vote for me."

"I always felt like that."

"Starkey," he said bluntly, his gaze as close to withering as be damned, "what the fuck gives you the right to sit there and be so bloody patronizing?"

I sat back. "My wife being held hostage because of a bomb you planted."

He snorted. "We're both in the shit."

"Yeah."

"And you're the only one with any hope of coming out of this smelling of roses."

"I don't mind if I come out smelling of shit, Brinn, as long as I come out, and at the moment that's entirely up to you. You have an answer for Coogan?"

He shook his head.

"He wants to hear soon. So does my wife."

"I know this sounds harsh, Starkey, but I can't put your wife before the country."

"It doesn't sound harsh, it sounds stupid. Think of her as the country. Save her, maybe you save the country."

"Now who's being cryptic?"

"Fuck cryptic, Brinn. Make your mind up."

"Okay. Okay." He moved thin fingers up to his brow and rubbed at it vigorously for several long moments. He shook his head again. He folded his arms. He looked at the door. At his books. Out over the lawns again. Down at the photo of the peace rally. At me. At my denims. At my hair. In my eyes. Finally he stood up. The moment of truth. "Wait here," he said quietly. "I need to ask my wife."

He stopped as he opened the door. "If I pay, do you think that'll be the end of it?" he asked. His hands were trembling.

"I don't know."

He nodded slightly and left.

I phoned Coogan. "He wants to sleep on it."

Coogan laughed. "Just who the fuck does he think he is? Sleep on it!"

"He has a lot to think about."

"Well, sleeping won't fucking help that."

"It's a turn of phrase, Coogan. I don't think he'll be doing much sleeping. Give him a break for God's sake."

Alfie Stewart showed me to a bedroom. He didn't say much. I didn't say much. The room was as spartan as rarely used guest bedrooms are, an artificial tidiness failed by a thin layer of dust. Alfie didn't wish me a good night. I lay on the bed and watched the dawn come up over the marina, grey to blue. Several times I heard raised voices, too distant to distinguish them properly other than as male and female, but it wasn't difficult to guess who they belonged to. I felt dirty and it wasn't just from lack of a shower.

Patricia and Lee were hostages to a gangster and their fate lay in the hands of a bomber, all because of an adulterer. Coogan would dispatch them with the same callousness with which Parker had entered the next world. Brinn had to deal.

Alfie had told me to stay in my room. He didn't want me wandering about Red Hall in case anyone not in the know came across me. As a precaution he locked the door, but it was more to keep strangers out than me in. Not that I could have picked the lock, but the window was open and it wasn't much of a jump to the ground below. And I still had one good leg to land on.

It was still early when Alfie entered the room. "Knock, knock," he said, closing the door behind him. He had a tray in his hands. "Breakfast is served," he announced with a flourish and set it down on the bedside table. He looked like he'd been up all night. "And don't worry, I didn't spit in it."

"I wish I could believe you, Alfie."

"Of course you can, Starkey, I'm in politics."

I pulled myself up from the bed. "Well?" I asked. "Any word. Do you bring me tidings of great joy?"

"No, I bring you scrambled eggs and Brinn'll be down in a minute."

He hovered by the bed as I poked at the food.

"You make this yourself?"

"Sure."

I left it. "I've not much appetite. Sorry."

"No skin off my nose, Starkey."

I shrugged. "He's told you about the tape?"

"He has."

"And you're sticking with him?"

Alfie nodded. "Through thick and thin."

"You must have wavered."

"Maybe. But I've made my decision. I don't change my colours that quickly, Starkey."

"Brinn did, bomber to politician."

"Don't try to provoke me."

"I'm not. I'm just saying. You must have thought about it."

"I'm here, aren't I? Doesn't that tell you everything?"

He lifted the tray and left the room. It told me everything. Everything about a man shown a glimpse of power reluctant to let it go. Brinn left me for another half-hour. Cars began to arrive outside: party workers for the most part, but also TV crews for their final pre-election interviews. The BBC and Ulster Television were there, ABC and NBC from the States, French and Italian. I recognized a couple of newspaper reporters, hanging around in the car park looking victimized. I thought briefly about opening the bedroom window fully and shouting my story to the world. But only briefly.

When Brinn appeared he looked even worse than Alfie. His eyes were puffy, like he'd been in a fight, his customary pallor had deepened; it would have frightened a mortician. A bone in his bent nose shone white against the bridge, as if illuminated from within. He was wearing a pale-grey suit that didn't do him any favours.

232

"I have a busy day ahead of me," he said quietly. "Final preparations. Interviews. I'm even going walkabout in the city centre."

I nodded.

"I've been up most of the night," he continued.

"So I heard."

"Yes. As you might suspect, she's not very happy with me."

I nodded again.

"But she's sticking with me."

"So's Alfie. Two out of two isn't bad. So far."

"So far, of course." He fell silent and we watched each other for half a minute. Finally he said: "I've decided to take the chance. Pay the man. It's all I can do. Agnes agrees."

I gave him a little reassuring smile. "I think you're right," I said simply.

"I have to trust it's the only copy of the tape."

"You will."

"Which isn't easy."

"No."

"It'll take me a while to get the money together. I'll have to arrange it in such a way that it doesn't arouse suspicion."

"Of course."

"Let Coogan know then."

I let Coogan know. "Time?" he asked, bluntly.

"Yeah, time. It's a lot of money."

"Not for him."

"Still."

"Yeah. Okay. Tomorrow then."

"Tomorrow."

I got Alfie to call Brinn in after the first of his TV interviews. He was wearing makeup. It wasn't much help.

"Tomorrow. He wants you to hand it over in person."

"Me?"

"You."

"Tomorrow? But it's election day, I . . ."

"But nothing . . ."

"Yeah. Yes. Okay. Tomorrow."

"Tollymore Forest. At dawn."

Brinn shook his head, but, again, it wasn't a negative response. "He's being a bit melodramatic, isn't he? Dawn in a forest?"

I nodded. "I think it's his style. He has a Hollywood approach to things. A meeting in a forest at dawn between two historical characters has a certain epic quality to it. It's *The Prisoner of Zenda*. It's *The Thirty-Nine Steps*. It's *The Godfather*. He's creating the Legend of the Paper Cowboy."

Brinn looked at Alfie, who shook his head. He turned back to me. "What?"

30

One of my legs was blue.

Cold sweats, hot sweats. Too much perspiration does things to denim. Metaphorically I wasn't attached to my adopted look at all, but, literally, my jeans were becoming attached to me. I peeled them off and scrubbed at the dye under a hot shower. The bullet wound was healing nicely. Alfie brought me some replacements. Not new, of course, someone else's again, but light and refreshing. Grey slacks, a sports jacket, a white shirt, a paisley tie which I rejected. Alfie didn't say who they belonged to. It was good of him to bring them, seeing as how he hated me. Perhaps Brinn told him to.

Both of them were away for the day. Alfie insisted that I stay in the upper, barely populated part of Red Hall, so I had access to Brinn's library, but I didn't have the concentration to read more than a few lines of anything. I kept thinking about my wife. And Lee. And Margaret. And everything. Agnes called on me towards lunchtime and asked if I wanted to go out into the garden.

"I don't think I'm supposed to," I said. She was wearing a light summer frock. Her hair was clean again, her mouth composed and inviting. "I might be recognized."

"Sure it doesn't matter much now, does it?"

I shrugged. "The world's press might have their cameras trained on the garden, Agnes."

"There's a secluded wee bit round the back no one can see

235

into but the birds. Even the guards can't see in. There's only a couple of the staff about anyway. They follow him about like an Indian encampment. I thought you might like some fresh air."

"I could do with it, right enough."

"Well, come on then." She turned. I followed. She led me down the stairs and out through the slippery-tiled kitchens to an enclosed yard at the rear of Red Hall. It was crazy-paved, which suited me down to the ground. There were two sun loungers already laid out and between them a table with a little sun-shade umbrella clipped to it. There was an icebox with the Coca Cola logo on the table. The sun was pouring down. She had prepared everything. I took my jacket off and straightened the back of one of the loungers and sat upright. There's nothing so ridiculous as a man sunbathing fully clothed. But there was no point in lying back. I wasn't about to disrobe because my leg was still partially blue. Agnes took off her dress. She wore a deep-blue one-piece swimming costume. She lay back on her lounger. I gazed studiously away from her figure. Everything was quiet. No seagulls laughing. No lap of the waves. No tapping of the masts.

"Have a beer," Agnes said, waving at the icebox.

"Don't mind if I do." I stood up and opened the box. There were about half a dozen cans of Harp. I lifted two. I offered her one. She had on very dark sunglasses. She didn't respond. Her head was pointed in my general direction but I couldn't tell if she was looking at me.

"Do you want one?"

"What? Oh, no. No, thanks. I'm trying to lose some weight."

"That's okay," I said. "I'm trying to gain it."

I took both cans and sat down again. I should have put one back, to keep cool, but I'd had enough things taken off me in the last few days when I thought they were safely in my protection not to trust letting go of it for an instant: Margaret, the tape, my wife.

"Nice and quiet, isn't it?" I opened the can and took a long drink. Nice. "I heard you, last night. Shouting."

She lifted her sunglasses up to look at me, then dropped them down again. "So?"

"Nothing. Just saying."

High up, a seagull circled. If it had been Africa it would have been a vulture, which would have been altogether more appropriate.

"I thought you might have gone with him today," I said, "on his rounds."

She lifted her glasses again, looked at me for a moment, then took them off completely. She folded the arms in and reached up to set them on the table. "I see," she said with a slight sigh, "that you don't believe in keeping the peace."

I shrugged.

"No," she continued, "I didn't go with him today. He has too much to do, too much to worry about. And I don't make a very convincing liar, so I would have had difficulty speaking at all. So I'm at home holding my tongue." She made a little pretend play at holding her tongue and smiled across at me. I smiled back. "Everything we do from here on in is a lie, isn't it?"

"That's a matter of opinion," I said, and her eyes half-crossed in mild despair. The great journalist sits on the fence. "I mean, everyone lies. It only matters to those who're caught out."

"And you think we won't be caught out? Come on, Starkey."

"I don't imagine your husband has gotten as far as he has without having some sort of plan up his sleeve. I think he's unlikely just to keep paying Coogan money for the rest of his life. But then Coogan will have thought of that, I presume."

I picked up my second can and offered it to her again. She reached out to take it. She pulled back the ring-pull and tossed it on to the crazy paving. "My diets never did last very long," she said. She took a sip, then a longer slug, and set the can back on the table.

"Are you relaxed?" she asked.

"No," I said.

"Neither am I."

I nodded.

"Maybe I should get out of this swimsuit."

I let that one sink in for a moment. I wasn't looking anywhere near her, but I could feel her eyes on me and I could feel

237

redness inching up my cheeks like a sponge cake rising in an oven. I took another drink. It was cold. It turned to steam. I turned to her. She hadn't made any effort to strip. I pointed up into the bluest of blue skies. "See that bird?"

She followed my gaze. "What, the gull?"

"Whatever."

"Yeah. What of it?"

"I have reason to believe that that may not be a gull at all, but a CIA robot bird equipped with a spy camera designed to take incriminating photographs of the wives of important politicians."

"I see," she said. "Perhaps I shouldn't then." She took another long drink of her beer, this time resting the can beside her sun lounger. She looked across at me thoughtfully. I dredged up the gumption to look back, although not quite directly into her eyes. Into her lids, which was close. "But if it was the CIA," she queried, her brow scrunched up, along with her lids, "wouldn't it be much better for them just to have a tape of that important politician confessing to a horrific bombing?"

I nodded. "Of course." She was quite right.

We drank the cans and she got six more and a bottle of wine. Political offices are always well stocked with alcohol. The sun remained hot and after a couple of hours I had my shirt off and my trousers rolled up to my knees, well short of the blue smudge on my thigh. I made Agnes promise not to take her costume off. I wasn't sure if I was disappointed or not when she agreed. It was neither the time nor the place for any of that nonsense, which meant it was in a crazy-paving kind of way.

The promise didn't stop the straps from slipping off her shoulders, revealing a little more than was comfortable of her breasts. Comfortable for me, that was. There wasn't really anywhere else to look. An enclosed courtyard shorn of decoration; a blue sky with only a blinding sun and the occasional gull. Her sunglasses were back on and her head was turned towards me, but again I couldn't tell if she was looking at me; but she could tell when I was looking at her; she could tell when my eyes darted to those big hints of breasts every few minutes. I felt like I was thirteen. Fourteen. Fifteen. And on.

Her head was getting a bit loose on her shoulders. It lolled back from time to time as she laughed and seemed to have some difficulty coming forward again.

"What will you do if it doesn't work out, Agnes?"

She moved her whole upper torso forward and the head came with it. She bent her knees and rested her head on them, turned towards me so that I could see one glassy eye through the side of her sunglasses. "What will I do?"

"Yeah."

"What does it matter about me? It's him you've to worry about. There's not a hell of a big gap between being most loved and most hated guy in the world, y'know. I expect he's about to find out how small it is."

"But what about you?"

"I'll keep the home fires burning. Which is a pun to be proud of, is it not?" She giggled. A nice girlie giggle. "You know I used to be a journalist, Starkey?"

"You did? When?"

"Oh, way back when . . ." She hiccuped. "Oh dear." She took her sunglasses off and dropped them carelessly on the ground, then sucked in a deep breath and held it for longer than seemed advisable, then let it out with a big rush and breathed sharply up through her nose. "That should be it," she said, still holding her breath, squeezing the words out between her teeth, like cheese through a grater. Then exhaled. "Aaaaaaah." She took another drink of beer. Then a sip of wine. "Yeah, me, a journalist. Oh, not for very long. I worked for a weekly paper. That's where I met the love of my life. He was only young. Just starting out."

"On bombing?"

She giggled. "That's uncalled for, Starkey. On politics. Just making his way. But he was very charming. I knew he'd go far. Although I didn't let him go too far that first date." The giggle developed into a big throaty laugh. Then she clamped her hand over her mouth. "Sorry!" she hissed, her eyes wide and moist but still brimming with laughter.

239

"He is a bit of a charmer though, isn't he?" Her hand fell away from her mouth, her lips tightened. She nodded. Tears sprang from her eyes. I took another slug of beer. Her eyes were imploring, drunk, suffocated, depressed, maudlin, mesmerizing. The only place to look was her breasts, which was less than gentlemanly under the circumstances. I was too drunk to look at her lids. She pushed her arm across her face, smearing the stream of tears. "I'm sorry," she said.

"It's okay. I understand."

She sniffed up, a big man's snorter. Half giggled at it, half cried. She apologized again. I shrugged. "He told me about your wife."

I shrugged again.

"I remember, a long time ago, days now, I met you in the garden and asked you what was troubling you. You should have told me."

"I was a bit confused."

"And you're not confused now?"

"Oh, I'm still confused, but so's everyone else. It's nice to have company."

"Yeah. Confusion reigns. Nice way to launch a new country, isn't it?"

"The only way."

She pulled the straps up on her costume. It was about time. "You love your wife?" she asked.

"Yeah."

"But you were having an affair with Margaret McGarry."

"Yeah."

"So you couldn't have loved your wife."

"I don't follow your reasoning."

"You couldn't love your wife if you wanted to go off and have sex with someone else."

"Love isn't quite as clear-cut as that, Agnes. You love Brinn?"

"Yes. Of course."

"And you've never been unfaithful?"

"No."

240

"What about threatening to take your costume off earlier? What do you call that?"

"Sunbathing."

"Ah."

"So?"

"What about dear Brinn? Has he never been unfaithful?"

"No. Of course not."

"Not Mr. Charming himself? Who has half the women in Ulster eating out of his Y-fronts?"

"He wouldn't." She shook her head and took a hasty gulp of her wine. There wasn't much left, in glass or bottle. "I would know," she stated flatly.

"Like you knew about the bomb?"

She snapped the glass down sharply on the crazy paving. It shattered. She stared at me. I stared at the interesting red brick wall that surrounded us on three sides. Then at the blue sky. "That's not fair," she said. She got up from the lounger. I tensed. I was going to get whacked. She towered over me. Blocking out the sky. That only left the wall to glare at. "I'm going for a pish," she said quietly and strode unsteadily away. The sun put his hat back on again.

While she was gone I walked back into Red Hall. I went through the kitchen and into the entrance hall. There was no one about. I found a phone and looked up a number, then dialled.

It was answered third ring.

"Hi, is that the American Consulate?"

"Yes, sir, how may I help you?"

"It's okay. It doesn't matter."

I put the phone down. The man in the black uniform beside me indicated that it might be better if I terminated the conversation by pressing a revolver to my scalp. I agreed.

"Sorry," I said.

"Don't worry about it. Away out and entertain the missus again, why don't you? I was enjoying the conversation."

"Okay," I said.

31

I don't remember much about the journey itself. I know we didn't talk much. There really wasn't anything to say. My role was clear cut. I was the courier delivering the goods. Brinn was the goods, but he was also the courier, delivering the money. I drove. We listened to some music on the radio. Brinn stared resolutely ahead. He looked better in the dark, his long nose cut down to size by shadow, his white eyes sharp, predatory, his thin lips fixed impassively, politically.

I remember more clearly leaving Red Hall in the full blackness of night, a damp lough breeze easing around our legs like a hunched cat. Agnes in the doorway in a white nightdress, her hair jaggedly wild, her eyes damp, her face grey, stale alcohol on her breath. Brinn, his hands in his wife's hair, kissing her goodbye, promising her everything would be different once he was elected. Alfie, upset that he had to stay behind, handing over the case of money to Brinn and watching us drive off with the feisty petulance of a retriever on a lead.

Percy French, the popular but dead songwriter, wrote movingly about the Mourne Mountains sweeping down to the sea. Some of them do. Others have at their mossy feet Tollymore Forest, a thick expanse of National Trust pine that exudes charm and welcome in the bright heat of summer but broods under cloud and mist for most of the rest of the time. It was a forty-minute journey from Bangor, a fair distance away too from Coogan's headquarters in Crossmaheart. There was no obvious Coogan connection with Tollymore, other than providing a suitably intimidating background. And it would be easy for him to disappear off into the trees if something went wrong.

There were no security checkpoints and blessed few cars on the road. Dawn was just beginning to break, the mountains peaking through the light mist like hazelnuts in a decaying blancmange, when we stopped at the gates to Tollymore. They were closed. I looked over at Brinn. He looked back. I shrugged and got out. I pushed at the gates, but they were firmly locked. I looked back at Brinn and shrugged again. Then someone said: "Ah, the man with the money."

A bulky figure stepped out of the gloom. He had a pistol in his hand and a balaclava on his head, but what little there was of his face was unmistakable.

"Mad Dog," I said, quietly.

"Just Mad, to my friends."

He pushed the barrel of the gun into my stomach and checked me over with his free hand. When he was finished he took a little torch from his pocket and shone it through the passenger window. Brinn stared straight ahead. Mad Dog gave a little whistle and said, "The man himself," with a little inflection of mock awe. He rapped on the window. "Okay, chuckles, out you come," he said and pulled the door open. Brinn climbed out of the car and stood to attention with the case of money on the ground in front of him. Mad Dog searched him, then shone the torch round the inside of the car, checking under the seats and in the glove compartment. He turned to the case, opened it up, then turned his half-masked face up to me. "Few quid in here," he purred, then snapped it shut. Abruptly he stood up and said: "Change of plan, mates, just in case you're thinking of something. Get back in the car and continue along here for about a mile. Coogan'll be waiting for you along there. He'll make himself known." We got back into the car. "Goodbye," said Mad Dog, closing the passenger door behind Brinn, "and may your God go with you."

"Thanks," I said.

"Don't mention it."

Brinn hadn't opened his mouth. He rested the case on his knees.

"Well," I said, starting the engine again and reversing back, "it keeps life exciting, doesn't it?" Mad Dog had already disappeared into the gloom. Brinn didn't move his head, but his eyes swivelled briefly towards me and then hit front centre again. "Drive," he said.

We moved off.

A couple of hundred yards further on car lights flashed on and off. I slowed the car. A green and white Land Rover was wedged up against one of the lichen-scored dry-stone walls that ran up either side of the road. About fifty yards short I stopped the car.

"Well," I said, "this must be it." It was more to break the eerie silence of the early morning than anything. Brinn nodded his head slowly.

"You ready?"

He nodded again. I moved to open my door, but he put a hand on my arm. "I'm sorry about all this," he said quickly, giving my arm a little squeeze.

"Yeah," I said. He was a couple of decades late. His hand lingered on my jacket for a moment, then he let go. He looped his arm through the case handle and pushed the passenger door open. Up ahead the Land Rover's doors swung open. Coogan, wearing a khaki combat jacket and bottle-green trousers, climbed out from behind the wheel. On the other side, the neanderthal Seanie emerged. From the rear his companion, the relatively erudite Malachy Burns, appeared. Seanie was carrying a shotgun, Burns what looked like a machine pistol; Coogan carried himself, with ease, flanked on either side by his gunmen.

We met about halfway. Brinn set the case down and positioned his legs protectively on either side of it. It was a bit silly really. He didn't have much to bargain with. I had even less. Coogan had a little smirk on his face.

"Nice to see you again," he said.

"Likewise," I said.

"I'm not talking to you, Starkey."

"It's been a long time," said Brinn.

"Yeah, things have changed a bit, eh?" He put his hand out and Brinn grasped it. They held each other's gaze for a long moment. Brinn let go first, then Coogan asked: "Where did all that revolutionary zeal ever go, eh?"

Brinn snorted. "We both grew up. In different ways, of course."

"You into the wonderful world of politics."

"And you into gangsterism."

"Ach, sure that was always in the blood, you knew that. My growing up was turning professional at it."

"You've done well."

"And you even better."

"Maybe. It got me this far. To a lonely country road with a couple of gunmen and a dipso reporter. Yeah, I've surely arrived now."

"But by tonight, all this will be yours. All this country. That must be a pleasant thought."

"Pleasant if I get to enjoy it, Coogan. I presume you don't intend to let me do that, do you?"

Coogan spread his hands, palms up, before Brinn. "Aw, come on now, what's a few pounds to an old mate, eh? You can spare that, can't ye?"

Brinn stepped back and pushed the case towards Coogan. "This you can have with my compliments, Coogan. Enjoy it. It's all you'll be getting. Once I'm installed — I hear a word from you, you're a dead man. You know that, I know that. I'll be bigger than you." It was a playground threat, that simple, that real, and, somehow, even scarier than adults at war.

"Of course you will." Coogan bent to lift the case. He weighed it, dropping it from one hand to the other. "Feels about right," he said.

"Is there any point in me asking for the tape?" Brinn asked.

"You'll have others."

Coogan's smirk slipped into a grin. "Don't you trust me, mate?"

245

Brinn just looked at him. Coogan turned to Burns. He held his hand out towards him. Burns undid the zip on his black Harrington jacket and removed a Walkman. He handed it to Coogan. "As a symbol of my largesse you not only get your tape, but something to listen to it on as well. How about that for two hundred and fifty thousand?"

Brinn reached out and took the cassette player. He slipped it into the left-hand pocket of his jacket without comment.

"Do ye not want to take a wee listen, make sure it's authentic? There's powerful good sound through those headphones. Top of the range, I'm told."

Brinn shook his head slightly. "It's the little cruelties you enjoy most, Coogan, isn't it?"

Coogan shook his own head. "Oh, I think you'll find I enjoy the big ones as well." Seanie sniggered.

Brinn nodded to me. "You staying here then?"

I looked at Coogan. "Ball's in your court."

Coogan turned to Burns. "What do you think? Keep him for a while or let him ride home with the boss here?"

Burns regarded me silently for a moment, his head moving almost imperceptibly from side to side, as if he was tossing a very fragile salad of conflicting argument. "He writes well," he concluded with a little smile to match Coogan's. They were nothing if not happy gangsters.

"But he's been a pain in the hole," Seanie contributed, uninvited.

"There's that," said Coogan. "A pain on the whole, and in the hole, Mr. Starkey. But all things considered, I think we'll hold on to you for just a little while longer, eh?"

There wasn't much I could say, nothing I could do. The pen, again, was not mightier than the sword.

Brinn turned away without a word and walked to the car. He stopped by the driver's door.

"I better give him the keys," I said. Coogan nodded and I jogged down after him. "You'll be wanting these," I said.

He turned to me. It was a bit of a shock. His face, for so long a fixed wooden mask, had brightened, his eyes looked alive, Parker keen.

"Jesus," I whispered.

"It ain't over, till it's over, Starkey," he said quietly. He opened the door. "Sure you don't want to come with me?"

I looked back up at Coogan and his crew, their ghostly figures shrouded in mist. I shook my head. "He has my wife," I said.

"Pity," said Brinn. He got into the car and slammed the door. He crunched the car into first gear and moved off.

As he drew away Mad Dog hopped over the opposite drystone wall. He watched the car's progress for a second or two. "Well, that's that," he said, to no one in particular, and began walking back up towards Coogan, who remained standing in the middle of the road with Seanie and Burns. I fell into step behind Mad Dog. As he reached his companions he said: "He accepted our gift then?"

Coogan nodded. Seanie nodded. Burns nodded. They kept their eyes on the car.

Mad Dog turned to watch it as well. "You think he'll listen to it soon?" he asked.

"I'll be very disappointed if he doesn't," Coogan replied.

"You think the batteries in the Walkman are strong enough?"

"I should think so."

Seanie tapped me on the shoulder. I was watching the car as well. "There's no tape player in the car, is there?"

"There's a radio. That's all."

"That's okay."

It was a long, straight road, curving away eventually to the right and the holiday town of Newcastle. Brinn was nearing the curve when his car disintegrated in a ball of fire.

I watched, mesmerized, as the flames were rapidly enveloped by thick black smoke until it looked like an old angry thunder cloud had descended to earth to wreak havoc on one particular individual. Seanie clapped his hands and let go a triumphant whoop. Coogan was biting absentmindedly at a thumbnail, his eyes trained on the war cloud. "They do say it's dangerous to listen to a Walkman while driving," he said quietly.

I shook my head free of the destruction and turned abruptly towards him.

"You are one complete cunt, Coogan," I shouted and aimed another of my famous punches at him. He leant back expertly and I flailed past him and attacked Seanie's gun butt with my face. I sank to my knees. My nose filled with blood.

Coogan stood over me. He tutted. "You should have learnt by now, Starkey, that a cunt's a useful thing."

Above the ringing in my ears I heard a metallic click and felt something cold and hard against the back of my head. Seanie asked: "Finish him?"

I looked up into Coogan's face. Only he had two faces and I didn't know which set of eyes to look into. I remember that time now as the longest ten seconds of my life: longer than school, than first love, than standing on a balcony waiting to be pushed, than finding a girl dead in her bed. I remember the sounds more clearly than The Clash, more refined than digital tape: the slight swish of the pines against the morning breeze off the sea; the crackle of flame from way down the road; the slight nasal whistle as Seanie snorted up air excitedly above me; the extended *t* of another tut from Coogan.

"No," he said.

A click, and Seanie said disappointedly: "Ach, boss."

"Sure he has a story to write."

Burns's voice then: "He won't be writing about this, Pat. No way."

A chuckle from Coogan: "Not now, no. One day. When it doesn't matter any more to us. Then he can write it. Maybe he'll understand a bit better the way things are."

They turned away from me then and I sat back on the grass shoulder and as my eyes slipped back into focusing I watched them move up the sloping road back to their Land Rover, Coogan marching purposefully ahead, his companions moving at a more leisurely pace, almost crab-like as they kept an eye on the burning wreck far down the road behind them. Coogan climbed behind the wheel. Seanie and Mad Dog hauled themselves into the back and Burns took the passenger seat. Coogan put the jeep into gear and executed a perfect two-point turn. As it began to pull away up the hill Mad Dog leant out the back and gave me the V-sign. I wiped blood from my nose and gave him the fingers back. He lifted his gun and trained it on me, kept it on me for half a minute then let it drop. I thought he gave me a little smile.

As the Land Rover reached the top of the hill, it exploded.

32

S tarkey."

I opened my eyes. A local accent, but neither here nor there, imprecise. A plump man in a half-ironed shirt. A faint whiff of tobacco. Neville Maxwell. Central Office of Information. A century before he had asked me to guide a foreign journalist around Belfast. He stood a couple of feet back from my bed. The sunlight streaming through the window split behind his head, making him look very slightly angelic. I squinted at him and he moved out of the light. My head was sore and my nose was blocked with dried blood. I had on a pair of stripy pyjamas. The dying fizz from a half-drunk can of Coke on the bedside locker was too loud. The crumbs from a Twix bar moved like freelance freckles in the little v-shape at the top of my tunic when I shifted position.

"Does this mean I've lost the job?" I asked.

He folded his arms across the jacket of his pinstripe. Without replying he turned slightly and spoke to the soldier standing against the door. "You can leave us, corporal," he said. He'd been there as long as I'd been more or less awake. Every thirty minutes or so another soldier had opened the door and given him three or four puffs on a fag and then taken it back. The soldier nodded, changed his rifle from left to right hand and pulled the door open. He joined his colleague on the other side of the frosted glass.

"Are they looking after you, Starkey?"

I nodded.

"Nothing you need?"

"You are joking, I take it?"

"No. Not at all."

I pulled myself up into a sitting position. I still had a touch of the dizzies, but I'd stopped being sick. He had a pained expression on his face, but it looked as if it had more to do with gastronomic overindulgence than any exasperation with me. Which was a nice change. "Maxwell — Neville, whatever," I said. "I've been given a free helicopter ride, medical treatment, good food, a nice bed. All of these things I appreciate. But perhaps you can tell me how all the people who have dealt with me have been struck dumb?"

Maxwell found himself a seat, a red plastic effort sporting a series of burn marks that allowed the yellow foam rubber within to poke out. It looked like an Edam cheese with legs. He took out a packet of cigarettes and offered me one. I declined. He lit up and took a long drag. "You're not normally supposed to smoke in hospitals," he said, "but the military wing's a bit behind the times."

I nodded and waited. He blew smoke out of his nose in one long stream. It hung around like an indoor haze.

"You'll be pleased to know," he said, leaning forward, "that your wife is okay. She has been in our care for a while actually."

"She's not hurt?"

"She's fine. There was a little, ahm, unpleasantness for a while until certain facts were made clear to her captor. He is currently recovering in another part of this hospital."

"What are you going to do with her? She wasn't involved in anything. You must know that."

"Yes, we know that. She will perhaps need a little time to recover. Then she is free to go home."

"The girl that was with her?"

"Oh, yes, fine too."

"And Brinn?"

"Good news and bad news. He was elected prime minister with a landslide at 2 A.M. this morning. Unfortunately he was declared officially dead at the scene of that explosion at 9 A.M. yesterday morning. He had of course been dead for quite a while by that stage. And we kept the news back until after the polls closed."

"The others?"

"Patrick Coogan. Michael Angus. Seanie Murphy. Malachy Burns."

"Yeah."

"Dead."

I nodded. I sat back. I thought about the coolness of the grass shoulder, lying back and watching the smoke from infernos at either end of the road rise and mingle high up in the blue. I remembered trying to pick out shapes in it. I thought I saw my mother's face. A vague horse and trap. I know I saw a map of America and watched helplessly as it fell apart as helicopters clattered through it. So much death. So much death around that I was laughing as the soldiers in black-face gathered around me. I sniggered at the cavalry come too late.

I was aware of Maxwell's intense gaze, but I was thinking of Agnes. I was thinking of Lee, and Margaret, and Patricia. I was thinking of mass peace rallies and sudden death. And then I was thinking of me. I could see them all, all their faces, as if they were at different points on a spider's web, some on the periphery, some close to the centre. What was I, the fly caught in the web or the spider that connected everything?

"Well," said Maxwell, smiling nervously, his capped teeth to the fore, "you're alive, which quite frankly surprises me, so you should consider that a bonus. Your wife is alive, which is another. There is a faint possibility that you could be charged with manslaughter over Mrs. McGarry, but frankly I think that that is unlikely — as long as you are cooperative, that is."

"Meaning exactly what?"

"You know a lot of things, Starkey. A lot of things that should remain out of the public domain for the immediate future. Things are very fragile out there at the moment, very fragile indeed. It wouldn't take much to tip them one way or the other."

It never did. "Just tell me what you're proposing."

252

"Okay." He rubbed his hands together briefly, then eased them down his trouser legs. He wasn't happy. He wasn't comfortable. "The agreement must be this — I tell you what I can about what has happened to you and why, and you agree that it's off the record. In other words, no story."

"Maxwell, I lost interest in stories a long time ago."

"I hope so, because this one doesn't need to get out."

I gave him a hand to get started, because he was plainly in no hurry. "Okay," I said, "in the beginning was the tape."

"No," he corrected, "in the beginning was the bomb. The 1974 bombing of the Paradise restaurant which killed eight people."

"Which was planted by Brinn."

"Which was planted by Brinn but whose detonation was organized by Coogan."

"Aha."

"Aha, indeed. Coogan was in command of a six-man IRA unit which organized the campaign in that particular area. Brinn was the youngest member, but an ambitious wee bastard nevertheless, even then. He was becoming something of a thorn in Coogan's bum. Coogan was more of a businessman than Brinn liked. The bomb on the Paradise was a hit on a police function, sure, but it was also because the owners refused to cough up enough protection money. We believe Coogan had a good idea that the police had already transferred their dinner before he ordered the attack. Anyway, Brinn was starting to catch the ear of some of the high-ups about Coogan's profiteering just around the time that the bombing took place. The bomb went off early, early enough to catch Brinn on the way out and give him some pretty horrific injuries."

"And he thought Coogan set it off early, deliberately to shut him up."

"Something like that."

"And did he?"

"We have no way of knowing. Brinn was in hospital for months during which time he underwent a conversion to democracy."

"A miracle indeed. And he was never suspected of the bombing?"

"No. We'd no reason to. Our information then wasn't what it is now. He was fresh on the scene and hadn't made it into those scabby little manila folders we used to have on prime suspects. As far as we were concerned then he was just an average punter who happened to be in the wrong place at the wrong time."

Maxwell took out another cigarette for himself, offered me one again, lit up. "So, all burnt-up and high on drugs, Brinn gives an emotional interview on TV condemning senseless violence which goes all over the world."

"And so the personality cult started. I know all that."

"Okay. So from patient to politician. And a good politician at that."

"But with a few skeletons in his closet. Eight, in fact."

"More."

"More? You mean yesterday's . . ."

"Well, yes, bringing it right up to date, but before that as well."

I shook my head. "Before when?"

Maxwell pushed another smile on to his face. Blew out a little more smoke. "Let's go back to Coogan. He's still in charge in bandit country, he's gotten rid of the little thorn. He moves progressively further away from Republicanism to concentrate on making money for himself. Eventually his unit is disbanded by the Army Council of the IRA, but he still remains the power in that part of the world, particularly in his stronghold in Crossmaheart. Follow?"

"Follow."

"Right. So Coogan and his new gang reap the profits, occasionally working hand in hand with the IRA, but mostly not. He watches Brinn's rise with some amusement apparently, appears happy enough to leave him alone in his new career, while he builds up a fortune in his. But then things start to happen that get him worried. There are a couple of failed attempts on his life. IRA men start getting hit. But there's nothing random about the hits; the gunmen are acting on very precise information. Within a couple of years the four remaining members of the original cell which organized the Paradise bombing have been shot dead. And you know as well as I do the way that cell structure works in the IRA. Only the members of that particular cell would have access to that sort of information."

"You're not saying Brinn killed them."

"No. He didn't kill them. But he fed the information to whoever did. The UVF. We believe he surprised himself with the success of his politics. He knew it would only be a matter of time before word leaked out about his past, so he did some leaking himself."

"He turned Deep Throat."

"Deep Throat and deeply depressed. The rumours had already started . . . he felt he had to take some action."

"So Coogan gets suspicious."

"Coogan doesn't get suspicious. He makes a decision and then acts on it, right or wrong. That's the thing about Coogan, he makes his mind up one way or the other, then gives it one hundred per cent. He sets out to get Brinn. But Brinn is already one step ahead of him. He got word, through whatever channels, that Coogan was going out for a bit of fun, a bit of cattle rustling. It's what he does to relax. He gets it to the UVF, who sit in wait for him. Unfortunately there's an informer on the UVF side who leaks the ambush to the police. The UVF gets offside sharpish, but Coogan gets caught in the act of rustling. He has everything in the book thrown at him, all the banks they know he did but can't really prove, in the hope that something will stick."

"But only the rustling does."

"Right. So he gets fifteen years, which is way over the top for the actual offence, but that's Diplock Courts for you. Not that I'm complaining."

"It wouldn't do to criticize the law," I said. "And with our cock-eyed remission system and good behaviour he's out in five and out for revenge."

Maxwell smiled wanly. "In a nutshell," he said.

"What an apt description."

"And about the same time the pressure of being at the top, of knowing what he knows, gets to Brinn, just the once. The wrong time, the wrong place, again. The story of his life. He lets his hair down to a traitor with a tape recorder."

"A pity for him that the two events coincide. Coogan getting out, the tape becoming available."

"Well, it's not quite as simple as that."

"Oh, I know that. I come in and fuck up the equation."

"Well, yes. You do, if you'll pardon the expression, and with all due respect to the late Mr. Parker, become the nigger in the woodpile."

"That's not showing much respect at all."

"It was only an expression."

"Expressions get you killed here."

Maxwell's head slumped and he gave what he thought was a pained expression. "You don't . . ." he began and then stopped. His caps appeared over his bottom lip for a second, about as far away from a smile as teeth can be, like the forced grin you get on a skull after the flesh has rotted away. "Don't be so combative, Starkey. It doesn't help. I know you've been through a simply horrid time and I will try to take that into account."

I pulled at my bottom lip, exposing a little of my own teeth. "That's very generous of you . . ." I could tell the sarcasm grated on him.

"We were . . ."

"If you don't mind me asking, Neville, who's we?"

"Central Office of Information. You knew that all along."

Of course I did. I knew everything. I just didn't know that I knew. "I always thought you were just some kind of press officer."

"I am."

"You must have fuckin' huge terms of reference."

He took a leaf out of my book. He shrugged. "Press. Information. The same thing really," he said dryly. "We were aware of the tape's existence. We were aware McGarry was trying to sell it."

"So why didn't you just nip in and nick it off him? Wouldn't that have been the wise thing?"

Maxwell gave a little sigh, folded his legs. Blew some more smoke out. "Starkey, you have to understand, sometimes it's better to watch and wait."

"To gather information."

"Sometimes these things have a way of working themselves out if you leave them alone."

"Brinn is dead. You knew something that could have saved the life of the prime minister, for God's sake."

"And would it not have been worse if he'd been unmasked as a killer while in office? Think about it. His . . . charisma, whatever . . . got his party into office. They're there now, by popular demand. They have a chance to change things."

I shook my head. "Do you know what happened to the Sex Pistols when Johnny Rotten left them? Did they survive and prosper?" He looked blankly at me. I persevered. "Cut off the head and the body dies, Neville. Think about it."

"Prune a rose bush, it flowers again. Better than before. You think about it, Starkey — we have a popular government in power, a famous gangster is dead, a political fraud has been removed. There's hope again. There's little real harm done."

I put my head back on the pillows, closed my eyes, and asked him if any harm had come to Margaret McGarry.

33

Scout's honour, I won't tell a soul. Except I was a Boys' Brigade boy from way back. Maybe Maxwell with his Central Office of Information didn't know everything.

I had four days of what he euphemistically called debriefing. It sounds like something vaguely humorous, like a Whitehall farce, but my interview sessions were ill-tempered shouting matches. He didn't say a lot himself, he had a team of experts to do that for him, but he was a brooding presence over it all, a probing, wistful spirit intent on entering every cranny of my mind in search of buried treasure, but shrouded in a perpetual gloom because nearly all the crannies were empty, or half full of a poisonous, swirling bile. They gave me drink and hoped it would loosen my tongue, but they were wasting their time because there was nothing more to tell; I was not privy to any secrets; I was not involved for any reason beyond my own stupidity; I was a fool first and journalist second and neither had overlapped during the whole episode.

During working hours they interviewed me. During lunch I interviewed Maxwell. "Who decided to let Brinn die?" I asked. He shrugged. We both picked at our hospital food, a wooden tray each. We sparred between swallows.

"The decision was made."

"How did you know there was a bomb in the car?"

"There wasn't a bomb in the car. There was a bomb in the cassette recorder. The unusual aspect is that the bomb was designed only to go off as the play button was activated. I mean, there was no timer or anything. That's the only thing that set it off. Could have gone off anywhere. Coogan's sense of humour, I imagine. Not something I can very easily relate to. Perhaps he knew Brinn that well that he could depend on him playing the tape. But he could very easily have gotten away."

I had clothes. My own clothes. Members of his team brought them from the house. I felt the same sort of bond with the clothes Alfie Stewart had given me as with the denims Parker had bought me. None. It was an amicable divorce in which I got fashion and Oxfam got back what was rightly theirs.

Maxwell handed the clothes over to me personally. A black sports jacket, black jeans, a white shirt, black Oxford shoes. The shirt was expertly pressed.

"Do this yourself?" I asked.

"No," he said, and after a moment added, "Your wife did."

I looked at the clothes again. "Recently?"

"Day before yesterday."

"You mean she's home?"

"She's home."

"And she didn't come to see me?"

Maxwell shook his head.

"I see."

He stopped shaking his head. Just watched me.

"Any message from her?"

"No."

"But she did press my shirt, so there's hope for me yet."

"Perhaps. You've put her through a tough time."

"It wasn't intentional, Maxwell. None of it was."

"So very little of it ever is." It was a cryptic turn of phrase, but I was prepared to let it pass.

I sat down on the bed and began to take my pyjama jacket off. All of a sudden he looked a little sad, as if his own revelation that not everything always went according to strict plan had rebounded on him, wounding his bureaucratic sensibilities. "What's wrong, Maxwell? You're not suggesting there was a cock-up on your side as well?"

He sat on the bed beside me, which made it impossible to get my arms into the shirt, but I let him be. I could sense a confession coming on.

"We lost a very fine agent over this."

I nodded beside him. We both looked at the ground for a while. "Parker was a good man," I said.

Maxwell's head twisted sharply towards me. The kind of twist that would give me a crick, but he was a well-oiled machine. "Parker? God, no!" he spluttered. "He was an incompetent of the highest order. Blundering about like . . . like . . ." He opened his arms, waved his hands with an exasperated flourish. "Like you . . . Starkey . . . and we have an excuse for you. He was supposed to be a professional . . . no, I'm talking about a very fine man who died along with Coogan."

I have never seen my own brows furrowing, but I could tell that they were. "With Coogan?" Their faces flashed towards me. Whole faces. Noses. Cheeks. Eyes. Skin. None of them burnt. An identity parade of the dead. There was only one logical candidate. Only one who had shown any sign of intelligence or compassion. "Malachy Burns? Your own man was Malachy Burns?"

Maxwell shook his head.

"Not Seanie," I exclaimed, aware of the shrillness in my voice. "He didn't have the brains of . . ."

He shook his head.

I looked him square in the eye. "You're not serious." It wasn't a question. It was a statement.

He let out a little chuckle; it sounded like an empty Coke can rolling down subway steps. "Like I say, Michael Angus, Mad Dog to you, was a very fine man. Very professional. Very brave. He trod a very thin line."

"Jesus." I shook my head. "He didn't give much away. The last time I saw him he gave me the fingers."

"Like I say, he was very good."

"He was very good, but you were prepared to let him die."

260

"No. Not quite." Maxwell clasped his hands before him, although they weren't quite set for prayer. "Starkey, you see, in the information game, you can never quite know it all. Ultimately, it's what you don't know that makes it interesting. One door leads to another, or one door leads to a whole block of flats. We knew about Coogan's bomb for Brinn and were prepared to go with it. We didn't know about Brinn's bomb for Coogan. We were quite happy to have Coogan still around, he had his contacts with the IRA which Mad Dog could pick up on easily enough, and at the same time he was a divisive element in the Republican movement. But Brinn slipped that one past us. Someone supplied him with the bomb; I couldn't tell you who. Yet."

I stood up to complete my dressing. "The same way as you can't tell me who killed Margaret? Coogan thought it was Billy McCoubrey."

He unclasped his hands. "I think it would be fairly safe to say her killer came from the Loyalist persuasion. But naming someone? No. Again, not yet. It will surface one day. Quite possibly it was McCoubrey or one of his soldiers. I doubt we'll ever be able to prove anything. But we'll know, as we so often do. I know it's not much compensation, Starkey, but these things do have a way of working themselves out. Eventually."

"Like Brinn."

"Like Brinn."

And then it was time to go. Maxwell booked me a taxi. He never mentioned paying me for all my hard work with Parker. I wasn't up to asking in case he hit me with the bill for a nationwide manhunt.

He didn't say goodbye. One of his men told me the cab was on its way and I was free to move on. So I stood in the sun waiting for it to arrive, a soldier on guard duty motionless and quite possibly asleep beside me. Wispy white clouds flecked the blue. The excited cries of children enjoying their summer holidays all but drowned out the steady hum of traffic outside the meshed wire of the Musgrave Park Hospital's military wing. The half-circle frontage of the King's Hall across the way advertised a gospel revival show. I was free. But not free. Healthy but scarred. Happy but desperately sad.

The taxi drew up in a diesel roar. I climbed into the back and the Belle of Belfast City grinned round at me, her yellowed teeth sharp as a shark's. Her voice was a sea elephant's bark: "Thought I recognized the name. How the fuck are ye? Yer gob's been all over the box this last few weeks, hasn't it?" She roared out into the traffic. She lit a cigarette, turned right, spoke into the radio and spat out the window all in the one graceful movement. "The wee man at home told me I shoulda called the fuckin' peelers about givin' ye a lift once before, but I sez to him, 'Billy, fuck up. I don't squeal to the fuckin' peelers about nothin.'"

"I'm grateful."

"Never you bother yer head thankin' me, mate. Long as ye pay yer fare you're okay in my book."

Musgrave Park is only ten minutes in heavy traffic from the Holy Land, but in the daze of my release it felt longer. I tried to imagine how I used to be, coming home from a shift on the paper, or sitting at home trying to be literary, waiting for Patricia to come home from the tax office. Did I get a little tinge of excitement every time I saw her? Did I welcome her home with a kiss and a hug and a "missed you dreadfully"? I couldn't really remember. But I suspected not. What did I do, storm through the door, open a can and flop in front of the box with barely a hello? Did she charge through, moaning that I hadn't put the dinner on? Dinner, beer: normality. I couldn't imagine it. How long since I'd sat down for dinner with my wife? How long since we'd made small talk over my burgers and her salad? Was she the love of my life any more now that I had slept with Margaret and she had screwed Cow Pat Coogan? What if I came through the door and she gave me that most terrible of all male/female murder phrases, the demotion with shame to the lowest of the low: I want us just to be friends. She would say it with alarming alacrity, flaunting her femininity and new-found independence. She would ask me to move out of our house, but she wouldn't be nasty about it. In my own time.

262

And then I thought of my shirt, crisply ironed. If all was not forgive and forget, would she have ironed my shirt? If there was hate she would have found some means to express it through the shirt: she would have ironed a rubber snake into the top pocket or removed a paunch-revealing button. But it was clean and smelt good and fitted me like a glove, or, indeed, a shirt. She would be there to greet me. We would fall into each other's arms, swap apologies and declare undying love. We would make love and neither of us would think of our dead, fleeting partners, or if we did, it wouldn't show. They would be consigned to memory with all the other horrors of the previous days. We would begin to live again.

I did not think of politics or the state. Of Brinn and the lionization that was already roaring into place. I did not think of the book I was to write that would make the propagators of his false martyrdom an endangered species. I did not think of the senseless deaths and the needless cruelties. I thought of Patricia. I thought of Margaret saying, "The best part of breaking up is when you're having your nose broken." Of telling her, no matter what, that I loved my wife. I'd always been honest about that. I thought of Margaret again in her cold grave in a field of death, a gentle slope on the outskirts of Belfast, and of the day I would go to see her, to say farewell, to say sorry — sorry for something. But only when things were right with Patricia. She came first. She had always come first, even if I hadn't always known it.

The Belle brought the taxi to a halt. She was a couple of doors short but I didn't have the gumption to tell her.

"It's taken care of, by the hospital, I take it?" I asked.

She looked back. There was at least an inch of ash on her cigarette; as she spoke the fag shot up and down in her mouth, but the ash stayed in place, as if it was scared of falling off. "Aye," she said, "the fare is."

I nodded and opened the door. I got out, then leant back in. "I'm sorry," I said, "I've no money on me at all."

Her yellowy eyes bore into me, miniature, distant suns that were too close for comfort. I wrenched myself free of their hold and slammed the door. I heard her words clearly through the window: "Big fuckin' head, tight fuckin' arse."

She was gone in a flash, her taxi belching one last insult back at me.

I had no key. I stood and looked at the door. I thought briefly about how to knock it — three quick, urgent thumps to summon her quickly; or a tune — tum, tumtumtum, tum tum, tum — to let her know it was me, back from the wars, all in one piece? As I stood there, the door opened, and she looked out. "I heard the taxi," she said. "They told me you were coming."

I nodded and tried to read her eyes. I had forgotten how to read them. Emotionally dyslexic. She wore jeans, blue, faded, housework jeans. A black jersey with a white T-shirt underneath. Her face was pink: a mixture of makeup and embarrassment, an odd concoction that reminded me of an animated marshmallow. Patricia all over: sweet, soft, full of calories and bad for your health but absolutely loveable.

"Are you going to come in?"

I nodded again and she stood aside. I crossed the threshold. The house was cool. A nice breeze blew through the kitchen window, into the hall and round the house. It smelt of polish.

I went into the living room. Tidy. Records neatly stacked. Elvis Costello was singing "Good Year for the Roses."

"Is that for me?" I asked.

"I couldn't find 'Eve of Destruction,'" she said. No smile. I nodded again. I sat on the settee. She sat beside me. We leant back.

"Anything much on the TV later?" I asked.

"No," she said.